I0577975

THE VESSEL

By:

Russell Nohelty

Edited by:

Leah Lederman

Proofread by:

Katrina Roets

Cover by:

Lee Kohse

Additional cover design work by:

Hannah McGill

ISBN: 978-1-942350-34-7

First Edition, June 2017

Printed in the USA

www.wannabepress.com

PROLOGUE

"Sir, Sir, Sir!" Penelope's heels clomped against the Center's sterile, marble floor as she chased a dark figure in the distance. "Sir! Would you slow down for one second?"

"They call me Wind for a reason," the shadow replied.

"Yeah," Penelope closed the distance to her boss. "because you're full of hot air."

"I could have you killed for that, you know."

Penelope poked Wind in the chest. "You really think the guards care about an old gas bag like you?"

"Well, you found me. I thought I could escape that ghastly meeting and get a moment's peace. I should have known better than to try and hide from you."

"When was the last time you had a moment's peace?"

"I think there was a day a few thousand years ago." Wind cracked his aging back. "I'm sorry. I get crankier as I age. I can't wait for a new body."

"Unlike most of us, who get just one. I pity you, really." Penelope handed Wind a tablet. "The press release is ready. Are you sure you want to do this?"

"I've been ready for a few thousand years." Wind's fingers glided across the tablet's glass. "Would you take my place if you could? Would you live forever?"

"Absolutely not! I barely want the one life I have. Most days I want to rip the force field in half, run outside, and let the radiation take me, you know?"

Wind grazed Penelope's hand as he gave the tablet back to her. "Soon, that may be an option."

Penelope touched her skin where Wind's hand had been. "We can hope."

Wind walked off down a dark corridor, his loafers clacking on the marble surface. "Often, that's all we can do."

*

Time mattered little to Wind. Years passed like minutes to him. It was a function of being very, very, very old. After all, he was one of the Five, chosen to live a life of eternal rebirth millennia after millennia. He'd grown from a testosterone-filled youth to a decrepit old man more times than he could count, and hated it every time.

He wished they had created the Transference machine to work when the brain was fully formed at twenty-five, instead of during the ridiculously malleable teenage years. Of course, it was only in that sweet spot of youth that consciousness could be transferred properly—when the brain was developed enough to withstand the imprint, yet nubile enough to recover from the trauma.

Wind longed for it to be over, though. He couldn't wait until the decades didn't flash in the blink of an eye, when a century didn't pass in the span of a day, and when he could finally close his eyes for good and rest.

But that was not his life. He'd accepted his lot. Most would kill to be in his position. Some did, back in the day. He had certainly thought it was a blessing when they had chosen him. Like most blessings, though, it was equal parts curse. Nobody knew about the horrors he faced, the horrible decisions he made, and the secrets buried in his ancient mind.

*

Wind opened the door to his quarters, unchanged since the Incident. It was his comfort, his sanctuary, and his prison—just like the City, which housed them all. Of course, it was everybody's prison in a way, but Wind felt it more acutely. He'd spent centuries shackled inside its walls, maintaining the Bubble that kept his citizens protected from harm while simultaneously sealing them off from the universe. Wind was their grand protector and heartless warden rolled into one.

He sat down at his computer and peered over at a picture on his bedside, the one of him and Penelope smiling like fools. She had insisted that they smile, even though Wind hated to do it. There was little to smile about, even on the best days.

A sound caught his ear and he whipped his head around. "Is something there?"

It was over in an instant. The intruder swung his arm out of the shadows and stabbed Wind through the eye. He wasn't captured by fear, anger, or even pain in the moment of his death. He was blissfully content.

Finally, Wind thought, I can find peace.

BOOK 1

The Journey

CHAPTER 1

"Just let it go. You're never gonna figure it out," I yelled at Jake as he slammed his meaty palm across the broken tractor.

There were few things in life I hated more than watching somebody royally screw up. It's the sort of grating hatred that made me want to punch somebody right in the mouth, especially when it's Jake— a major, world-class, screwer-upper of things. I'd been watching him fix his family's tractor for six hours and it was not even close to being usable.

"I hate you so much right now," I shouted, dangling my feet from Jake's woodshed. "Do you know how much I hate you? I hate you more than anything has ever hated anything in the history of the universe."

It was true. The only thing I hated more than watching somebody muck up was if they refused to let me fix it. He'd failed seventeen times already; I'd counted. I could get that stupid tractor working in three minutes if it weren't for his stupid, male pride.

What got me was how confident he was each time he failed. Men are always so confident, even if they don't have a reason to be.

"I got it this time. I know I do."

I wanted to leave, but knew I'd be stuck fixing it eventually. In order to do that, I had to know exactly how bad he'd screwed up, which meant watching this train wreck even if I had a dozen other chores to do.

"I'm so hungry, Jake. Can't we just go eat now? I mean you clearly don't know what you're doing.'"

He was as stubborn as he was clumsy, and he wouldn't listen. I couldn't believe Daddy wanted me to marry this man.

Jake popped the clutch and put the battered tractor into gear. It sputtered, fizzled, and fell silent. "Dang it!"

"I told you before, it's a stopped-up intake. That tractor isn't going anywhere unless you remove all that build up."

"Oh yeah? And what do you know anyway?"

What a stupid boy. "What do I know? Well, I know we aren't eating until this gets fixed, and I know you aren't going to fix it, and I definitely know how to fix a stupid intake. And I know I'm starving!'"

"Please, girl, you don't know anything."

That pissed me off. I had fixed everything on this ruddy farm, from the baler to the water heater, and he still didn't trust me. Even though my dad had taught me everything he knew, it didn't matter. I was still a girl. I didn't know why having a vagina prevented me from knowing how to fix stuff.

I'd had enough of listening to him. I hopped up from my hay bale and opened the intake valve. After a few seconds, I pulled out a wad of mucky slime. "I told you. Try it now."

"It's not gonna work," Jake insisted.

"You say that every time you try to fix it yourself and every time you fail. Can you just trust me for once already?"

He stepped on the clutch and turned the ignition. The rusted tractor turned over and purred like a kitten. "Dang you, Althea. Can't you just be wrong this once?"

The truth was, I couldn't be wrong. Not about this sort of stuff. I knew these farms inside and out. I could sleepwalk my way to fixing anything within a ten-mile radius. "Where's the fun in that?"

"The fun's in letting the man be the man for once in your life."

"You find me a man and I'll let him be one, alright? Now come on. We're late for supper and I'm starving."

I wanted to like Jake because Daddy wanted me to like him. I mean, I liked him more than any of the other boys, but that didn't mean much since I hated all of them with the fire of a thousand suns. Maybe I could grow to like him enough, love him even. That's what Daddy wanted.

"Come on!" I shouted to Jake.

I didn't like to think about that sort of stuff though. That was a worry for the future. I just wanted to feel the rush of the cool, fall night on my skin. It felt so good. We liked it cool in the Fifth ring. We were bred for it.

There were six rings in all and they radiated out from the Center where the Five lived. The Five have been around since the dawn of time, moving their consciousness from person to person every generation.

The First Ring, where the richest and most powerful lived, was closest to the Center, and therefore closest to the Five.

The Second Ring was where your family lived if your body was chosen as a Vessel for the Five. If that happened, then every need for you and your family was taken care of for eternity. The Third Ring was full of bankers and businessmen. They handled all the money in the City and made sure everybody got paid.

All of that made up the Inner Rings. A big moat surrounded the Inner Rings to regulate the Outer Ring's population from going there. The only way in was by train, and there were only four trains in the whole City. They all started at the Bubble and made their way in from all four directions, taking soldiers out and bringing goods in. The trains were way too expensive for anybody except soldiers to use, but I often hoped I could get on the train one day and see the Center myself. They say it's beautiful.

The Outer Rings were where the City made stuff. The Fourth Ring warehoused all the raw materials and processed them into food and consumable products. The Fifth Ring, where I lived, made all the food the City needed. The Sixth, well, you didn't want to go to the Sixth. That was where they mined all the ore, and it was dirty and smelly. Farmland stayed dead for a hundred miles from its edges. People from the Sixth were mean and hard.

Every Ring had its people; the Five had bred them from birth, generation after generation, to do a specific job. For instance, I'm a farmer, just like everybody else in the Fifth. That's what I know. That's who I am. We are practical, humble, and no-nonsense people, who don't mind hard work or getting our hands dirty.

I would say that I'm a pretty average Fifth. I'm tall and broad with long hair and dark eyes. I run pretty fast, but not too fast. Just fast enough. Some people say I'm pretty, but not pretty enough to be noticed. I like to think I'm kind too, but not kind enough to be taken advantage of. I'm just right, Daddy says, average in the middle. That's what you want to be, average. You want to fit like a glove. If you don't fit, they'll find you. You don't want to be found.

"Hurry up, slow poke!" I shouted over my shoulder to Jake. "They probably ate all the good stuff already."

Jake looked a little like me, except he was a boy. Like most Fives, Jake was hearty, strong, and confident. The Five needed us stronger than oxen. They relied on us to feed the entire City, and the City was hungry.

*

Our house wasn't big or flashy, but it got the job done. My great-grandpa built it with his own hands two hundred years ago. It was a good house even though it was a little drafty, the walls were paper thin, and the floor creaked horribly. Mama said it had character. That's what people say about something when they don't have anything nice to say.

"Mama!" I shouted, rushing through our front door. "Sorry we're late. Hope dinner's not cold."

Mama knew I would be late. I was always late. They all just went on without me. If there was no food left it was my own fault, but they always left me enough. My family was like that. We watch out for each other.

They weren't in the kitchen when Jake and I ran inside, and they were always in the kitchen when I got home. We weren't that late. The dinner table was full of food, too. We never left food on the table. "Mama! Is everything alright?"

The sound of the TV blared from the family room. Our TV never stayed on when it was dinnertime. We had strict rules about even glancing at the TV room until the food was cleaned up. Something was wrong.

I found them in the family room. Mama was crying messy tears. Dad and my brother, Bobby, were silent. They stared at the TV like zombies. "Mama. What's going on?"

"Shhhhhh," Dad responded, barely able to move his lips.

An elegant, poised, beautiful lady was on the TV. She was somber and dignified. It was Earth, one of the Five, the patron Saint of the Fifth Ring. Earth came from the land and had built all of the agriculture after the Incident. It was because of her that there were farms and land, and Mama and Daddy and Jake and even my disgusting brother Bobby.

"I regret to inform you," Earth said, "that early this morning, we found Wind, dead."

CHAPTER 2

The Five were as eternal as the City itself. They were the protectors who watched over us. Their bodies were human, but their minds were forever. The Five always were and always have been. Now, one of them was dead. Everything I knew about the world was thrown into upheaval.

"It is with a heavy heart," Earth said in her most solemn voice, "that I relay the news of Wind's sudden death. He was an old friend, my oldest friend. I never thought I would see the day when one of our own was brutally attacked...and in our own home, no less."

I couldn't believe it. None of the Five had ever died before. Not for real. They left their old bodies for new ones, but they always were, and were always supposed to be, until their mission was fulfilled, and we could leave the Bubble for good. But we were still trapped inside the Bubble, like we had been for generations, and now Wind was dead. He was never coming back. Not ever.

Earth choked back her tears. "This is a cold, hard realization that we are mortal in body though immortal in spirit. With that in mind, we have concluded this predator could strike again, at any moment. If they do, we must be in peak physical shape to survive. Which is why, even though it is not due for decades, we are initiating a new Transference protocol."

A new Transference? I was supposed to worry about potentially sending my daughter to the Center, but not myself. In one more year I could avoid it; I'd be too old. But right now, I was still seventeen, the last year I was eligible to compete.

Dad shot me a look before I could even think, and Mama's eyes would not leave my face. They were speaking clearly without saying a thing: *Don't even think about going.*

Earth's voice trailed on from the television, "I know this is unexpected, but we decided on this protocol ages ago, should this situation ever arise."

Why would they have planned something like this if they were immortal? I couldn't ask Mama, although I desperately wanted to know. Even if I asked, she wouldn't have told me. They always clammed up when it came to the Five.

"For your safety, for the preservation of the City, it must be done. We must continue to serve and protect this great City from the outside world. If anything should happen to us, the world, as we know it, will descend into chaos. We are vulnerable. And if we are vulnerable, all of you are vulnerable as well."

Each of the Five had their specialty. Earth grew the crops that fed the City; Arrow bred the people that inhabited it. Stone, before her nervous breakdown, had maintained the power generators. Time made sure everything ran properly and promptly. Wind...Wind had handled the Bubble, the force field around the City that protected us from the outside world's deadly radiation.

"I know I cannot force you to send your sons or daughters. However, I urge you to fulfill your duty. We must have the absolute best candidates available in order to serve you properly. This is not about your family; it is about our family. This City is our family. Please understand just how much your City needs you."

It was true that they couldn't force us to go. We had to volunteer. There were plenty of reasons to go, though. Some went because they believed in the Five, others because their parents demanded it. Some just needed the money. It didn't matter why you went, but it was essential that you did.

"All public transportation will be free for the next two weeks. After that, the judging will commence. Those chosen as our new vessels will have their families cared for, for the rest of their days. Those who are not chosen will return home, no worse for the wear."

The most powerful motivator to enter was the money. You could make a lot of money in just a few days of work. That's how they convinced the farmers and miners to enter their children, even though they were needed at home. It was the cash infusion tiny farms like ours desperately needed and in the poorer Sixth Ring, it could keep a child from working in the mines for good. It could save their families from a lifetime of black lung.

"This is your civic duty," Earth said. "I hope you take it seriously. I trust you will make the right choice. Hope be to us all. By the will of the Five."

With that, the broadcast ceased. Dad turned off the TV. He looked directly at me. "You're not going," he said in a clipped tone, "so get that notion out of your head right now."

"I don't think it's so bad," I said. "To go, I mean."

Mama and Dad looked at each other. They shared a thought in that moment they wouldn't speak out loud, the kind they had thought too often when I was younger. I thought we were past that. I thought they considered me an adult, not a child.

"Can you at least tell me what's so bad? I mean, I'll make some money and be home in a couple of weeks."

"Unless you're not," Mama replied in spite of herself.

"Esther!" Dad shouted. "No!"

"Harold, we can't keep her in the dark forever."

"We could, if you just—"

"What?" I said. "What are you keeping from me? Just tell me what's so bad and I'll shut up about it. It's not like I even want to go."

"It's none of your concern," Dad replied. "It doesn't matter anyway. We have plenty of money. We put food on the table. We eat well. We have a simple life by the will of the Five. Can't you just be happy with that?"

I was happy with it until that moment. Now, I wasn't so sure. Not when I couldn't trust my own parents to tell me the truth and not when they treated me like an infant. "I'm going to my room," I snarled at them. "Don't come after me."

*

Why was I so angry? I didn't even want to go to the Center. I was happy staying home and being on the farm. I loved the simple pleasures of working with my hands. I could do it forever, but for some reason, being told I couldn't do something made me want to do it really badly.

My room was on the second floor overlooking the barn and our cornfields. From my window, I could just make out the crest of the Fourth, where white smoke plumed into the air. I wondered if they were processing our grain at the moment, or ore from the Sixth.

I'd been to the Fourth a couple times with Dad, riding shotgun in our pickup truck as we dragged a thousand pounds of grain behind us. The people of the Fourth Ring were...nerds. I suppose that's the best word for them. They were fastidious, clean, and very particular. They took great pride in being the smartest people in any room.

Fours thought they were better than Fivers and Sixers because they were closer to the Center. That's stupid, of course. No doubt the Fifth was the most important. We had all the food and the politicians and merchants in the Inner Rings couldn't go very far without food. Plus, without food everybody would starve. The Fours only had their numbers and words. We could survive without them, but they couldn't survive without us.

"Looks like the door will survive the pummeling you gave it," Dad said, caressing the door hinges. "That was quite a performance."

"I don't like being lied to, or treated like a kid. We're not supposed to have secrets in this family."

"When you get a little older, you'll see most of life is keepin' secrets for the good of others."

"There aren't any good secrets."

"Really? No good secrets? I suppose you told Jake you don't want to marry him then?"

"Dad! That just isn't true."

"Now you're just lying to me. I'm not an idiot. You're warming up to the idea, but it's not what you want. And that's fine. We do things we don't want all the time. Jake's a good man and you'll grow to love him. Still, you don't talk to him about it because you don't want to hurt him. That's a lie of omission, kiddo."

"So what? It's right to keep a secret like that?"

"I don't know if it's right. I can't speak to that. There ain't no easy answers in this life. I can only say that maybe you can understand where we're coming from since it's for your own good. Maybe you can do that. Maybe you can trust us a little. I think we've earned it. Now get dressed. It's time for church."

"Why are we even going? You hate church."

"We all gotta do things we hate sometimes, Thea. That's another big part of life."

*

I hate church worse than Daddy does. Not only is it a bunch of boring, old men talking about loving the Five—or the Four, I guess now—but it's long and hot and you have to wear really uncomfortable clothes. I hate dresses, I hate heels, and I definitely hate putting bows in my hair. And yet, when we go to church, all of that is required.

Did I really need a crusty, old guy telling me it sucked that Wind had died? We all knew it was crummy and saying "by the will of the Five" a hundred times wouldn't make his death more bearable. I mean what does that even mean, really?

But we had to go. There was no denying it. Even if Daddy saw it was unnecessary to show our face at church, there was no talking Mama out of it. I understood it, even if I didn't agree.

Wind was a good man, and he deserved our respect; we should at least acknowledge his death after all he did for us. He deserved that much, even if he wasn't much of a god after all.

The church was more packed than I'd ever seen it before. Most of us were holiday observers at best, but Wind's death, having been so sudden and so scary, had brought people out of the woodwork. I guess everybody needed help figuring out how to feel.

We took our seats in the back as the organ music began a brooding tune. Then, we stood up as a gangly, old priest shuffled down the aisle waving incense, and we sang in monotonous unison with him.

> *Praise to the Five. They gave us life. They protect us from harm. They are everything. They are the only. We are only here by their will. By the will of the Five we will find truth.*

The priest stood at the pulpit as his horrible singing came to an end. He cleared his throat. "Good evening. By the will of the Five!"

We all knew the response. It had been engrained in us since birth. I hadn't been to church in seven years and I still knew the response by heart. I vomited it out just like the rest. "Praise be to them."

I say vomit, of course, because it's all bile: the Five, the church, all of it. Dad had told me years ago that I should think for myself and be my own person. He hated the idea of kowtowing to anybody, especially the Five. I don't know why he was so bitter towards them, why he hated them so much.

And even though Mama wasn't a fan of religion either, she had nothing on Dad. His face turned purple at the very thought of the Five. His face was already beet red and the priest had barely said two words. There was no way he would make it through the whole service without blowing up.

"Please be seated." We complied.

"What happened was a terrible tragedy. In this time of great turmoil, I think it fitting for a reading from Wind chapter twelve, verse thirty-nine. 'And lo there will be a time when the harvest is sowed without being reaped and hope is lost. In those moments, do not despair. Try harder. Love longer. Be comforted.'"

I didn't like the *Book of Books*. Each of the Five had their own Testament interpreting what had happened since the Incident and how we should live our lives until the Bubble opened and we could see the outside world. They were crap, though, full of flowery language and stupid expressions. I had to study it for years in Sunday school until Mama let me stop. I hated every minute of it.

"It's very important," the priest continued, "to understand that life is fleeting, and that even after his ascendance into the cosmos, Wind still looks down on us."

And if I had to choose, I liked Wind's Gospel the best. His passages were hopeful. Earth's were more practical while Stone's were grim and barely intelligible most of the times. Arrow's were full of fire and brimstone while Time's testament was philosophical and flowery in the most boring ways possible.

But, it was crazy how different the Gospels were, contradicting each other at every turn. And yet somehow, we were supposed to believe that they were all the truth? I didn't know how anybody could follow five "different" truths at the same time without going crazy. Some tried, though.

Thankfully, they did all agreed on a couple of things, at least. One of the shared beliefs was that the Five had descended from a higher plane, had taken shape in human form for our benefit and that they would ascend back into that higher plane once the Bubble opened again. It was a great sacrifice to remain as they did in a human form.

"So today, we decide not to mourn Wind, but to celebrate his return home. He is with the stars now, as he was before the Incident. It is up to us to continue living in his image. He would want us to continue on in the traditions of the past. With that, I implore you all, in your civic duty, to send your children to the Transference. The Five gave you life, and they ask for so little…"

Dad leaned over to me. His face was purple, like he'd been holding his breath for an hour. "Come on, we're leaving."

*

Dad didn't speak the whole way home. When we got there, he stormed upstairs and as he slammed the door, Mama ran up behind him. I heard them screaming at each other through the thin walls.

This was my fault. I had ruined our perfect family. I turned to my brother Bobby. I wanted his advice about what to do, but he was already halfway out the door. I couldn't blame him. He was a doer, and not one for deep thought. Transference didn't concern him because he was too old, so he hadn't given it a second thought most likely.

I didn't have that luxury.

*

I couldn't sleep all night and eventually I gave up trying. I got up and finished everybody's chores while it was pitch black. I wouldn't ever admit it out loud, but I enjoyed doing menial tasks. It got me out of my own head, and tonight, I desperately needed that.

I never really bothered with the ways of the world before Wind's death; I was always content with what I had. There was plenty on the farm to worry about, and plenty of stuff to rattle through my head without thinking about the big outside world. But now, that world kept crashing into my thoughts over and over, even while I was feeding the chickens and milking the cows.

After chores, I tried to go back to sleep, just lying there until I couldn't stand the thoughts racing through my mind any more. So, I went back downstairs and saw the table was set for breakfast, but Dad and Mama were nowhere to be found.

This wasn't necessarily unusual. They started early, milking the cows and gathering eggs from the chickens before sunrise. Most everything we ate came from the farm and it took time to gather everything each morning. But I'd already done that and left a basket on the counter, so what could they be doing?

It didn't take me long to find them out back having a fight. They didn't usually fight. They were blissfully happy. Sickeningly happy, even. But this business with Transference had brought out the worst in them somehow.

"I don't care if we could use the money," Dad hollered. "She's not going."

"I'm not saying she should go," Mama replied. "I'm just saying wouldn't it be nice to have some money, so we didn't always have to worry about losing the farm?"

"What do we need money for?" Dad said. "We have everything we need right here."

"Electricity isn't free. Land isn't free. You know we aren't harvesting what we used to, Harold."

"We can get it back. Bobby marries Noel and Althea marries Jake. Then we'll have three farms, baby. We'll get by."

"By the Five! You always just wanna get by," Mama shouted. "Don't you ever want more than that?"

"I'm happy, by the by."

"So, you're happy to sell our daughter off so we can get by, but you won't let her go do something that could actually help us get ahead in the world. How dumb are you? Honestly."

"It's not dumb to want to secure your family's future. We don't do that, we starve, and our line dies out. Is that what you want?"

"What I want is for you to quit acting like a fool and grow up. I'm not saying she should go. What I'm saying is we could sure use the money. Otherwise the City will take back our land. Then we'll be out on our ass, just like the Johnsons last year. Do you want that?"

Dad looked toward the ground. "No. I don't want that."

"Then can you at least agree we could use the money?"

Dad sighed. "Alright. We could use the money. You happy? The money would be nice. But we aren't auctioning our daughter to the fates for a chance at money. We're better than that. The last time—"

"This isn't like the last time! You know they're going to pick those dolls from the Inner Rings who think it's some sort of perverted honor. They always pick those kids."

"Unless they don't. You remember—"

"I know there's a chance," Mama said. "And I agree she shouldn't go, but that should be her choice, shouldn't it?"

Dad sighed. "What if she makes the wrong one?"

Mama threaded her arms through his and squeezed his waist. "Then we'll deal with that, alright?"

I made up my mind in that moment. I had to go to the Center. My stomach turned in knots just thinking about leaving the Fifth, but at least my mind was clear. I couldn't let my family fall into poverty and lose everything. Not if I could help it. If I didn't do anything, they would always resent me. More importantly, I would resent myself.

CHAPTER 3

I shouldn't have said anything. I should have left like a thief in the night, but I couldn't do it. I needed them to know I was going. I needed them to know why. I thought they would listen to me. I thought I could reason with them.

I'm an idiot. Dad was less than pleased when I told him the big news.

"I absolutely forbid it!" he shouted. "You will not go to that horrible place and that's the final word I have to say about it."

I asked why they were being so hardheaded and stubborn. They wouldn't tell me. Mama and Dad had never been this unreasonable about anything. They let me get earrings when I was eight and that only took three weeks of convincing!

"I don't understand!" I shouted.

"No, you don't," Dad said. "And you don't have to. That's one of the benefits of being a child."

"I'm not a child!"

Mama held up her hands. "That's not what he meant. All he meant was that—
"

"Don't tell me what I meant, Esther!" He turned back to me. "I meant what I said—you're a child. You don't pay for this house or the electricity. You get to live in the magical fantasy of childhood. The world is a harsh place, much harsher than you know. I mean, when we," he began, but then changed course. "Just forget it."

"When you what? What are you hiding from me?"

Mama sighed. "We were in the last Transference."

"What?" I gasped. "Why didn't you say anything about it before?"

"We...were ashamed."

"Why would you be ashamed of helping out your family?"

"That's not why we did it," Dad said. "We did it to escape. Escape our lives for the luster of the Inner Rings."

"And you think that's what I'm doing?"

"Not exactly," Dad said. "Listen, the Center, the Inner Rings...they change you. They make you hard. The people...they're not like us darlin.' They play for keeps. We did things...saw things..."

"We don't want you to go through that," Mama said. "It's a horrible, miserable place that saps your innocence. It makes you cold and bitter."

"I won't let it do that to me," I said. "I can handle myself. I heard you out back. I know we need the money."

"Forget what you heard. That wasn't for your ears. We ain't gonna send our baby girl off for our own selfish gains." Dad looked at the clock. "Now hurry on before you're late for school. I don't wanna hear another word about it."

Why do they keep telling me they won't allow me to do things? Every time they do, I just want to go more. Since I can't talk to them about it, I'm just gonna do it under their nose.

*

It was a long way to school; two miles across flat land, through nothing but thorny wheat fields that tugged on my clothes with every step. It was a boring walk, but I was thankful to have time with my thoughts. That is, until I was interrupted by my brother's girlfriend. Usually I was happy to see Noel, but today I wanted to be alone.

"Wait up!" she shouted. Noel was sweet and kind; the type of person you hope joins your family. We'd been friends since we were babies.

"Hurry up," I told her. "I'm late!"

Noel's skinny legs scooted faster than her small frame allowed. Noel was a little short for a Fifth, and she wasn't that strong either. She was enough to get by, and not much more. When she finally caught up to me, she was winded. "Oh god. That is tiring."

"I don't have time to wait for you today."

Noel held her side. Everybody loved her, even Bobby. He took a while to warm up to her, but she grew on him until they had become inseparable. Now they were engaged and getting married the moment she graduated. "Fine. I'll just deal with the stitch in my side then."

"If that's what you gotta do."

We were in the same grade, but she was a few months younger than me. We were both eligible for Transference, so I knew the same thoughts were going through her mind.

"Are you gonna go?" Noel asked.

"Go where? There isn't anywhere to go."

"Don't play dumb. I'm not some boy you're trying to impress."

I couldn't fool Noel. We'd known each other all our lives. "Mama and Dad forbid it."

"That's not an answer, girl. Are you gonna go or not?"

"Are you?"

"No, but not because Mama and Papa forbid it. It's because I just don't feel like it. I know there's only a real small chance I would get picked and zapped by one of them, but I don't even like them odds. Besides, I got Bobby to think about."

"I have Bobby to think about, too," I replied. "And Mama. And Dad. There's a lot of money on the table, Noel."

"What do we need money for? We got three farms once you marry Jake and I marry Bobby. We can make everything we need and barter for anything we can't."

"I wish I could see things as simple as you, Noel."

*

That night, I went to bed early and waited. Once everybody had fallen asleep, I would leave for the train.

When the murmurs had finally died down, I packed my backpack and threw it out the window. My eyes got teary as I kicked one leg and then the other out the window and jumped down to the ground.

Don't cry, I told myself. This is hard enough as it is. Besides, it's not like I'm never coming back. There's going to be about four thousand people at the Center and they only pick four. The chances of me being chosen are really small.

It wasn't hard to get through the fields in the dark and find my way to the train station. I knew the farms even in pitch black. Even though I'd driven past the train with Dad a few times, I had never used it before. Fastest I ever went was down a straight away on Route 37 when Jake stole a truck without asking, when he'd been trying to impress me. It worked, for a bit at least.

Somehow, I had convinced my body that it would be okay although my mind still didn't believe it. But I always found that if you do something even when you're scared, your mind just ends up falling in line. I had to look forward and fought the urge to turn back and look at my dark house one last time. If I looked back, I'd never have the strength to keep going.

*

The train station was cold and dark, and the wind whipped hard against my cheek as I approached. How was it that the wind could be so harsh now when it was so pleasant in the light of day? It was as if the Fifth didn't want me to leave.

Maybe I was an idiot. I was leaving everything I knew and loved. What would be waiting for me when I came back? What would Dad and Mama think? They could hate me or disown me, even. Would they see that I was doing this all for them?

"You weren't even gonna say goodbye?" The voice came from behind me.

I turned, startled to see Jake and Bobby standing on the platform. I scrambled to my feet, my backpack jabbing into my arm as I spun to meet them. "I'm not going back with you guys."

"Relax," Bobby said. "We're not here to take you back."

"Then why are you here?"

"We're here because we love you and want to say goodbye," Jake said.

"And also, to warn you Mama and Dad are on the way," Bobby added.

"What? How?"

Bobby chuckled. "You're like a bull in a china shop, Thea. Everybody heard you leave. I snuck out while they were hollering and slit one of their tires, but you don't have much time. Daddy can change a flat lickety-split, y'know."

The track rumbled, and the loud horn of the train blared in the distance.

"The train's here. Please, you have to hold them off for a couple more minutes. Then I'll be on the train and they can't do anything."

Dad's voice blared from the darkness. "We're not going to let you go, Thea. I don't care if we have to lock you in a room until this stupid thing starts, you are not going!'"

"Dad, I'm sorry. You gotta understand—"

Mama stepped forward to join him. "No, we don't. I thought you could be trusted with a decision like this, but your father was right. You are just a little kid. Now come with us, right now."

The train rolled into the station. "I just want to help, Mama. You've got to let me help. I'm sorry for running off. I'm sorry for everything, but I'm not going home with you."

The train squeaked to a stop in the station. "I'm getting on that train. You can say you love me and wish me well, or you can yell at me. But I'm getting on that train all the same."

"No, you are not."

My eyes got misty again. "Don't make it end like this. Please."

Dad stomped forward. "Do not disobey me, child. You come with us this instant!"

The train doors slid open and I bolted for them as Dad lunged at me. He latched onto my backpack and dragged me back. I fought free of the straps and ran inside the train. Dad fell back with nothing but my backpack in his arms. He tried to stand but Bobby held him down.

"Let me go," Dad shouted, "or I'll kill you, boy!"

I'd never heard Dad talk like that. His thunderous voice boomed through the station, but Bobby held firm and yelled back, "Just let her go! It's her choice! Let her go!"

Mama ran toward me, but Jake picked her up off the ground. She kicked the air as Jake struggled to hold onto her. She cried and shrieked into the heavens. The train pulled away as my heart broke in two.

Why did they have to be like that? Why couldn't they let me go? I was doing this for them, after all. The Center couldn't really be as bad as they made it out to be, could it?

CHAPTER 4

The train wasn't designed for sleep, that's for sure. There were sleep cars in the front for VIPs, but I wasn't allowed up there. I was just a little P, so I was stuck with the tattered seats in the back. Why would the seats be nice anyway? It's not like anybody of consequence ever used them. It was all soldiers coming to and from the Bubble and massive payloads of ore and grain, neither of which needed luxury.

I often wondered why soldiers guarded the Bubble. After all, it was impenetrable. Thousands of soldiers guarding the wall seemed like overkill. Dad told me it was because every government needs an army to keep their citizens in line and the Bubble was an easy point to call soldiers to action against their own citizens. Dad was very pessimistic, but Mama never argued with him.

I curled up for an hour, but sleep was impossible. Even if I could get over the ragged seats, my mind raced with thoughts of home and the look of pain on my parents' faces as I rode away. I wanted to leave, to leap off the train and head back. I wanted to apologize to my parents and promise to never leave again.

That was impossible. I'd made my choice. If I turned back now, I would always know I was a coward.

Since I couldn't sleep, I went to the dining car, though I didn't have any money for food. All my supplies were in my backpack, which Dad had ripped off me back at the station. Now I didn't have clothes, money, or a phone. All I had was what I was wearing and a bit of gumption. Gumption doesn't feed a starving belly though.

"You headed to the Center?" the man behind the counter asked.

"Yeah."

"You want anything to eat?"

"I'd love something. I don't have any money though. I'm just gonna smell it for a while."

The man reached under the counter and pulled out a peanut butter and jelly sandwich. "Here, this was my lunch, but I don't need it much as you."

"I can't take that from you."

"Nobody should go hungry. Not where I come from. So, eat. I'll be all right. I got a whole cart full of food."

Nobody should go hungry. That was our motto. It was ingrained in the Fifth that nobody should starve. We were built that way.

It made us work harder when the crop yield was low, and even harder when the crop yield was high. There hadn't been a food shortage in 200 years. The Fifth was very proud of that. Without us, everybody would wither away. Without us, the City wouldn't exist.

*

I talked to the nice man behind the counter for the next hour. His name was Thomas. He was from the Fifth, but the government had found out he was a Mutie. Being a Mutie was worse than anything in the City. Being a Mutie meant your birth wasn't approved.

Every birth in the city had to be approved by the Ministry of Maternity. If a couple wanted to have a child, they needed to fill out the proper forms, get blood drawn, and have a home visit from a minister.

Usually, births were approved without an issue, but sometimes...well sometimes, there were problems. It could be that the parents weren't biologically compatible, or one of them had a hereditary disorder that would affect the child, or any other of a thousand little issues that could lead to an impurity in the genetic line that Arrow had cultivated since the Incident.

Still, love was a powerful thing, and lots of people risked it anyway. The Ministry had a lot of babies to look after, and paperwork often got lost in the shuffle...either because of bureaucratic incompetence or for the right price.

Sometimes, those babies grew up to be fully functioning members of society and nobody was ever the wiser. But other times, the Ministry discovered the deception, and came down hard on them. In those cases, the baby was labeled, branded, and forced to live their life as an outcast in the margins of society as a Mutie.

There weren't many choices for Muties in the City. They could live in squalor in the Third or sell their soul to the military. Either was a miserable life. Thomas, though, seemed happy enough riding the rails.

"They wouldn't let me get along doin' what I was supposed to do, so I had to find work doin' something else. There ain't no shame in that. People gotta get from one place to another. We all the same on this train. We all proud of what we doin,' too."

Everybody working the train was a Mutie. Of course, they were. How else would the train get from the Bubble to the Center every day? No ring bred people for that—only the Muties could do it. But they were the lucky ones. Most Muties lived on the fringes.

I'd heard a lot about them but had never seen one. They were supposed to be the scum of the earth, but Thomas seemed fine to me. I mean it wasn't their fault they weren't approved. Lots of people looked down on 'em though. Everyone needs somebody to look down on, I guess.

*

Trains started at the Bubble every day. They picked up soldiers done with their duty, made their way through the Inner Rings and into the Center, where they picked up fresh soldiers, and then returned back out to the Bubble.

Most people wouldn't dare leave their ring for a dangerous life on the Bubble, which explained why so many of the military were Muties too. They could find purpose and hope in the military. The Bubble offered them some sort of redemption.

Maybe that's why Thomas seemed so happy. Everybody that rode the train was like him. Except for me, I guess, and the other kids headed toward the Center right now.

I finished my sandwich and headed to the front of the train, which was packed with teenaged Sixers. They were covered in soot and grime from working the mines. Their sulfur smell burnt my nose and the soot forced me to cough.

Sixers had no shame in their dirt. It was a way of life in the Sixth to be dirty even when you were clean. The mines caked every acre of their ring in a fine layer of dust. It was so dirty there that it wafted miles over into the Fifth, polluting thousands of acres of farmland. This drove some of the Fivers crazy, but Sixers wore their soot proudly. They worked their fingers to the bone all day and night.

My people worked hard, too. Fivers did hard, callused, backbreaking work, but it wasn't nearly as dangerous as the work done by Sixers. Sometimes the farm was even fun. Not like the work of the Sixth. The Sixth had dangerous work. Most wouldn't survive to see adulthood. Those who did weren't as much excited about surviving as burdened they were so "lucky."

It was a hard life in the Sixth, and it showed in the lined, cold faces, narrowed eyes, and slumped shoulders of the teenagers on the train.

We were in the Fourth now, passing rows and rows of empty warehouses. I found an empty seat across from a Sixer and leaned my head against the cool window and watched him as he flicked something metallic open and closed over and over again, almost entranced by it. His face was softer than the other Sixers I had seen, but it looked old just like the rest of them, like he'd lived his whole life in a few short years.

The train came to a stop. The conductor shouted out "All aboard!" and a flood of nerdy kids in glasses marched down the aisles. I kicked my feet out across my row of seats so none of them could sit next to me.

Fours were so dainty. I watched them as they took their first whiff of sulfur and winced. The smell wasn't even that bad anymore, barely more than a faint odor. Pansies.

The people of the Fourth weren't known for grit or determination; they were all in their heads—bookish, logical, hyper-rational, and analytical. A Four would kill their own mother if they could justify it on paper.

They were important though, and notoriously meticulous. Millions of pounds of food and ore ran through their centers daily, and it was their job to keep track of it all and process it into something the whole City could use. They were very good at it. Nothing was ever lost. *Every detail accounted for and everything in its place.* That was their slogan.

There wasn't much to see in the Fourth, mostly silos, warehouses, and processing centers with smoke pluming out of them. The Fourth was the heart of the City, storing the blood that kept it alive and distributing it perfectly. It was a marvel of efficiency...and incredibly boring to watch.

I made the mistake of curling up my legs, so I could better look out the window and regretted it immediately. A curly haired boy with glasses sat down next to me without asking.

"Don't worry about the smoke," he said. His voice was nasally and high pitched. "It's not toxic."

"I wasn't worried," I replied. "I was enjoying being alone. Go away."

He didn't. He just kept talking, lost in his stupid words. "You see, the condensers in the sky convert the carbon dioxide from the smoke stacks into rain that waters the fields in the Fifth, which is where I'm sure you are from since you aren't covered head to toe in soot. It's the circle of life, you know."

"Fascinating. You know I didn't ask you to sit down, right?"

"Yes, but I walked throughout the train and determined this was the most comfortable seat available. It has the most padding and least frayed edges. I find that if you just do things, people won't complain that much, but if you ask, they will yell at you."

"It's kind of a jerk thing to do, ya know?"

"I'm willing to take that risk. You see I'm probably never going to see you again. So, my need of finding a decent seat until we reach the Center is the bigger issue when you compare it to the slim chances of me needing anything from you in the future." He took a breath. "Have you ever been to the Inner Rings before?"

At this, the Sixer turned around. Two things became immediately clear: the first being that the thing he'd been flicking was a knife, and the second being that the boy was actually a girl. "I'm gonna need you to shut up, alright? This is a quiet car."

"Oh really?" the boy replied. "It didn't say anything—"

She held out her knife. "I'm saying it now. So, either shut up or I'll cut out your vocal cords, alright?"

The fire in the girl's eyes said everything. She wasn't kidding. The boy must have seen it, too, because he didn't say another word until we neared the bridge separating the Fourth from the Inner Rings.

*

If I had to break down the difference between the Inner and Outer Rings, it's that the Outer Rings produced things and the Inner Rings financed things. The Inner Rings was where the money circulated. Us folks in The Outer Rings took care of the basic needs of food and shelter and in return, they took care of paying us and making sure the system didn't come crashing down on our heads.

A river that measured a hundred miles across separated The Inner and Outer Rings. The sun glistened off of it and shimmered into my eyes. I had never seen anything so beautiful or wondrous as the City's crystal-clear skyline, backlit by the sun, and the river flowing so sweetly and calmly at its feet.

"It's beautiful, isn't it?" the boy asked under his breath so that the Sixer couldn't hear.

I nodded. "I've never seen anything like it."

"You know how they make the—"

"*Shhhh.* Just let me enjoy it."

Captivated by the beauty of the approaching city, I watched in awe as it grew in front of me, becoming more wondrous with each turn of the train's wheels. Until that moment, I had never known such splendor. I had made the right decision to come here. For the first time, I felt true happiness. I felt peace. Then it all came crashing down.

I didn't hear the clicking of the tracks until it was too late. A pop. Two beeps. And then a thunderous explosion sent me shooting backwards. My head crashed into the back of my seat. We shook and skated along the track, thumping along the way.

Our cabin swung out over the water and the train let out a guttural moan as it tilted toward the water below. My stomach crashed into my throat as we hit the water full force.

I slammed against the window and water gushed over me. Everything went fuzzy, then dark.

CHAPTER 5

When I regained consciousness, I was waist-deep in water, gasping for air. Blood and water blurred my vision as a murky mixture of water, coal, soot and engine oil crashed over my head and threatened to push me under forever. Screams echoed up and down the narrow chamber.

Somebody yelled above me. "Bill! Get up, Bill!"

"Harriet! Oh my god! Come on! We have to go!" another person shouted.

I blinked and struggled to think clearly. *There was an explosion, and then we fell into the water.* But, with each second, the water gushed higher and higher. I had to get out.

The train was sinking vertically, further and further down into the depths. The only way out was climbing up. I could survive this. I could survive anything. I reached my right arm toward the seat behind me, but it seared in pain from a deep gash in my shoulder. I saw blood oozing into the water. Grinding my teeth against the sting, I pulled myself up onto the next seat.

My vision fogged from the pain and I was dizzier than I had ever been in my life, but I kept going. I fought through it all. I climbed and climbed, foregoing the pain in my arms and soreness in my bruised legs. I had strong legs from lifting hay bales out of threshers and into trucks my whole life. Thank the Five for that.

"Give me your arm," a voice cried from above me. "I'll pull you up!"

It was Thomas from the food cart. His eyes were panicked, and he was panting. His voice cracked, "I don't have all day! Let's go!"

I threw my arm towards him and it slipped through his hand. I tried again but couldn't reach. He bent down further. "Try again! One more time! Then I'm leaving you!"

I swung again and missed a third time.

He looked down at me. "I'm sorry."

Thomas dove out of the train. I couldn't blame him for saving his own hide, but I finally understood a universal truth I'd heard Dad mutter under his breath at least once a month: people only look out for themselves. Would I have done any different though? Probably not, but that's little comfort when you're about to die.

The water had filled the train car up to my neck now. I gasped for air until there was none left. The water burned my lungs something awful. *This is it, I guess.* So much for the Center. My tears joined the water when I considered the way I'd left my parents.

Then, something smacked me across the face— an outstretched arm from a lifeless body. I hesitated for a moment, but I wouldn't fail to save myself a second time, no matter how gross the salvation.

I grabbed onto the back of a seat, lunged, and latched onto the arm. I struggled against my own weight until I pulled myself above the water line, exhausted.

The exit door lay sideways next to me. The water bubbled under my feet. I sucked in a great puff of air and rolled out into the deep. For a moment, I floated motionless in the water. The train crashed and careened onto the sea floor. How many bodies did it drag down with it?

I didn't have time for an answer. My lungs burned, my body ached, and my arms throbbed in pain. All I wanted to do was die—and I'd come so close—but I had to live. I forced myself to kick my legs toward the surface.

It took all my might, but I eventually emerged above the water. I was spent. I could have fallen back under the surface right then if a hand hadn't grabbed my butt. I was about to smack it until I realized it was a dead body floating to the surface; no doubt a victim of the crash that paid the ultimate price. There were dozens of bodies in the water around me. I should have died like them, but somehow, I had survived. I thanked the Five in that moment for my life.

*

It took me over an hour to kick my way to the shore. It was slow going, but the heat of exercise warmed my freezing body. I kicked as hard and fast as I could. I thought of home, of Mama, of how I would tell Dad he was right, how I would never leave home again, how the world was cruel, fickle, and mean. The Inner Rings *were* dangerous. All I wanted to do all day was lay on the grass and let the wind whip against my face.

I used the last of my strength to pull myself onto the grassy shore. There were a couple dozen other survivors there, along with multiple ambulances. I recognized the Sixer I'd sat next to on the train, the nerdy boy who stole the seat next to me, and Thomas from the food cart, who made good on saving himself at my expense. He came over to me after a medic finished tending to him.

"I'm so sorry," he said.

How could I respond? There was nothing to say to somebody who didn't value my life enough to stay around another minute and help me. But who was I to judge? We all did what we had to do to survive.

He had been kind to me once. He looked like the sort of man who would be torn apart if I gave him a cold look and I couldn't live with that on my conscience, so I cracked a tiny smile. I didn't know if I could smile anymore, but I fought against the horrible feelings inside to force one out.

*

Medics gave me warm blankets and dry clothes. "You're lucky," one of them said. "Another few minutes in that freezing water and you might have lost a toe."

"A toe," I replied. "That would have been a tragedy worse than death."

Some of the survivors went with the medics when they left. Others went with the military police for questioning. Eventually, all that was left on the beach was a pile of wet clothes, the Sixer, the nerd, and me.

"Where are you headed?" she asked me.

"Ummm...the Center. For Transference," I replied.

"Cool. I'm headed that way too. Are you ready to get your mind sucked out?"

"I mean the chances of that are small, right? I mean the odds are like—"

The nerd, whose name was Henry, chimed in over the water lapping onto the shore. "The average Transference has ten thousand boys and eight thousand girls. Of that, four are chosen. I would bet that this time there are half that, since it's been planned in such a rush. Given that, there should be roughly nine thousand possible Vessels to choose from, which means chances you are chosen would be roughly point-oh-four percent."

The Sixer whipped around to Henry. "You're that nerdy dude from the train. The one I almost eviscerated, right?"

Henry gulped. "I doubt it would have come to that, but yes."

"I'm shocked you didn't die. Most Fours are pussies. They would've drowned in that train crunching survival numbers without ever taking action, but not you. You survived." She smiled. "That shows balls, and saying dumb stuff, like what just came out of your mouth, shows that you don't give a care about what other people think. I like that."

"Thanks," Henry said, confused. "Well, in that case, I think it makes sense for us to travel together, since we are all going to the same place."

"Why does that make sense?" the girl asked. "Do you have any idea where you're going?"

"Some," Henry cocked his head toward me. "Do you?"

I shook my head. "No, but I'm sure there's a map somewhere. I mean it's in the center of the City, right?"

"Wow, you really do need my help. Fine. We can go together." She stuck out her hand. "I'm Joan."

CHAPTER 6

I didn't understand the Third. It wasn't like the Outer Rings at all. There were big buildings, loud noises, and everybody seemed angry. Actually, that last part I got. If I lived somewhere so densely packed, I would be angry all the time too.

And the homeless people. There were so many homeless people everywhere. The Third's lush parks and sidewalks were crammed with hundreds of shanties constructed of metal and cardboard, each filled with dozens of wretched looking people huddled together. It was almost too much for me to bear, and after all I'd just been through, I could bear a lot.

We zigged and zagged through the city streets like old pros. Joan walked in front of us, guiding Henry and me through the throngs of people moving their way through the streets. They acted like it was the most normal thing in the world to be constantly touching complete strangers.

Joan was being modest when she said knew the Third a little bit. From what I could tell, she knew every square inch.

"The shanties are exclusive to the Third. The Outer Rings don't have them and the rings closer to the Center won't allow them." Joan shrugged. "So, they all end up here."

"Why are there so many Muties here?" Henry asked. "It would be more prudent to disperse them throughout the City. There are thousands of miles of uninhabited land in the Sixth."

I thought back to Thomas. He wasn't living in squalor, from what I could tell. He got out, somehow. Clearly, that wasn't normal.

"I don't know why they're all here," Joan said. "I'm not a tour guide. It does suck to be them, though. They can't find jobs because of who they are, and nobody will rent to them because it's illegal. It's tough when you're a Mutie. Nobody wants you."

Muties had it worse than anybody in the City because they were an affront to the natural order. In order to breed officially, you had to fill out an application. DNA tests were administered to test for anomalies and ministers conducted interviews with the candidates. If they were compatible, permission was granted to procreate. If not, they were rejected. If you were rejected but still wanted kids, or didn't want to go through all the hassle, you tried to have a kid and hide it. It never worked. They were always found.

Muties tainted the bloodline to the Five. There was a genetic reason why their births weren't approved. If they were allowed to breed, it could cause defects for generations to come. We don't have a lot of people in the City, and it's not like we can just migrate to another town somewhere across the horizon to find new blood. We were stuck breeding with the people inside the Bubble, so even one small mutation in a single person could lead to disaster for all of us.

Worse, they were a constant reminder of what happens when citizens rebel against the Five. The Five demanded complete obedience from their flock. We were at the mercy of their whims. The Muties were the embodiment of defiance and a constant reminder to the Five that rebellion was possible. Thus, they had to be dealt with swiftly and harshly to serve as an example for all of us.

"It doesn't make much sense, though, does it?" Henry said. "The Inner Rings are meant for financiers, not Muties. There's much less room here than in a similarly sized camp in the Sixth."

I looked down and saw a young woman with a symbol branded into her arm. It was the shape of the seven rings. I knew what it meant immediately. She was a Mutie.

"Yeah," I broke in, "but then they'd be out of sight and out of mind."

"Then why not just kill them?" Henry asked.

"They can't just go killing everybody," Joan said. "There has to be some illusion they care about us, even if it's not true."

We stopped at the tallest tower in the Third and I recognized it immediately; I'd swum toward it after the crash. The building seemed even more impossibly big standing in front of it. I craned my neck, but even squinting, I couldn't make out the spire I'd seen from the river.

Joan walked inside. "From the top, we can see everything. Then I'll be able to get my bearings."

The security guard at the front desk laughed when he saw our frizzy hair and the poorly fitting clothes we'd been given. It also didn't help that we smelled like wet dogs from hours in the water. We certainly didn't look like the businessmen and tradesmen he was used to greeting.

"State your business," the security guard said.

"We want to see the top of the tower."

"Thirty each," he stated.

"We don't have any money," Joan said. "We're coming from the Outer rings for the Transference and well...we were on the train...you know, the one that went boom."

"I'm very sorry to hear that," the guard said. His expression softened. "I'll tell you what, twenty each then."

"You aren't being very fair, sir," Henry said. "We are just children, and we have gone through a terrible ordeal. All we want is to see the top of the tower and we'll be on our way."

I could tell by the guard's eyes he wouldn't be swayed by logic, and Henry was all logic. Annoying, constant logic.

"Look," I said. "We could be picked for the Transference, lose our consciousness, and never get to see anything again. All I wanna do before that happens is to see the City from the top of this building one time. Is that so much to ask?"

Tears bubbled in my eyes. I always knew, intellectually, that I could be chosen, but saying it out loud made it so real. What if I became a hollow husk for the Five? The thought of it suddenly was too much. I started sobbing.

Joan saw an opening. "Do you see what this is doing to her? Can't you just let her up this one time?"

"I could lose my job," he said, glancing down the hall.

"And we could lose our lives. What about that? Aren't we all supposed to sacrifice for the greater good? What have you done for the greater good today, huh? Have you ever been as selfless as we are?"

*

Moments later we were in a glass elevator shooting up to the top floor. I had never been in an elevator before. There were no buildings in the Fifth more than a few stories tall. The butterflies in my stomach mingled with my terror. I watched the City grow smaller and smaller as we rose into the clouds.

"So, this thing could just fall right now?" Henry asked. His annoying voice grated my ears, but his words disconcerted me.

"It could," Joan replied. "But it won't."

"But what if it does?" Henry asked. "The odds of a crash are miniscule, but still possible."

Joan shrugged. "You already survived one disaster today. What are the chances of a second one? Not very high."

The elevator dinged on the top floor and the doors slid open. We stepped out into the glass tower. The walls were made of huge, glass panels that looked out over the entire city. My heart pounded, but Joan showed no fear, rushing both of us toward the window.

"Wow! It's so beautiful. Check it out. You can see all the way to the edge of the Bubble from here!"

I inched forward, and Joan pulled me close. Sure enough, in every direction I could see the blue hue of the Bubble as it ascended from the edge to a point above us. I had seen glimpses of the Bubble from the farm but was never able to make out the top of it before. Being several hundred feet into the air, the gridlines converged at a point in the sky right above us.

Henry pressed his nose to the glass. "They say there's a laser in the tip of this building that keeps the bubble steady and gives the outer shell a point to shoot for."

His words barely registered. I studied how the rolling darkness of the coal mines bled into the vibrant pasture of the farms, which crashed into the silos and warehouses that drained into the factories and finally into the river.

My eyes tracked to the smoking chasm in the bridge, where the wreck had been, that led to the Inner Rings. Robots and workers worked hard to fix it. They had to work quickly. There were only four crossings in the Inner Rings, one in each direction.

Joan pointed at a huge building in the middle of another island nestled inside the Third. "There it is. The Center. Everything in the whole City spreads out from there. It's kind of a dump if you ask me, though. They haven't updated it in forever."

The Center was enormous, big enough to be a ring all by itself, filled with buildings of every size, shape, and variety. In the middle was a glass dome, and to its left stood a processing plant. On the other side were twenty silos for storing food.

Henry pushed his glasses to his nose. "It's completely self-sustaining, you know, just in case of a disaster. The Five...well Four now, could live for the rest of eternity without ever stepping a foot outside."

That would be my life if I were chosen. I would never see the outside world. I would never see the Outer Rings, or my home or anything else, again. I would be a shell.

After we got our bearings, we left the building and walked outside into a sea of citizens crashing on us. Joan pushed against the waves of people stampeding into her. Hundreds, thousands even, flooded the streets simultaneously, flanked by guards corralling them toward a single point in the distance. I'd seen this sort of herd mentality before when cows were led to slaughter. "What is going on?"

Joan pulled us into an alleyway. "Don't move. They're headed toward the Square. Something must be happening—something bad. Keep quiet. The guards have better things to do than check every alley for stragglers."

I didn't ask questions. I knew enough to stay quiet. Henry wasn't as quick to comply. "I just don't under—"

Joan wrapped her fingers around his jaw and squeezed his mouth closed. "I said *shhh*."

I crouched down into the grimy darkness. It smelled like piss. Thousands of feet passed me. We watched the boots and feet go past until they trickled to a stop. Once it was quiet, Joan stood. "I think we're clear. Let's see what the hubbub's about, bub."

Joan pulled open the door to a nearby building. "Quietly," she whispered. We climbed up the stairs and onto the roof. Two blocks away there was a park with thousands of people gathered in front of an open stage. Military police stood guard around the park. Behind the row of officers guarding the stage, the miserable wretches screamed and clawed to get out. An officer nailed a crying woman with the butt of his gun. Blood streamed out of her nose and made her wail harder.

The Third was the financial capital of the City but this was more like a madhouse. It was hard to believe all the money in the City flowed through these streets. The Thirds were supposed to be cunning and powerful, but they looked more like sheep than captains of industry.

*

Once the crowd calmed into submission, a military Jeep drove into the Square, parting the crowd like a sea. Four soldiers flanked the Jeep on either side as it drove up to the stage and stopped.

Earth stepped out of the Jeep and stomped up to the stage. I could tell it was Earth, even from a few hundred yards away. Nobody else wore a purple dress like that except Earth, and only when she was delivering important news. You couldn't even buy that color purple without being arrested. It was the same color she wore to tell us Wind died.

Guards pulled three prisoners, wearing orange jumpsuits and hoods over their heads, out of the Jeep and pushed them onto the stage behind her.

"This isn't good," Joan whispered, scratching her exposed arms. I looked down and noticed a huge scar on her forearm.

"How did you get that scar?" Henry asked.

Joan pulled her arm away. "In a mine accident when I was ten. Machinery gets hot down there. I was careless and stupid."

Two hovering televisions popped up on either side of Earth, broadcasting her face across the Square. "Good morning, citizens. I wish I came to you under better circumstances. It is never pleasant to be unpleasant."

The guards behind Earth forced the prisoners onto the ground, then stepped back and aimed their massive guns at the prisoners' heads.

"This morning there was an attack of terror carried out on a train bound for the Inner Rings...a train that carried military men, a train that carried children... to the Center. This was a despicable act carried out by cowardly members of our society."

"The unwanted, the sullied, or Muties, as you may know them, have been shown enormous generosity over the millennia, even though they are an affront to everything we stand for in our beautiful City. We care for them, we wash them, we give them shelter, and by all accounts we should kill them. Yet we do not. Do you not think that magnanimous of us?"

The group collectively groaned a "yes." It was unenthusiastic by even the laxest standards.

"And yet, Muties continue to commit atrocities upon us, even as we give them everything! Look at the cowards who committed these horrors upon your people!"

The soldiers pulled the bags off the prisoners' heads, revealing dirty, frightened, beaten, and piteous faces.

"We are one people in this City. One people that survived for thousands of years by working together—and only because we worked together. A hand cannot function without a face, nor can a heart without a brain. We are one organism and at a time when we are recovering from such a deep wound, these animals have done the unthinkable. While we grieve for Wind, they plot brutality. It sickens me."

The image on the screen switched from Earth to the guards behind her. They cocked their guns and pointed them at the prisoners.

"So, let me make this clear to anybody who would try to wound us, to anybody who would try to stop this beautiful machine from working. We will find you. And you will feel our wrath."

"They aren't actually going to kill them, are they?" Henry asked. It was the first useful question he'd asked, and I wanted to know the answer as well.

It didn't take long to get one. The bullets rang across the square, and the three traitors lay dead on the ground. I screamed when the bodies hit the stage floor, but the crowd didn't even flinch.

Joan clasped her hand over my mouth and tackled me to the ground. "You can't scream. They'll hear us. We do not want to be found."

I'd never seen anyone killed before. I had seen a dead person; I'd just never seen anyone actually die. It was brutality at its core.

Henry didn't scream, but he didn't speak, or move a single muscle either. He was in shock. If he could be brave and silent, I could too. I calmed my heart and breathed deep.

A moment later Joan let go of my mouth. I sat and looked down at the unfazed crowd. "I don't understand. Why isn't everybody freaking out?"

"They see it all the time. It's old hat to them. That's why I like the Outer Rings. You don't see this crap in person. You— we get to live in blissful ignorance."

Earth's voice boomed again. "I'm sorry you had to see that. It breaks my heart every time. The Five created you in our likeness. The death of one is the death of all."

Earth breathed deeply. "However, we cannot stand idly by and let this City rip itself apart. Justice must be swift, and it has been swift. These deaths do not take away those innocents lost on the train, but if they can prevent more deaths in the future, it is worth it. Thank you."

After it was over, Earth got back in her Jeep and drove off like nothing had happened. The police disbanded, and the people moseyed away, like it was another normal day. But it wasn't normal for me.

I mean there was death on the farm. Cows, chickens, pigs were slaughtered all the time. I even slaughtered some of them. People died in the Fifth too, some even suddenly. However, I'd never seen a person killed like an animal. "How have I never seen something like this before, in the hundreds of hours of television I've watched?"

"I've seen it a dozen times," Henry said. "Never up close, though and never in real time. Sometimes businessmen from the Inner Rings would come into the warehouses and show videos of it to my dad, like it was funny. Dad pretended to laugh with them. What else could he do? It was his job."

I placed my hand on Henry's to stop his trembling. "That's horrible. I've never seen it in the Fifth."

"They don't want you to see it," Joan said. "It's a whole different world in the Inner Rings. Out there we can be naïve. You do your job. You do it well. You keep the machinery working. Keep everybody fed, clothed, and on track. But, here it's different. They don't do anything. They are consumers. They are gamblers. They work with their minds, not their hands. It gives them more time...time to rebel. It gives them more need for harsh justice—even if it's unjust."

"Unjust?" I asked. "But those guys blew up the train. Don't you resent them?"

Joan shook her head. "Did they though, Althea? Or were they just brought in for swift justice?" she asked, cocking an eyebrow. "Come on, we have to go if we want to make it to the Second tonight."

*

Joan was right. The Inner Rings weren't like the Outer Rings. You could walk from the Bubble all the way to the tip of the Fourth if you wanted. But things were different in the Inner Rings. People from the Third never saw people from the Second, and they never interacted with people from the First. Each of the Inner Rings was a completely segregated society.

"The Outer Rings do their jobs and do them well," Joan told me. "You don't aspire to anything else. Here, nothing would get done if the Third didn't aspire to the Second. You can't aspire to something if you don't see it every day."

After the explosion, the Center shut the trains down throughout the entire city, meaning we could only get to the Second by ferry until they told us otherwise. The problem was that ferries were hard to come by in the Third. The Second wasn't rolling out any welcome mats for us.

"Why would they make it so hard?" I asked. "I mean they invited everybody into the Center for Transference."

"Based on Joan's supposition, it seems they want people in the Inner Rings as segregated as possible to prevent insurrection," Henry surmised.

"Yeah. That's one reason. They do a good job acting inclusive, don't they? What do you think would happen if every Mutie could get to the Center, huh? It would be chaos."

The sun set over the water on the pristine Second Ring as we got to the ferry. It wasn't full of high rises or skyscrapers. It was a peaceful beach village, pleasant and calm, unlike the dock that led us there. The line for the ferry stretched a quarter mile and wrapped around the next dock. People shoved and shouted at each other.

"What's going on here?" Joan asked loudly.

"They're all waiting for the ferry," Henry said, pointing to a schedule on the side of a building. "The next one should begin boarding any moment."

Joan approached a miserable looking sod sitting on a barrel. "How long have you been here waiting?"

"Two days," the man responded. "I'll probably be waiting a couple more at this rate."

Joan walked back over to us. "I don't have four days to wait."

Henry's eyes rolled in his head. "Well, if we count the amount of people here and weigh it against the possibility of getting on a ship, then we should only have to wait a day, maybe two at most. Based upon this schedule at least."

Joan chuckled. "I don't have that kind of time, either. Come on. I have a better idea. We're going to wait for them to start calling names and slip past them."

"That's crazy," Henry said. "What if they find us?"

"Then you go home or find another way to keep going. Simple as that. Agreed?"

I nodded along with Henry, "I don't have anything better," I said.

We walked up to the barge as a fat woman with a clipboard waddled alone across the plank. We inched forward through the sea of people until we were past her.

"Bryant! Cumberland! On the boat!" She continued calling names over and over in a monotonous tone.

After the first few shuffled on board, Joan pushed me over the stern and then hopped over it herself. "Come on."

She grabbed my hand and pulled me up the stairs and into the cargo deck. Henry leapt on board behind us. We hugged the wall and prayed we wouldn't be seen. In the darkness, I could barely even see Joan. I felt her head tuck into my shoulder. "Go to bed. It's a long, slow ride."

I didn't need another word of convincing. I rested my head on Joan's and drifted off to sleep.

CHAPTER 7

It was harder to sleep on a boat than a train. I actually longed for the uncomfortable chairs of the train—at least those had a little support and were designed for sitting. The ship was unyielding, and it swayed unbearably. My eyes popped open before long and I couldn't force them closed again.

"Go back to sleep," Joan muttered.

"The boat is making me nauseous. All this musty air and rocking."

Joan pulled her head off my shoulder. "I guess that means I can't sleep either."

"No. Please don't stay up because of me."

"It's fine. We've been on this boat for a while. It won't be long now."

"How do you know that?"

"I know because I grew up in the First Ring, alright?" She sighed. "My mom and dad...they thought they were above the law. They didn't even apply to have me. The Five didn't like that. Nobody is above their rules."

I feigned surprise. "Oh?"

Joan's eyes dropped. She instinctively rubbed her forearm. "Yeah. Mom and Dad paid a lot of money to send me away. They smuggled me out of the Inner Rings and told me never to come back. I drifted through every ring trying to find my place, but there was no place for me, even in the Sixth. When I heard about the Transference I decided to come back and try my luck."

"But they'll lock you up when they find out."

"Oh, I'm not going to the Center. I'm going to see dear old Mom and Dad. Ask them why they did this to me."

I rubbed the scar on Joan's forearm. "This isn't from the mine, is it?"

Joan shook her head. Tears streamed down her face. "I've...never...told anybody...that. You must...hate me..."

I didn't. I should have, maybe, but I didn't. I'd heard my whole life that Muties were the worst form of evil—that they weren't even people but animals. I had watched Earth execute three in front of me and nobody batted an eye. Yet, Joan was kind, and nice, and savvy and I liked her, even though she was a Mutie.

"I really couldn't care less where you're from."

Joan smiled. "Thank you."

That's when the dry heaving started. I held them in at first. I thought I could control them, or that I'd get over it. Then the retching took over. My body began to spasm until it became unbearable. I ran out of the cabin and heaved over the side of the boat.

*

I vomited until we reached the shore. Between heaves, I looked out onto the clear ocean and up into the hazy morning sun. It rose over the cozy beach city of the Second. Twofers were merchants. They owned the means of production. They were regal, headstrong, and entitled. All of the money flowing through the Third came from the Second.

The crisp air from the cold sea chilled me to the bone. I wanted to be inside, but I couldn't walk back into the hold without the spins taking over.

"It's pretty, right?" a nasal voice asked. It was Henry. "You know they don't actually have a sunset or sunrise here. It's all programmed at the Center—same for the heat you feel, and the cold. It's all in our minds."

"Why do you have to ruin everything, huh? This was such a nice, peaceful moment."

"I don't know. It irritates my mother to no end. We all know about these things in the Fourth, but don't talk about it. It's fascinated me since I was a kid."

I laughed for the first time in a long while. "You really have no filter on that thing, huh? Just shut up, Henry and look out at the water. Real or not, it's beautiful."

"How do you know? You've never seen anything else." He paused for a moment. "I'll shut up now."

*

The citizens of the Second walked around with big old smiles on their faces everywhere they went. They stood tall and proud. In the Fifth, we wore our burdens heavy on our backs. Our feet clomped, and our backs sagged. I had never seen anybody stand so tall as they did in the Second. It was like they didn't have a care in the world.

The streets in the Second were pristine, with no signs of trash, dust, or grime anywhere. Everything gleamed bright and wondrous. It hurt my eyes to stare too long.

A pair of guards stood on every corner, protecting the streets filled with retail shops and restaurants. The smells from the bakeries and sweet shops tore at my stomach. I hadn't eaten since the sandwich on the train. That was days ago.

"I'm hungry," Joan asked. "Are you hungry?"

"Oh my god, I'm so hungry."

"I am famished as well," Henry said. "But the river swallowed my money along with all my earthly possessions."

Joan smiled a sneaky smile. "Don't worry about that, just go into the alley and wait. I'll be back in a couple minutes. I got this."

We waited for Joan in an alleyway that smelled like lilies. Most alleys were dingy and smelt like trash and piss. But, in the Second, the allies were cleaner than my own house, even after I'd scrubbed the whole thing.

I didn't know what Joan was doing, but she was taking forever to do it. I was starting to worry she wouldn't come back, and I couldn't take much more of Henry's facts and figures.

"The Second is the only Ring that doesn't have a specialized group of people," he said. "Or I should say, they have many specialties. Since this is where families of Transference winners move once their child's brain is zapped, there are farmers, logistics specialists, financiers, and even miners living, eating, and working together. It's the only place in the City where that happens. Isn't that fascinating?"

"What about along the Bubble, or in the military?"

"Well, yes, but since they are Muties, they technically don't count for—"

"I would stop talking now," I growled. "Just sit there and wait. In silence."

I stared down the alley, expecting Joan to materialize any second, but she never did. Maybe she'd realized she was sick of me and bolted. Or maybe she was sick of Henry. That I could understand. Getting to the Center was possible without Joan, but it would be way less fun.

I wondered what it was like to bounce from ring to ring, never finding your place. The people of the First weren't known for their survival skills and Joan's parents had condemned her to death by sending her out into the cold, dark world. They didn't pull the trigger, but to think somebody from the First—with no life skills or proper breeding for manual labor could make it in the Outer Rings, devoid of friends or a way to make money—was cruel and heartless. Yet, she'd survived, despite everything going against her.

I wished I could be there when Joan knocked on that door. I would love to see the look on her parents' faces when they realized their daughter was alive. Would they be elated or horrified? That's a question no child should ever have to wonder. Thankfully, my family had never made me feel like that. They had always made me feel safe, secure, and wanted.

Finally, Joan appeared, racing across the street with a bag full of food.

I took a few steps toward her—or toward the food. "What took you so long?"

"*Shhh*," Joan said. "Just keep going."

A scream erupted behind her. "Somebody stole my food!"

"Crap!" Joan shouted. "Run."

I took off behind Joan as two military police officers broke into a sprint after us. We crossed between the alleyways, bolting down one after another. The officers clipped our heels at every turn.

"I can't believe they care this much about a little food," I yelled at Joan between gasps of air.

"They care about everything here," she shouted back. "That's how it's so pristine. It's a police state and a euphoric police state at that. The citizens don't know any better. Outsiders hate coming here because they rule with an iron fist. You can't do anything here without being shot on sight."

"Why would you risk steal something then?" Henry asked and this time, I couldn't find fault with Henry's logic.

"We have to eat. I figured if I waited until just the right moment, we'd get away with it. I mean, everything's a calculated risk, right?"

Joan turned a corner and I stopped short when I heard an officer shout. "Stop right there!"

As Henry and I backed up in the shadows of a big dumpster, I realized that the policeman couldn't see us.

"Go," Joan whispered from the side of her mouth.

"I'm not—"

"Go!" she whispered again before taking a step forward. "Officer, can we talk about this?"

Joan had proved to me that she had known best in every situation thus far, so I listened to her and pulled Henry down an alley. I prayed to the Five she would be fine. I prayed for Wind to watch over her.

Two gunshots rang out and Joan's body hit the pavement.

The Five were worthless.

*

I should have stayed away. It was a huge risk going back, and Joan would have hated me for it, but I didn't care. Not even if they shot me on the spot. All I cared about was my friend.

I didn't ask Henry to come with me, but he tagged along anyway, his face solemn. Joan had meant something to him, too. It was the second experience of death we'd had together. Too bad everything that tied us together was so horrible thus far.

The alley was empty when we ran back into it. Empty, except for Joan lying on the ground whimpering in a pool of blood. Big wet tears rolled down my face as I kneeled down.

Joan smiled at me through the blood that lined her mouth. "Don't worry about me. I've had worse."

I smiled at her through my tears. I couldn't help it. Even in her worst moment, she tried to comfort me. "You made it all the way out to the Sixth and back again. You are so close. Stay with me."

Joan rummaged through her coat and pulled out a picture. Her hand smeared it in blood. I glanced down at it. The picture was of her parents, smiling, holding her as a baby. On the back, I could just make out the address under Joan's blood. "Give it to my parents, okay? Tell them I still love them. I just wanted to make them proud. I think they'll like that."

"You're going to make it. You're going to be fine."

Joan smiled at me for a moment. "Liar."

She slumped back as the life drained out of her face. Only cold, dead, lifeless eyes stared back at me.

I wept. I wept until I had no tears, then I wept until the tears came back. I stayed there beside her until I heard the noise of police officers coming back to dispose of her body.

"We can't stay here," Henry said through ragged breathing. "We...have to...go."

I allowed him to drag me to my feet. Then we ran. I ran away and left my friend...forever. If I hadn't asked her to come with me, if I had just let her leave, she would still be alive. I would never get over that.

*

The world is a cruel, dark place. I'd heard that my whole life but never believed it. I didn't want to believe it, either. Now it was right there in front of me. A bag of food had meant more than Joan's life. An unsanctioned birth was a death sentence. They hadn't even made the food—we reaped it in the Fifth—but they had no problem killing my friend over it.

I wanted to stop and go home, but I knew couldn't do that. I'd come this far, fought through so much; I'd risked everything and seen so much wanton death. If I gave up, it would be a slap in the face to all of them. It would be a slap in the face to Joan.

I held Joan's picture in my hand the rest of the day as Henry and I stared out at the river. For once Henry was silent. There was nothing to say. I liked him when he was silent. I even let him lean his head on mine.

*

Public transportation wasn't an option to get any closer toward the Center. Additionally, I was covered in Joan's blood. Until I crossed into the First, I would have to stay on the back roads.

I had told Henry to leave me and go on alone, but he wouldn't. "We started this together. We owe it to Joan to see it through to the end. Wouldn't you agree?"

I did. I didn't like Henry much at first. He wasn't much to look at and he talked too much, but he was sweet, and he had a confidence that allowed him to keep going even in the face of great danger. I let him take my hand in his as we walked out of the Second and toward the Center.

*

There was no industry in the First. The entire ring was reserved exclusively for the descendants of the first Transference, those without any genetic interference from the Five. The first of our kind, the entire world was built in the First's image. They were praised in the Book of Books and their lives were written into our songs. We celebrated their birthdays with fireworks.

Joan would have been one of them if her parents had played by the rules. Instead she'd been cast out. If she had been birthed the right way and lived a normal life, we might have celebrated her birthday in schools. Her picture would have been in my textbook.

But if Joan had grown up in the First, I would have hated her for being an uptight jerk with silver spoons dangling from her mouth. But at least she would be alive. If she had been in the First, if her parents hadn't abandoned her, Joan would still be alive.

A butler walked Henry and I inside Joan's old house, an ancient mansion, and sat me down in a palatial living room. He didn't comment on the blood-stained clothes I wore. Actually, nobody had commented on them as we snuck our way through the First. They were too busy feeling better than everyone else to glance down at the urchins scurrying past them.

The living room was bigger than our whole farm and taller than the steeple of our church. Heck, with its gilded and ornate walls, the room was fancier than our church, too. The detailing of the marble must have taken ages. I knew I didn't have any right to be here, but I was here for Joan. I wrapped my hands tightly inside Henry's and looked him in the face. His eyes brought me strength.

After a couple moments, an elegantly dressed middle-aged couple glided across the room and took their seats across from me. I quickly noticed they didn't have a single wrinkle between them. By the time people in the Fifth were their age, years of backbreaking work in the hot sun had cracked and browned our skin.

"I hear you have some information for me," the man began, tight-lipped, his words fast and short.

"And be quick about it," the wife added. "I have tennis lessons in ten minutes."

He tugged on the lapels of his jacket as he nodded in agreement, his moves graceful and fluid. Even more perfect than the Twofers. You can't teach elegance-- that kind of sophistication was bred into you. I didn't know how to say the words. I didn't know how to say that Joan was dead. I couldn't. Every time I opened my mouth, the tears started. So, I pulled the picture out of my pocket and held it up. "Is this your daughter?"

The man looked intently at the photo, his face expressionless. He didn't even flinch at the bloodstained paper. "Why? What do you want from us? Is it money? I won't be blackmailed if that's what you're after."

"No...no, it's— I met her. She helped me. She gave me this picture before— before—."

Tears welled in the woman's eyes. "Before what? Is she okay?"

The man gave her a stern look and she tried her best to pull it together. That's not how an elegant lady behaves, losing themselves in their emotions.

I opened my mouth to answer her, but nothing came out. I fought back tears. Luckily, Henry was strong enough for both of us. "She's dead."

The woman gasped as tears streamed down her face. "What?" she whimpered. "How?"

The man snatched the picture. "Does it really matter how, dear? She's dead." He tossed the picture to me. "We won't be needing this."

"Are you sure about that?" I asked. "Joan was a good girl. She helped me over and over again and taught me things. She survived really well, until she didn't. She even asked me to tell you that she loved you. All she ever wanted was to make you proud."

The man's eyes showed no mercy. They were cold and calculating. "That's enough. Take the picture back."

Henry jolted up. "You are bad people. You brought your daughter into this world and don't care how cruelly she left it. I should report you to the Center, but I won't. I won't because Joan wouldn't want that. She only wanted to say she loved you. That's all. I'm sad my friend is dead, but very glad she never saw you again. You would have broken her heart."

It was everything I wanted to say, but couldn't, and yet Henry said it without a moment's hesitation. I loved him for that, and for pulling my jellied legs up to leave. I left the picture on the table. "She wanted you to have it. It was her last request." I looked at the woman. "I'll leave it to you to throw it out, if you want."

It pained me to leave the picture. It was all I had left of Joan, but I made a promise. The man reached for the picture, but the wife snatched it away. I could tell it was an act of defiance she didn't risk often.

Joan would have approved.

*

Henry and I walked the rest of the way to the Center, our hands clasped together. The air was cold, but it felt good against my warm cheeks. I curled under Henry's arm for warmth. I remembered how he'd told me that the temperature was an illusion conjured by the Five and it wasn't real. Possibly, I wasn't even cold. Nobody alive today except the Five even knew cold. They had manufactured and bred us all to be perfect citizens, so cold could mean whatever they wanted it to.

It seemed like so long ago that Henry had told me that, but it was only yesterday. Leaving home had felt like it was years ago, but it hadn't even been a week. Joan was the best friend I'd ever had, and we'd only just met.

It hurt to think of her. I could barely stand the thought without collapsing, but I couldn't turn away from it either. I didn't want to. Remembering Joan made me feel alive, if only for a moment and that was worth all the pain a million times over.

We crested a ridge and the Center came into view. Hundreds of buildings in every imaginable size, shape, color, and type lined the horizon. Lines of teenagers stretched for miles in front of two huge openings shining brightly in the darkness.

"There it is," Henry said. "The Center. We made it."

We tumbled down the hill and came face to face with a wall of military police. My throat clenched. I once saw them as a welcome sight bringing order to chaos. Now, they were only murderers, and I was drenched in the blood of their victim.

"Are you here for the Transference?" one of them asked.

I couldn't think or speak. I just nodded. The guard sighed, rubbing her temples. "Age?"

I blanked. It actually took me a moment to remember how old I was. My lips didn't want to part, but I forced them open. "Seventeen, ma'am."

"Third line. Not second or fourth. The third line."

My hands shook when I parted from Henry. He was in the fifth line full of seventeen-year-old boys. This was it. I wouldn't have any more moments with Henry. I wanted to hold him, kiss him, to feel his skin for one more moment. I might never have the chance again. But I didn't do any of that. I just smiled and said "Goodbye." He just smiled and nodded.

I took my place in the third line down the row, not the first or the second or fourth. I counted four more times just to make sure. There were lines of kids so young I couldn't believe they had traveled alone. Most of them wore infinity necklaces, a symbol of their devotion to the Five. The young girls didn't know better and seemed happy to serve. They didn't understand the heavy burden they were carrying.

The older girls in line with me weren't so naïve. We didn't smile or laugh because we knew any of us could be chosen. We knew that the world was cruel, and life wasn't fair. If it were, none of us would be standing here in the first place.

Transference should have happened when we were all old ladies. Instead, it was happening right at that moment, and we were a part of it.

The shimmering lights of the entrance grew in front of us, and there was a murmur amongst the younger girls. They looked shocked and excited. Those of us in the third line stared straight ahead with vacant expressions. There was no hope. There was only fear and resignation.

There was no turning back now.

BOOK 2

The Center

CHAPTER 1

Turn around! There's still time! Just turn AROUND!

The words ran through my head over and over again as I stood in the monumental line to get into the Center. I couldn't believe I was waiting for a chance to give myself over to the Five. *Was I crazy?* Of course, I was. After what I'd been through, there was no other way to explain why I was still moving forward.

My heart beat in my ears whenever the guards passed. The thought of being inside the Center, the biggest complex in the City, gated off from the rest of the world, "protected" by the type of guards who'd shot three innocent people and my best friend, felt like a death sentence.

They had shot Joan like a diseased animal, just for having the balls to steal a little bit of food so we didn't starve. That was the kind of thing they did in the Inner Rings— shoot people like dogs for minor offenses, all to keep the peace.

Run. Just run. You still have time.

We trudged through the gates one at a time. The rhythmic clapping of our shoes on the concrete streets nearly lulled me to sleep more than once, even standing up. I was so tired. I'd hardly slept since leaving my warm bed at home.

Once inside, the warehouse was underwhelming to even the most optimistic among us. It looked like a regular warehouse, the same kind the Fourth manned.

Its ceilings were hundreds of feet high and fluorescent bulbs dangled down over a registration desk manned by dozens of pale and joyless workers, all clad in tunics and simple glasses. No one made eye contact. There were no smiles. We just moved forward.

The dark-skinned girl in front of me, a Sixer no doubt, walked up to an angry, badger-faced woman. I had caught the coal in her nails as she flicked them nervously. I wanted to care about her, but I didn't. I didn't care about any of them. I just wanted to do my bid and get out.

"Next!" a blonde-haired woman shouted. She wore thick glasses that partially hid the dark bags under her eyes. As it was my turn, I walked up to her gingerly. "Name!"

I breathed deeply, pulling a smile from the depths of my bowels. "Althea Clark, ma'am."

"Outer Rings, I assume."

"Um...that's right. The Fifth."

"Farmer. Got it. Age?"

"Seventeen, ma'am."

She jotted down "17" in her book, stamped it below a thousand other stamps and a thousand other names. Then, the exasperated woman sighed loudly and pointed down a row of tables. I saw the Sixer who'd been in front of me already there, picking up her towel and tunic.

"Next!" The crabby lady shouted, and I was on my way. I scooted down the line toward the Sixer.

A beady-eyed woman smiled at me when I picked up my tunic and towel. "Head behind that curtain over there and strip down. Then follow the line around."

"Excuse me? I'm not stripping down."

The woman looked up. "Yes, you are. Or you can leave. It's your choice."

She flicked her wrist and two guards walked forward. They flanked me on either side. "Is there a problem?"

"This girl doesn't want to strip down," the woman said.

One of them scoffed gruffly at me. "Is that true, girl?"

This was it. I was going to be shot. I knew it. I shook my head and muttered the Five's prayer under my breath. I heard a gun click behind me, and the barrel touched my thigh. "No. No. I just don't understand why I have to strip down."

"That's not important," said another officer. "Just do what you're told or leave."

I couldn't leave. I had to keep going. "Yes, sir."

The guards turned away. The woman smiled again. "Like I said, go into the room and strip down, okay? Once you're done, wrap yourself in the towel. Or don't. I don't care. But don't put the tunic on yet, okay? No more problems."

*

It wasn't much of a changing room. It was just a tarp that covered up to my chin. The taller girls shrunk down so their breasts weren't showing while the shorter girls disappeared under the curtain. I wished I could disappear under the curtain too. I wasn't so lucky. I was the perfect height to see over the changing station comfortably. I saw the humiliation on the faces of those waiting to change, and the tears of those stepping out in just a towel.

The girl next to me sucked in her breath when her bare feet touched the cold concrete. Her pants dropped to the floor and her belt clinked on the ground as she made a poor attempt to hold in her tears.

"It's going to be alright," I said, though I didn't believe it.

"Really?" the girl asked.

No, I thought, *of course not.* "Yes, of course. It's going to be fine."

I really didn't care if the girl felt better, as long as the crying stopped. I couldn't deal with it. It made me want to cry, and if I started crying, I would never stop. If I cried, I wouldn't be able to keep going and I had to keep going.

I undressed, shedding the bloody clothes that kept Joan close to me. Nobody had mentioned the blood stains on my clothes, as if it were normal for a teenager to come to the Center covered in blood. That's the only condemnation of the Center I needed. When I was naked, save for a towel, I pulled the curtain open and stepped outside.

"Just leave everything in there," a guard said. "We'll take care of it."

I watched them throw my clothes into a trashcan, discarding my last mementos of home, my last connection to Joan. Other girls cried as the guards ripped the infinity necklaces from their necks and threw away pictures of their loved ones, but I stayed stone-faced.

All of us were alone. It was a sobering thought. Nobody had any distinguishing features any more. Everybody was the same.

*

It took another cold hour, standing in nothing but a towel, before I reached the front of my second excruciatingly long line of the night, which wrapped around the warehouse like a snake.

Finally, the door popped open and a guard pushed me inside. Before I could protest, the door slammed shut behind me. Tiny, wet footprints ran out the back of the room and disappeared behind a wall.

"Put your tunic down," sighed a large woman. They all sighed so loudly. Why, I wondered? They were in the Center of the world, the greatest, most amazing place on the planet, and yet they sighed like they were watching a math documentary. I put down my tunic on a metal stool in the corner.

"And the towel."

I did what I was told. I exposed myself for the whole world to see, so long as the whole world was inside a fat woman's eyes.

"Step behind the door," she instructed.

A sliding door opened in front of me. The room I walked into was even tinier than the one I had just left, lined with tile from floor to ceiling. Twenty nozzles pointed at me from every direction.

A voice shouted at me from the speaker on the ceiling. "Hold out your arms!"

The room was cold enough to give me immediate goose pimples all over my body. My arms were all I had for warmth. I hugged my breasts as the hairs on my arms stood on end. "Why?"

"Because I said so. Now lift your arms or go home!"

I couldn't go home. There was only one way for me and it was forward. I lifted my arms and sighed loudly. *Maybe this is why they do it,* I thought, *because they are completely exposed all the time.*

Gears whirled behind the tiles and the nozzles spun to life.

"Do not, under any circumstances, lower your arms."

Like a jet engine, water blasted me from every corner. I fought against dropping my arms to protect my face. I prayed for it to stop, but when it did the cold was even worse than the water. It was so frigid I prayed for the jets to start again. They didn't. Not right away at least. Instead, puffs of powder rained down from the sky and stung my eyes.

"Don't swallow anything," the voice from the speaker shouted.

The second jet of water was heaven. I tilted my head so that the powder could wash away. The pressure hurt, but not as much as the powder's burning. Seconds later it was over, though there was still some powder on me. Huge air driers popped out from the wall and blew the water away. I welcomed the heat like an old friend, even as it singed my skin.

I wiped my mouth as I stepped out of the chamber, trying to rub the powder off of my face. It mixed with the droplets of water on the back of my hand and created a thick paste.

"You didn't swallow any of it, did you?"

"No, ma'am."

"Good, because it'll kill you."

"Then why use it?"

"Kills germs, too. We care more about killing the germs than killing you, I guess. Put on the tunic and head down the hallway. There will be a bunch of girls waiting there. Stop there and wait with them."

"For what?"

"For the next thing. Quit asking questions. NEXT!"

*

My damp feet slapped against the concrete hallway as I wandered along. Why was everybody in the Inner Rings so mean? They had everything. They were richer, and closer to the Center; they had better clothes. And yet, the closer I got to the Center the more everybody was just... so hateful.

There were angry people everywhere of course, and there certainly were some in the Fifth. But there was always a reason back home. It was always accompanied by the loss of their farm, or their wife, or a harvest that didn't go as planned. You could always point back to something. In the Inner Rings, though, it seemed like you could be angry just because. It was stupid, almost as stupid as hundreds of girls, all powdered, wet, and shell-shocked, milling around a hallway with no direction, feeling entirely alone.

I'd never felt so alone in a group of so many people. And it was so quiet. I was used to talking. There was always talking at home and at school. Here there was only a pained silence borne out of loneliness.

A clacking sound reverberated through the hallway. We turned in unison. A figure, wearing glasses and a scowl, came out of the light at the end of the hallway. She was draped in a tunic as well, but hers fit much more comfortably than any of ours did. It looked like she'd been born to wear it.

"You are my girls," she said. "All of you will be together for the remainder of the competition, until you are cut. And make no mistake— you will all be cut. Every single one of you will be cut. The chances of you even making it through the preliminaries are so small that I can comfortably say they are impossible. Making it to the finals will never happen, as only four out of thousands will make it. And none of them will be you."

This news deflated most of the girls, but not me. It brought me hope. She was right. I was going to get cut. I might be cut in the first event. I wanted the money. I wanted to do Joan and my family proud, but if they forced me to go home what could I say? I could be in my bed by the weekend. That would be wonderful.

"However," she continued, "you might win some money for your families, and you'll have a good story to tell your children when it comes time for their Transference."

At this, the woman's scowl broke into a slight smile. "Ah, well we have a McAllister in our ranks. Never mind, there is hope for one of you after all."

I tracked the woman's eyes to a blonde girl beaming from ear to ear. Even soggy and bedraggled like the rest of us, she was the most radiant girl I had ever seen.

"Although my given name is Penelope," the woman informed us, "you all will call me Chaperone. If you call me Penelope, you will be cut immediately."

"Why tell us then?" one of the girls asked.

"Because the sooner you are all cut, the sooner I can get back to the real work at hand. Follow me."

Three girls slipped up and called her Penelope before we even made it to our rooms. They were told to stay put until guards could find them and lead them away. It would have been so easy to slip up and call her by her name—a ticket home—but I kept my mouth shut.

The hallway never ended. For all the majesty of the Center's façade, the interior was nothing more than tunnels of ugliness filled with bitter people roaming the halls. I wondered how many people were lost in this maze. Penelope couldn't have cared too much. She walked too fast for the slowest to keep up.

Luckily, I was healthy and strong. I'd carried bales of hay across acres of our farm. Others weren't so lucky. Some, especially from the Sixth, wheezed and coughed the whole trip. Years in the mines did that to them. Others from the Inner Rings weren't used to hard work. Their chubby, stubby legs struggled to keep up.

*

I counted twenty-seven turns before we stopped in front of a metal doorway. Twenty-seven. Thirteen lefts. Fourteen rights. I was pretty good at memorizing directions. Being from farm country, it was important to know where everything was without a map. Most of our streets didn't have signs—those that did probably weren't right. You needed to know it was four rights and a left to the supermarket, and that you turned right after nine paces to get through the cornfields without getting a rake to the face.

Penelope turned on a dime in front of the steel door, one of a half dozen in the hallway. "And here you are. It's not much, but it's going to be home for the duration."

She grunted against the weight of the steel door as she slowly pushed it open. We funneled inside behind her and the groans started immediately.

"Don't dilly dally." Penelope clapped her hands briskly. "We have to get ready for the inaugural address. Everybody in!"

When I stepped inside, I understood the reason for the groans. Even for someone like me who was used to humble means, the room was sparse and crowded, filled wall to wall with identical bunk beds. No frills at all, each bunk had a little pillow and a thin sheet that covered an even thinner mattress.

Lines of at least ten girls deep had formed outside each of the bathrooms located in the corners of the square room. It wasn't a good idea to have just four bathrooms with over 100 people in a room, but I figured it was just another test. I was learning that The Five were sadistic like that. If we all killed each other trying to pee, then we weren't worthy of them.

"Now," Penelope said, "everybody has a bunk, and in front of that bunk is a cubby. In that cubby you'll find another towel, a toothbrush, toothpaste, and a comb. Get yourself clean. You have an hour before we go to the inaugural address. Not a minute more. Everybody is to line up here within ten minutes. Are we understood?"

Penelope didn't wait for an answer. She turned on her heels and left.

*

Girls clawed and scratched for the top bunk. I didn't understand why people cared about where they slept. I was just happy to have a bed, any bed. I sat down on the nearest one. After standing for the better part of a day, the bottoms of my feet ached with relief.

"You can't be there," I heard from across the room.

I looked up to see McAllister, in all her beautiful glory, fully dry and not a hair out of place. "I called that bunk."

"I don't see your name on it."

McAllister smirked. "Then you aren't looking hard enough. There are plenty of bunks."

"Maybe there is, maybe there isn't, but you seem like the kind of girl who always gets what she wants, and I'd like to see you lose for once."

McAllister snarled, indignant. "Do you know who I am?"

"No. People seem impressed with you, though."

"I am McKinsey McAllister. My family has been Stone's Vessels for five cycles. So, you watch out if you know what's good for you. I'm a Legacy."

"Congratulations. You are the only guaranteed dead person here. Kudos on all your family's success."

All eyes were on me. I'd stood up to the queen.

No, I faltered, not a queen. I knew a queen. Earth was a queen. McKinsey was just a very rich peon. The rest of the girls didn't know better. They were legitimately scared of McKinsey, as if she had real power.

I had seen real power and felt real fear. This girl could do nothing to me, but I saw it in her eyes. She would certainly try.

CHAPTER 2

I didn't even bother fixing myself up before we left for the auditorium. The lines were too long, and the girls were too catty. I might not have been swayed by McKinsey's power play, but my roommates gobbled it up. They dangled on her every word, and those words were about how awful I was for standing up to her.

"Doesn't she know who I am?" McKinsey asked. "I met *Stone* once. Who does that girl think she is?"

By the time we left for the auditorium, the whole room had turned against me. I was a pariah. They whispered about me under their breath, and one even elbowed me in the side just to get a chuckle out of McKinsey. I didn't plan to stoop to their level, though. I was here on a mission: Get the money and leave. That's all I had to do. I sure didn't need friends. I didn't need anybody.

The auditorium was packed when we finally got there. McKinsey made power plays throughout the entire walk, whispering insults in my direction and having her lackeys shove me into walls. Girls giggled and laughed. I just shook my head. I knew she just needed a swift punch in the mouth, but I couldn't do that. There were rules. So, I just let her pick on me. It was only one more day, after all. By tomorrow we would probably all be gone.

"Hey!" I heard from behind me as I shuffled into my seat. "I liked what you did back there."

I turned to see a little pipsqueak of a girl bouncing up and down on her chair. She couldn't be a hundred pounds soaking wet, her hair shaved almost to the bone.

I nodded at her. "Okay."

"Seriously," she continued. "Nobody has the balls to stand up to these scumbags from the Inner Rings. Everybody's scared stiff. But you... you did it without a second thought."

"That's true."

"You're a woman of few words, huh? That's all right. I just wanted to let you know that McKinsey McAllister can suck noodles. I mean, what kind of name is that? What drunkard puts two macs in the same name, huh? Don't they cancel each other out? I mean shouldn't she just be Kinsey Allister?" The little girl made a face at her own comment. "That's an even worse name, actually."

I didn't want to chuckle, but I couldn't help myself.

The lights flashed in the auditorium and the shaved girl sulked down in her chair. "We'll talk later."

I liked her immediately, which was bad news. I didn't want to like anybody. I had a job to do, and I had to be focused. Besides, I couldn't handle another Joan.

The din of the auditorium faded away and a very proper waif of a woman took the stage. She had perfect posture, but of course she did. She was from the Second. "Good evening, ladies and gentlemen. Welcome to this very special Transference."

Everyone applauded and as soon as it died down, she continued.

"We are very excited to have you in our midst. It is a great honor to be inside the hallowed halls of the Center. We who work here were hand-picked by the Five for this task and have studied our entire lives for this moment. We understand the depths of your sacrifice."

Why did we keep calling them the Five? There were only four of them. It made no sense. I guess tradition is tradition even if it's dumb.

"You are the continuation of a great tradition, one that dates back farther than any of us can remember. Back to those dark days after the Incident, when the Five delivered us from unmentionable evil."

Unmentionable evil. More like "unknown evil." No history book or textbook had ever talked about what really happened during the Incident. All we had were the accounts of the Five from the Book of Books, and even that started hundreds of years after the Incident. It's almost like the first 500 years of our history didn't exist.

"In a moment, you will meet each one of the Five."

The audience gasped. "Quiet down now. You will meet the Five, yes, but first we must go over some ground rules."

"First, although clearly stated, I will remind you that you must fall between the ages of thirteen and seventeen to participate. Additionally, please know you will be tested before you receive any money and/or move on to the quarterfinal rounds. So please if you do not fall within the proper age range, do us all a favor and leave now."

Girls and boys shuffled in their seats. There was rampant cheating that went along with the earlier stages of the Transference. Children as young as ten and as old as twenty-five used to enter, make it through a couple of trials, get paid, and then run off never to be seen again.

"Second, you must be a permitted birth. Honestly, if you think we can't spot a Mutie by now, you have another thought coming. If you do not come forward and we find you participating, the punishment will be severe—more severe than if you were found on the street. Examples must be made."

"Third, there will be no violence against any contestant for any reason. While you are here within these walls, you are considered a Vessel, and thus one of the Five. Any aggression against a Vessel is an aggression against the Five and will be punished as such."

I clenched my fists tight. That was the reason I couldn't hit McKinsey as much as I wanted to, and oh, how I wanted to hit her.

"Fourth, you must be a *virgin* in order to participate, no exceptions. You will be tested before you receive any monies and certainly before you move on to the quarterfinals. Is all of this clear? Yes, yes?"

Mumbling echoed through the chambers as we nodded.

"Good, good. Now you all know the payment. Every time you complete a task in the preliminaries you are granted a week's wage. There are thirty-six preliminary tasks and you must complete ten in order to move on to the quarterfinals. Yes, yes. So, in theory, you could be awarded up to ten weeks' pay.

"If you make it to the quarterfinals, you will receive an additional month's pay. If you make it to the semi-finals, you will receive an additional six months' pay. Should you make it to the Finals, you will be awarded an additional year's pay."

She paused and looked around the room, trying to build suspense even though we all knew how it worked. "Should you make it through and be chosen by one of the Five, your family will be endowed with money and status for all their days."

I'd never heard it talked about in such simple terms before. The more you win, the more you make. Suddenly, I had my goal. Make it to the semis, get forty weeks' pay. It would be hard, but all worthwhile goals are hard. It would be enough to fix our farm. We could buy better crops and make sure we never had to worry about a bad harvest again. All I had to do was beat almost every other girl in the auditorium with me. I turned around and looked at them. They didn't look so tough.

"And now, without further ado," the woman shouted, "the Five!"

The Five came out onto the stage with all the pageantry befitting gods. There were fireworks, music, cheers, and adulation, but I saw right through them. I knew they were just humans. I turned back to see if anybody else knew it, but they were all entranced. Well, almost all— the little, bald girl couldn't care less either. It made me like her more.

Time, tall, lanky, and bespectacled, appeared first, his long beard waving back and forth. He looked the same in every lifetime. He actually looked like an older version of Henry, or nearly anybody from the Fourth. Historically, most of his Vessels had been Fours.

Next was Stone, demure and fragile. She caved in upon herself, jumping at the sound of the fireworks and cowering from the music's crescendo. She was a McAllister in beauty, but not in stature. I looked over at McKinsey and saw her grinning. That was her aunt up there on stage, looking haggard and run-down. How could anybody take pride in that?

Arrow waddled across the stage like a tub of lard. His vessels always ended up portly. He loved to eat and had no respect for the bodies he chose. It was almost as if he took pride in destroying a body chiseled to perfection. He always went for the most athletic boy; content to watch them wither away under his care.

Finally, out came Earth to thunderous applause. Earth was an enigma. She never picked the same type twice. Pictures of her were tall, thin, fat, blonde, blue eyed, and everything across the spectrum. I think it's because she never wanted to get attached to the bodies she chose. If you see yourself in a Vessel, it's harder to make a rational choice. Earth was all about rational choice.

They all sat down next to an ornate podium, leaving a space in the middle for the deceased Wind. He'd always had kind eyes. No matter what the picture, somehow, he captured the same kindness behind the eyes of all his Vessels. Of all the Five, he had seemed the least likely to be murdered.

*

Time came to the stage first.

"This is not a time to celebrate," he began, "as it usually is when a Transference is upon us. No. This is a solemn occasion, a time for mourning and loss. But we must do what needs to be done. Wind was a great man, a giant among men, and he will be forever in our hearts."

I heard sobs and turned to see Penelope weeping. I couldn't believe it. She'd really come off as a mean, vindictive robot like you'd see in bad sci-fi movies, yet she cried harder than anybody else in the room.

Stone's words were short and to the point, although she spoke so softly into the microphone, I could barely hear her. "I look forward to the day when I can meet some of you in person and have a frank exchange of ideas. I would wish you good luck, except that luck is a statistical impossibility."

Why would Stone pick a McAllister? I wonder if it was for the same reason Arrow chose jocks. Maybe she wanted to take the most beautiful girl in the room and destroy them. Perhaps in a previous life she'd been homely and wanted that which came with a McAllister's innate beauty. She didn't stay radiant for long, if that was the case. Before long, her hair frayed, and her skin became pasty.

After Stone, Arrow approached the podium, all fire and brimstone. His jowls flapped as he screamed to the heavens. "We will strike down with vehement rage the evil that did this to our beloved friend. He will be avenged! Avenged I say!"

He was more funny than scary, as his face was very jowly and jiggled all over the place when he spoke. I heard it clap against itself more than once. How can you take somebody seriously when his face clapped?

The time had come for Earth's address. The last time I'd seen her, she'd executed people and by the end of this whole process, she'd effectively kill another person. One of the girls in this auditorium was going to die, her soul sucked away to be used as a Vessel for Earth, and three others would die to make room for the others.

"I have to say, you all are very brave for making your way here. Very, very brave. Give yourselves a hand."

The audience clapped awkwardly. "Come now. Don't be shy. We wouldn't be here if it weren't for the sacrifices of you and your families. So please, clap louder. All of you."

The barely audible applause rose into a thunder.

"Very good, very good. Yes, now we all know why you are here. We all know the rules, and we all know what we are going to do. You must give it your all. Do you understand?"

Heads bobbed throughout the audience.

"Good. Because there is a very compelling reason to cheat. Money is a fantastic motivator to do bad things. You must not allow that to happen. Our survival, and by extension the survival of our entire species, depends on you doing your best so that we can find the best among you. Do you understand?"

Again, nods from the audience.

"Too often we forget in this City that the world is a very, very nasty place. It is filled with things that will kill you—even the air will kill you. However, we Five protect you. We have always protected you, and we will continue to protect you for as long as we are able."

"So, I ask you, beg you, implore you, to do your duty. Do your duty as if your lives depended on it...because they do." With that, Earth sat back down to another round of thunderous applause.

The Twofer host came back to the stage. "And that, as they say, is that. Have a good night's sleep and—"

The woman continued to talk, but her voice no longer carried across the speakers. The lights went dim and a dozen video monitors popped on throughout the auditorium.

It was Wind, there on the screen. "Hello. If you are watching this, it means that I am dead. I am dead because of what I know, or more correctly what I am trying to do. All of you are being lied to and you are in danger. Leave, before the fickle hand of fate chooses you, too. I have a simple truth for you, a truth I have stayed silent about all these many, many years. Now it is time to come clean. The simple truth is this: we do not need the—"

The video cut out in the middle of Wind's sentence and the monitor fell away. I looked over to see Penelope's eyes wide in astonishment. A smile cracked across her face like she was holding in a belly laugh. The lights came back on and I squinted to readjust to the brightness. By the time I could see again, Penelope was composed as ever.

"Well," the Twofer said, "that was surely an adventure, wasn't it? I guess old Wind had something left in his sails after all. Good night, everyone, and good luck!"

*

Streams of children poured out of the auditorium like a sea, crashing upon each other.

"Althea!" I heard Henry shout from behind me. The welcome sound of his voice lifted my heart.

He broke away from his crew and ran to me. "I can't believe I found you. Isn't this neat? I mean that thing at the end with Wind was crazy, right?"

I squeezed him so hard he couldn't hug me back. "Thank you for finding me. I have to go, though. I don't want to get lost."

"Me either. This place is a maze." A long pause. "I'm kidding, of course. We took four hundred and thirty-seven steps to get into the auditorium—three lefts, eleven rights, and straight on 'til morning. The Center is laid out like a grid. If you just know where—"

I smiled. "We took seven lefts, and three rights. We must be closer than you."

"I'll remember that." Henry waved to me as he ran off. "Goodbye, Althea. Man, this place is great."

I wished I had Henry's enthusiasm toward the Center. I wished I had his enthusiasm for anything. He found life, even this place, so fascinating. All I saw was a prison. A prison everybody was going to escape from except four people.

"There you are!" Penelope shouted. "You're holding up everybody else. We have a schedule to keep. If we don't leave this instant, you won't receive the necessary eight-and-a-quarter hours of sleep required for peak performance."

"I was just—"

"We were all 'just.' You are lucky I don't just leave you. If it wasn't for your friend, I would have. She can be very annoying."

"I don't have any friends."

Penelope pointed to the girl with the shaved head. "She would disagree."

The group waited a few hundred yards ahead, cowering in fear of being lost or dragged toward their doom by the current of children. As Penelope walked me back to them, a shrill voice rose over the din. "Oh Penelope!"

The sea parted instantly. It was Earth. In the flesh. In Public. Close enough we could reach out and touch her, though nobody would dare.

"I was hoping to have a word with you."

Penelope pushed me away. "Go stand with the other girls."

I didn't move. I couldn't. I was frozen in place. Earth cleared her throat. "That was an odd occurrence today, wasn't it, Penelope? With Wind suddenly popping in, like he was a ghost. Ghastly business."

"Yes, ma'am. It was."

"And, where were you?" Earth pressed. "When all of this was going on?"

As Earth circled us like a vulture over prey, she looked every bit her age, even older if possible. The weight of the world weighed heavily on everything except her eyes. They were crystal blue and laser focused on Penelope.

Penelope stuttered. "I...I was right there, ma'am, next to my vessels."

"Were you? Curious. No matter." Earth cocked her head. "Do you know what I believe a god is, Penelope?"

"What, ma'am?"

"A being who has been around long enough to see everything an infinite number of times. They know every possible outcome before it happens. What do you say to that?"

"I believe in the Five. I always have. I always will."

"Very good because I have lived many lifetimes. I have seen it all before. Many times. Remember that."

"I will, ma'am. Thank you, ma'am."

Earth flicked her wrist at the girls from my dorm. "Your wards need their sleep. Take them to bed. I would hate to send them home because of your pitiful supervision and care, Penelope. I'll be watching you."

With that, Earth bent the sea of people to her will and walked away. The wave of kids crashed back upon each other as she turned a corner and vanished. That's when Penelope snapped back to attention and saw me. "Didn't I tell you to get in line?"

"I was—I couldn't...I'm sorry."

Penelope's eyes became slits. "Don't let it happen again. Now move."

She pushed me into the pack of gawking girls. They chattered away, asking me questions about Earth as they walked back to the room. Even though I hated her, seeing Earth in the flesh had been a thrill, even for me.

"Don't think that makes you special," McKinsey said. "I've actually touched one of the Five. More than you've ever done."

But it didn't matter what she said, all eyes were focused on me.

CHAPTER 3

People are so ridiculous and easily impressed. All I did was stand close to Earth for a minute. By any standard it was an unimpressive feat, yet it didn't matter; everybody wanted to touch me. They wanted to hear what I had to say.

No matter what she did, McKinsey couldn't keep their attention. That was the only part that made their adulation bearable. They would drift over to her, hear a story, then get lost in their starred-eyed adulation for Earth and turn back to me.

"What was it like?" one of them asked. "How did she smell?"

"I don't know," I said. "I wasn't really paying attention. I was just trying not to piss myself."

"I'll bet that she's going to pick you now. I'm so jealous."

"Me too," a girl sobbed. "I would do anything to be picked by Earth."

I furrowed my brow. "Why? You know it means you're dead, right?"

"But then you're one of the Five. Your consciousness ascends back to the Origin Point. The *Book of Books* says that when you give yourself to the Five as a Vessel you are immediately forgiven of all your sins and given a place of honor in the Heavens."

It was true. The last chapter was called Transference, and it spoke about why you would give yourself to the Five and what would happen if you did. One of the girls started quoting verses from the third chapter, "Lo, and those whom the Five choose will live for eternity at the right hand of the Five at the Origin Point, where all life began. They will want for nothing and need for nothing."

"And once that happens," the girl continued, having finished the verse. "We can be with Wind forever as the Five intended. Wouldn't that be lovely?"

"That's stupid. When you're dead, you're dead." I stood up and gestured towards her body. "This is just a meaty flesh vessel and you're going to give it away. For what? So, somebody can use it as a bag to walk around in for a couple decades?"

The girls gasped. "You don't believe in the Five?"

"Of course, I believe in them. I mean they exist. They're probably good people, but they're not gods. I'll suck my gross toes if they're more than just regular people we put on a pedestal."

"So," McKinsey said, smiling, "why are you here then?"

"Money." I looked deep into her eyes. "Plain and simple. Thousands of girls come here, only two of them are chosen. Lots of 'em get money, though."

McKinsey shook her head. "Oh. You're one of those. Well then, I'm sure Earth saw right through you and you'll be going home tomorrow."

I walked away from the group, their faces aghast. "Let's hope so. This place gives me the creeps."

*

I tried to put McKinsey out of my brain for the next hour, but it was no use. She took the only thing from me that I wanted—sleep. She was a diabolical genius.

I found the toothbrush and small canister of toothpaste in the cubby in front of our beds, just like Penelope had mentioned. But, of course, I quickly realized the canister of toothpaste wouldn't last a week. I mean, why would it when everybody in the room would be gone by the end of the next day?

I wondered what the toothpaste situation would be like for the people who made it onto the finals, though? Would there be some sort of golden toothpaste canister bestowed to them? They'd probably be forced to scrounge for toothpaste like a mutt, knowing the Five.

I had plenty of time to think about this while I stood in line for the bathrooms because even at midnight, the lines were impossibly long. Why they would only have a couple bathrooms for hundreds of girls was ludicrous to me, even if we were all going home soon. I mean, how much do a couple extra toilets cost in the grand scheme of things? Even if this was a test from the Five, it was a pretty terrible one. I shouldn't have to worry about my bladder exploding while I'm focused on losing my mind to the Five. That's psychotic manipulation.

The girl with the shaved head sidled up to me. "Hey."

"I don't have to pee that bad," I said. "If you have to pee really bad go ahead."

"No. I don't have to...well, I do have to pee but it's not an emergency. I just wanted to say hi. I don't get to meet a lot of new people where I'm from. I'm Cam. But, don't call me Cammie."

I shook her outstretched hand. Her nails were black from years of soot. "Nice to meet you."

She watched me put my hand back to my side without cleaning it. "You know, I appreciate the fact you didn't wipe your hand after shaking mine. Most people here do."

"Yeah well, I'm from the farm. We shovel horse crap there, literally. A few germs never hurt anybody."

"I guess that's true. I never really thought about it much. In the Sixth, it's so dirty from all the coal that we don't even notice the grime anymore."

"Yeah. That coal bleeds into the Fifth for a thousand miles. It's gross."

"Yeah. Imagine living in it every day. View's nice though. Only place in the city you can see the Outside, even if it is through the haze of the Bubble."

My eyebrows shot up. "Outside. You can really see it?"

"Oh yeah. I mean, not really. It's fuzzy and out of focus through the force field, but it's there all right. I like to go and look out into the abyss sometimes. Imagine what's out there."

"Monsters. That's what they say. Cannibals. Every horrible thing you can imagine."

Cam gave me a withered look. "You really believe what they say?"

I hadn't ever thought about it before, but I did. I believed that they wouldn't keep us locked up like rats if they weren't protecting us from something. Even Dad believed that, and he didn't believe anything the Five said. I had always trusted at least that to be true. Now I wasn't so sure. "I guess not, when you put it like that."

"Yeah. I can tell in your eyes. You don't give a screw about any of this, huh?"

"Not even a little bit. I just want to make some money and go home."

Cam smiled. "Not me. I could stay here forever."

"So, you believe in all this crap?"

"Oh God, no. To be stuck with somebody else in my brain? No thank you. Still. It would be nice to get out of my terrible smelling house and live in the clean air. Plus, the people ain't all that bad."

"Oh yes they are. Actually, they're worse."

The door opened to the bathroom and McKinsey sashayed out. Of course, it was her holding up the line.

"Took you long enough," I said.

"I'm not going to stop my routine just because I'm stuck here with you." She glided through the line and stopped in front of me. "You must think you are really something, being that close to Earth, huh?"

"That's not why I think I'm something, McKinsey."

"Well you're not, you know. You're nobody. You're nothing and you'll be gone tomorrow."

*

I woke up the next morning to the sound of snickering and the wetness in my mattress made my eyes go wide. The dewiness of my hand told me what had happened. I had a brother. I knew about pranks. I looked down at the floor and saw the bucket of water by my bed. The wet stain on my tunic. I pissed myself. I would have horrified me if I wasn't so pissed off.

"What's the matter, Fiver?" McKinsey said, stepping forward. "They don't teach you how to use the toilet in Hickville?"

"I'm gonna rip you apart!" I rushed McKinsey, but Cam pulled me back. I thrashed violently against her hold, but somehow, she was stronger than me.

"If you clock her, you go home," Cam said. "You know the rules."

"Your little, bald friend is right, Thea," McKinsey said. "Besides, can't you take a joke?"

The room roared in laughter. McKinsey was triumphant; she had regained her control of the gaggle. All I'd wanted to was to keep my head down and do my bid. I was the only one who had the guts to stand up to her and she handed me the most humiliating moment of my life—in front of a hundred strangers.

I pushed through the throng of girls waiting for the bathroom. I didn't care if they were mad I cut in line, I just needed some quiet, and to be alone for a few minutes. I needed to break down. I needed to make sure McKinsey didn't see that she won.

I pulled a stubby, little girl out of the bathroom and slammed the door. A hand blocked it from latching. It was Cam. She squeezed her way inside and shut the door. "You need any help?"

"I don't want you in here."

"Yes, you do. You just don't know it."

My eyes filled with tears. "I can't believe...what is this, third grade?"

"Yes. Yes, it is. It's more like sleep-away camp though. Did you ever go to sleep-away camp?"

"No. Who has money for that kind of stuff?"

"People in the Inner Rings, that's who. I read about them in books, and I've seen 'em on TV movies. You know, it looked fun. I guess it's not so fun."

"Well, I have a brother, and he has stupid friends, and my stupid neighbor is a stupid boy too, so I can say without a doubt this kind of stuff is *not fun*." I fought back more tears. "Where were you, anyway? I thought you were my friend."

Cam frowned. "I gotta sleep too, and shower, and get ready. This kind of beautiful don't just roll out of bed. Besides, it's not my job to keep my head on a swivel for you."

She was right. We weren't friends. At best we were acquaintances, and that's not good enough to win this game. Here, you need somebody watching your back. Otherwise, somebody's gonna stab you in it. "Can it be?"

"Oh really? You gonna keep your head out for me too?"

"Of course! That's what friends do, right?"

"Yeah. That's what friends do." Cam smiled.

There was a loud bang on the door. "Open up!" It was Penelope. "What's going on in there?"

Cam opened the door. She didn't say anything. Her eyes just scooted over to me standing there, nearly in tears, covered in my own piss.

*

"You know, it's really not that bad," Penelope said as she washed my tunic in the sink in her room while I sat on her bed wrapped in a towel.

Penelope took pity on me—there was plenty to pity. She'd dragged me through a few hallways and a heavy metal door, into her quarters. It was small, and I mean really small. There was barely room for a bed and a shower.

"It's not going to get any better," Penelope said. "You know that. Money and power make good people do crappy things and it makes crappy people do *really* crappy things."

"I thought it's not supposed to be about the money."

"Don't play naïve. You know money drives people here. Nobody would line up to be brainwashed just for the good of it."

"McKinsey would."

"They've brainwashed McKinsey's family with money and power for generations. They are all idiots."

"What happens when your family wins multiple times? Do you get more money or something?"

"Don't call it winning. Let's not demean people's sacrifice." Penelope stood and wrung out my tunic. "It's not going to be totally dry for a while." She walked over to her dresser. "You're about my size, right?"

"Seems like it." Under her tunic we probably were the same size. In fact, there were lots of things about Penelope that reminded me of myself. She had an old, oak cabinet for a dresser, just like I did. Her room smelled of wheat, and she had photos on her wall of farms. "Are you from the Fifth?"

Penelope pulled out a pair of underwear and handed them to me along with a tunic. "Yes. Before I was summoned. But that doesn't matter now. Go change."

"Why are you being nice to me?"

"Despite what you might think, I'm not a bad person. I'm just a person. People aren't just one thing. We just are. Now hurry up or you'll miss breakfast. Today is a big day and the mess hall is going to be crowded."

*

The mess hall stretched out as far as I could see and crested over the horizon in the distance. In front of us was an ocean of girls. Dozens of television screens were mounted to the walls. In the center of all the screens was a number: 4,496.

"What's that?" I asked Penelope.

"The total amount of girls. Underneath is another tally for girls that made the quarterfinals. Only about ten percent make it."

"That's not very many."

"You think that's bad? Semifinals are ten percent of those. Finals are ten percent of *those*. That's how we whittle down the best of the best of the best. It's served us well so far."

My stomach gurgled as I looked at the cafeteria line. Penelope nudged me toward it. "Go get some food."

*

Breakfast was three heaping helpings of green gruel, brown gruel, and blue gruel. Each one smelled terrible and tasted worse. What I would give for an apple and some eggs. This processed crap they fed us couldn't be healthy. I couldn't believe all our hard work in the Fifth turned into this garbage.

I sat down next to Cam and tried to eat. I really did, but I couldn't bear it. They only gave us a spoon. I never ate food with a spoon, unless it was soup. Even then, Mama made it so thick that you could eat it with a fork. It was more like a roast with sauce than a soup. "I can't eat this."

"You're gonna need your strength," Cam said.

"Then I'll suffer." I pushed my plate over to Cam. She wolfed it down.

I looked around the room, studying my competition. They were not a very intimidating lot. Many of them were from the Inner Rings, so they were chubby and soft, except for a few girls like McKinsey. They didn't stand a chance in the physical competitions. But the competitions weren't all physical—there were emotional and psychological challenges too. The Inner Rings were masters of psychological warfare.

A meek girl interrupted my line of vision. I recognized her from the bunks. She was one of the only girls that didn't laugh when I pissed myself.

"Can I help you with something?" I asked.

The girl shook her head. Her fingers had soot in them from the Sixth and she still flicked them nervously. "No."

"Thank you for not giggling with the others."

"I...I...," she stuttered, "I didn't think it was funny."

"What's your name?"

She smiled. "Violet."

"It's nice to meet you, Violet."

"Don't talk to her!" McKinsey's voice boomed over the conversations at the table. "She's going to get in your head, Violet. She wants you to fail."

Violet looked at McKinsey, then back at me, quizzically. "She does? Is that true, Althea?"

"No, I don't!" I shouted at McKinsey, not Violet, but the meek girl flinched just the same.

"Come on, Violet sweetie. Leave the shrew alone with her failure."

McKinsey's smug face was too much to bear. A fiery ball of rage exploded in my belly. I didn't care if they kicked me out; I was going to deck her.

I ran forward, fist clenched. I cocked my arm back and was ready to swing. That's when a pile of blue goop splotched right on my forehead.

"Food fight!" Cam screamed.

Nobody moved. They just turned to see Cam on the table with goop all over her hands. "No? Nobody. Not one person, huh? Man, I hate you all. All right then, I guess I'm gone. Jerks."

*

Two burly officers dragged Cam out of the mess hall, kicking and screaming. She knew the risks and had helped me anyway. We were supposed to watch each other's backs, and she had done her job. I failed mine.

Why were people I just met risking their lives for me all the time? Was I that pathetic?

I couldn't deal with failing somebody else. It was bad enough living with the guilt of leaving home and the guilt of killing Joan. The guilt of exiling the only girl in the Center I didn't hate was too much to bear. I had to stop it.

I headed out of the mess hall. It wasn't hard to follow Cam. She screamed loud enough to be heard across the City. I followed after her. The remaining guards were too busy keeping the other girls calm and didn't see me go.

I followed the path through the Center until it dead-ended into a single doorway. I cracked it open and the smell of outside flooded my nostrils.

The sky was bright in the morning. I hadn't seen light since entering the Center. When my eyes finally focused, I saw the two officers leading Cam across a wide-open square toward an ornately clad military police officer. She looked like the constable in charge of the Fifth.

Each Ring had their own police and their own constable. This constable was more ornate than the one in the Fifth, with hundreds of medals adorning her uniform.

With her hands perched behind her back in stoic silence, she stood there, stern, unyielding. Her eyes, even at a distance, scared me. I wanted to turn back, but knew I had to act. If I waited, Cam would be gone forever.

"Wait!" I shouted. Fear bubbled up in my belly. The military police were going to shoot me. I knew it. I was begging for a gun to the temple. But I couldn't stop myself. Adrenaline and guilt pumped through my veins. "She didn't do anything!"

The guns all trained on me at once. It would only take a weak moment, or a heavy sneeze and their hair triggers would gun me down. I fell to the ground expecting to die. "Don't shoot. I'm unarmed!"

The Constable raised her arm. "Lower your weapons, for the Five's sakes. She's just a little girl in a tunic. If she can kill me, then I deserve to die. You better have a good reason for this, girl."

The guns lowered. I felt the tension ease. I could breathe again. "I do...Cam...she didn't do anything wrong, ma'am."

The Constable stepped forward. "Oh really? From what I hear, she pelted one of the Vessels in the face."

I wiped some of the blue goop off my forehead. "Yeah, she hit me."

The Constable cocked her eyebrow. "So, it is. And you would speak for this girl?"

I stood to meet the Constable's gaze. "I would. She was just having some fun, ma'am."

"I'm sure you understand the seriousness of the accusations against this girl. Striking one of the contestants is akin to striking the Five."

"I know, ma'am. But I'm not one of the Five. Look at me—I'm no god, I'm a kid. And I'm not even hurt. It's not like she gave me a black eye or bruised anything. I just got a little stuff in my hair. It'll wash right out. I had worse after that gross powder you all sprayed me with yesterday."

"If I let this go, how do I know it won't happen again?"

"It won't. I swear it won't. And if it'll make you feel any better, I'll leave. I'll go back home. Right now."

"That's stupid," I heard from behind me. It was Penelope. "You're not going anywhere. Neither of you are."

The Constable's attitude turned from contempt to rage. "You dare tell me what will happen? As if you still speak for the Five. Your power left with—"

"I'm telling you a point of order, Constable. Althea wasn't struck. Law states there must be tangible damage. A bruised ego is not damage. We both know mashed berries can't do anything but damage your taste buds."

"I am in charge here," the Constable grunted. "Don't you forget. You are nothing."

"I'm not debating that, but this is a bad look. I mean what if she's the one Stone or Earth would choose? What if she's the Vessel they are looking for, and you don't even let them see her in action? She'll be gone soon enough, if she's not the right one. Let it play out."

The Constable let out a defeated groan. "Very well. But if this continues, it will be on you."

"Add it to the list of things that are my fault. Come girls. You're late." Penelope's hand hovered over the wall until it opened up. It was either some sort of magic or great security, but it was pretty neat.

She gave one last fearless glance to the Constable before the door closed. I loved her in that moment. She was my hero.

CHAPTER 4

I've seen seething hate before, like Dad's hate for the church, or Jake's hatred for this boy named Tommy who hit on me in school. And my hatred for the police was seething. But I'd never witnessed the level of seething hatred that the Constable had expressed when she'd stared Penelope down.

"Why does that police woman hate you so much?" Cam asked Penelope on the way back to the mess hall.

"The real question is why would I risk my neck to help you?" Penelope replied.

"That's a good question," I said. "A really good question."

"I know," Penelope smirked. "I said it. Now quit flapping your gums. You'll need all your energy today even though I doubt either of you will make it to the afternoon."

"So, I can't even fail one event?" Cam asked.

Penelope shook her head. "Absolutely not. Why would the Five want a loser?"

"What if everybody fails?"

Penelope pushed us into the mess hall. "Then I guess we'll just have to do it all again, won't we? Don't leave again."

The mess hall had emptied out as the girls were assigned to their tasks. Lists of people had replaced the numbers on the screens as names were blared over a loud speaker on a constant loop: name and number, name and number, over and over again.

Around the mess hall thirty-six doors sprung open. I hadn't seen them before; it was probably the same magic Penelope had used to open the door that had led us back inside.

Penelope walked back to us. "You're at door twenty-four, Althea. Cam, you're at door three. Good luck."

Penelope could have just left me to the Constable's mercy, and she could have left me to stand there in the mess hall hoping they hadn't called my name out. Why was she being so nice to me? I hadn't earned it. I didn't deserve her help. I deserved to be disqualified and sent home.

And yet, here I was, about to walk through door twenty-four and meet the first preliminary challenge. All because Cam had saved me, and Penelope had found me. I didn't have enough gratitude for all the people who had helped me.

*

During the first task, I sat at a desk in a sterile white room and while the heat had been nearly unbearable, the loud music was worse as a barely comprehensible voice screamed questions at me.

"If a tiger heads west at four hundred and thirteen kilometers per day, when would it intersect a train that was on its way from Andebarle to Metuchen?"

The voice sped up every time you got a question wrong. The only way to slow it down was to ask pointed questions. Of course, they don't tell you that. You have to figure it out yourself. "The tiger," I asked, "is it mechanical?"

"Correct. It is mechanical."

"And the train..." I didn't like to think about trains. The thought of them made my throat tighten. "Is it going in a straight line?"

"Yes. It is going straight between Andebarle and Metuchen."

"Those are two cities? How far apart are they?"

"Time is running out, miss." You were always rushed—what a whirlwind.

I'd heard of Andebarle before. It was a city near a lake that had evaporated after the Incident, according to Stone 12:13. Tigers were animals that also hadn't survived, as I'd read in Earth 4:31. They were impractical to our purpose after the Incident.

"Um...they don't meet," I began, "cause the Incident wiped them all out?"

A green light flashed and the round continued. All of the questions were from or about the *Book of Books*. "How many Testaments are there? Name them all!"

"Wind, Earth, Arrow, Stone, Time, Transference, The Beginning. Seven. Seven Gospels."

"Where did the Five come from?"

"The Origin Point."

The green light flashed when I was right, and the red light flashed when I was wrong. Finally, the timer on the wall clicked down to zero and the sealed door opened. "Thank you, miss. Have a nice day."

The cold air punched me in the gut when I walked outside. *Was it always this cold in the mess hall?*

Then Cam ran up to me, the sweat dripping from her brow. "Holy heck, Thea. What did you do in there?"

"I just answered some questions."

"You were in there a long time. I thought you were dead, or maybe napping."

The scoreboard behind us dinged. I looked up to see my face plastered on the board with a "1" next to my name. "Our first point goes to Althea Clark!"

Half the girls clapped, the other half scowled at me as Penelope shouted from across the mess hall. "Maybe you should skip breakfast every day."

Cam grabbed my arm. "Congratulations! Just nine more points and you're into the quarterfinals."

I smiled. I'd won the first point of the tournament. Even McKinsey couldn't take that away from me.

*

I didn't stay alone at the top for long. Soon, dozens of girls showed up on the billboard, along with a bunch of boys. Henry pulled two points in the first three events. McKinsey pulled three as well. At the pace they were going, they both looked like they would be able to relax after the first day.

The second and third events were not as easy as the first, but they were just as weird. One had me standing on a small platform catching balls being tossed from every direction. If you fell off the platform, it was an immediate disqualification. I spent the whole time simply trying to stay on the board. I don't think I caught a single ball, but at least I didn't fall.

I did better at the third event, an obstacle course through the muck and the dirt ...in our tunics. Mine snagged on a razor wire and nearly drowned me in the river. I mean it was legitimately dangerous.

A girl in front of me ripped off her tunic and finished in just her underwear. She was braver than me. Still, I finished fast enough to get a point. By the end of the third event I had two out of a possible three points and felt pretty good about myself.

The rest of the day's events continued at a similar pace. We took a written test to name all the capitals of the Old World. I did okay on that one. We also participated in a tight rope walking challenge that simulated being suspended ten thousand feet in the air, and a game where you had to redraw a picture from memory after only seeing it for a few seconds. And in one of the stranger events, we simply got x-rayed and left. That one was my favorite even though I didn't earn a point for it. It was just so easy.

I fared decently well the first day, picking up four points. Cam and McKinsey were tied for the lead amongst the girls with six points each. Only three other girls received points besides McKinsey and me, and one of them was Violet; she had two. At the end of the day they let us see the boy's scores. I smiled when I saw a five next to Henry's name.

"It's incredible," McKinsey mentioned to Cam at dinner, "that somebody with such ill breeding could be doing so well."

"Is it though?" Cam asked. "Every day since I was four, I've lugged huge rocks and equipment and I've worked in mines that could collapse any minute, while you've been laying at home eating bonbons. If anything, I'm surprised *you* can keep up with *me*." McKinsey didn't like Cam's response, but I loved it.

After dinner, as we trudged back to the bunks, McKinsey had a spring in her step. "My aunt only got four points on day one," she said. "My great-aunt only had three. I would say I'm doing pretty well."

I wanted to punch her so bad. Even the mindless drones that worshiped McKinsey grumbled at her cheeriness.

As soon as we got back to our room, I looked around and noticed how many empty bunks there were. Even though the disqualification toll was astronomical, Penelope was utterly pleased with our performance.

"Better than I thought," Penelope said. "I honestly figured you'd all be gone and there's nearly forty of you still here. That's impressive. Seven of the other chaperones have nobody left. Now they get to sleep for the next few days, of course, but this is good too."

Were the ones that went home the lucky ones? It definitely seemed that way. Those of us remaining seemed miserable and pathetic and to add to that, while we should have showered and brushed our teeth, we didn't. We were too tired. I crawled on top of Cam's bunk and fell asleep immediately. No way was I sleeping on the bottom bunk again. Not after last night.

*

The next morning, every muscle in my body ached. I had never felt such pain on the farm. I could bale hay all day, go to a barn dance, and wake up fit as a fiddle.

I bet it was the air—it was stale and recycled here in the Center. I realized how much I missed the cool freshness of the Fifth blowing through my hair. I longed for home and my family with each passing second. Were they worried about me, I wondered.

This whole time I'd been too busy to think about their pain, and I felt that alone made me a bad daughter. There was no getting around it. They must've heard about the explosion and knew I was on the train. But I hadn't even tried to contact them to let them know that I was okay. Now I couldn't since Transference had started.

Maybe when I came back with enough money to fix our problems, I hoped they would see that I meant well and would forgive me. Maybe we'd even have a party to celebrate me coming back from the dead and saving the farm in one fell swoop. It would all be worth it.

I couldn't avoid brushing my teeth, but I wasn't about to shower. There was no point. I was just gonna get dirty again. Besides, they'd left me a clean tunic in my cubby. A little water through my hair and a splash on my face was all I needed.

Even though so many girls had gone home, the line was still miserably long. All of us had been exhausted and waited for Penelope to rouse us twice before getting ready. Violet stood in front of me, yawning.

"Good job, yesterday," I said to her. I was being honest. She was one of the few girls there I could tolerate.

"Thank you. You are doing well, too."

I nodded. "Let's just hope we can both get through."

She smiled. "I'd like that."

*

The second day's events were just as difficult and weird as the first. I had to take a test on differential equations. What are differential equations? Who the heck could even get one question right in something like that? Henry. That's who. I bet all Fours aced that test. I missed every question, but at least I finished. You didn't have to pass every test to avoid disqualification. You just had to finish them.

I liked the physical tests best of all. I won a point for lifting a kettle ball over my head as many times as possible. It reminded me of baling hay back home.

I was convinced that the Five wanted me to go crazy though, since every physical challenge was followed up with a psychological one. Whether it was standing in a room listening and repeating a language I didn't understand, or spotting what was on some stupid inkblot, the mind screw tasks were the worst. I felt drained after them, even though all I was doing was sitting in a chair answering questions.

McKinsey went four for four that morning, making her first person to get ten points. I thought she was smug before, but after she got ten points, her attitude went from annoying to unbearable. Fifteen other blonde pieces of perfection from the Inner Rings pushed through right behind her. While the rest of us killed ourselves, they frittered the day away.

After the second day, ninety-one people had made it through to the quarterfinals. Violet was one of them, which was crazy to think about. She had started the day with two points and ended up acing eight straight events to qualify. I was really happy for her, and it was nice to see somebody who didn't suck make some money. I gave her a big hug when she got through.

I slumped that second day, only pulling together two points—the kettle ball toss, and during the very last event of the day, I stacked blocks to reach a key on the ceiling before the floor fell out from underneath me. After twenty-four events, I had six points. That meant I needed to secure four points during the last day.

Lots of people went home at the end of the second day, and not just because of disqualifications either. One girl made it through to the quarterfinals, only to be told that she was a Mutie after her blood test results came back. The poor girl hadn't even known! Her family had apparently never told her. When the call for the Transference came, she was so excited to help her family that she'd run away from home just like me. Now, she was going to be sterilized, marked, and forced to live in squalor or join the military and her parents would be jailed...or worse.

It was a shame... a crying shame. Suddenly I was paralyzed by a thought. Maybe it was the stress of competition, or trauma from the things I'd witnessed since leaving home, but I couldn't stop the paranoid thoughts that raced through my brain. *Was that my lot too? What if I was a Mutie? Was that why my parents didn't want me competing?*

*

By the end of the third day, I was so drained I felt delirious. I had completed thirty-five events total but had only mustered nine points. Cam, McKinsey, Violet, and five other girls from my room had already moved on to the quarterfinals.

I had one gate left. The third. I had to complete it and pray to the Five that I would place. I had already completed twelve physical and twelve mental challenges, so this was a psychological challenge for sure.

From listening to Cam and Violet, it was the worst challenge of the thirty-six. I had asked all the girls what they experienced inside. The weird thing was that everybody I talked to had had a different experience, so I didn't know what to expect. All I knew was this—it was an outlast challenge. The longer you stayed in the better you did, and I knew the time I had to beat. Twelve minutes. In order to qualify, I had to last for twelve minutes and one second.

There was nothing inside but a white chair and silence. The door slammed behind me.

"Should I sit?"

No reply. There had always been a reply in the other psychological tests. I pulled the chair out. The cushion squeaked when I sat on it, and it didn't stop, its slow whine filling the room.

All at once, each movement my body made boomed through my ears. I heard my eyelids flap, my hair grow, and my nose wiggle. The chair squeaked loudly. My hands throbbed and pulsated. My heart thumped rapidly. Every single sound reverberated off of the room's walls.

"Hello. Do you want me to do anything?" No answer.

A panel opened from above me. A single pin dropped from the ceiling and when it hit the ground it deafened me—the "ting" exploding in my ears. I needed it to stop echoing before it perforated my eardrums, but it wouldn't stop. I cupped my ears to deaden the volume, but the overwhelming sound of blood coursing through my veins, pulsating into my brain, drove me crazy.

Then, a new hole opened in a wall and a manual clock appeared, ticking rhythmically. The ticking grew louder and louder as the hands moved around its face. I squeezed my eyes so tight they hurt. When I opened them, I saw Joan sitting in the corner, blood covering her shirt.

"I'm glad you're having fun," she said.

"What are you doing here?" I asked. "You're not supposed to be here."

"I thought we were friends? Aren't you happy to see me?"

"Of course, but you're dead. You shouldn't be here."

"I know that. You killed me. Don't you remember watching pitifully as cops shot me like a dog?"

"I know. I know. I'm sorry. I wish I was dead and not you."

Then, Mama's voice rang in my ears. "Why would you want that? Don't you want to see us again?"

"Of course, I do. I love you, Mama."

"Then why did you abandon us?"

"I just wanted to help."

Joan's voice came back, stronger than ever. "Like you helped me?"

"No. Not like that at all. Stop. Please just *stop!*"

And suddenly the voices were gone. The clock stopped. My hair stopped growing and my heart stopped pounding.

The door opened. I crawled outside, crying. I never wanted to experience anything like that ever again. I collapsed into a heap outside the third gate.

Why? Why? Why would they do that to us? It was horrible, unbearable. Of the thirty-six gates, that was the only one I would never do again under any circumstances. I would rather die.

I tilted my head ever so slightly to the scoreboard to see my time.

Thirteen minutes and fifteen seconds. I made it. I made it! I don't know how I lasted so long. It felt like a second—an excruciating, agonizing second—but I had made it.

*

"It's just going to be a little prick," Penelope warned me. "Don't flinch."

That's a thing people say when they aren't scared of needles. I couldn't help it. It was a natural reaction to being stabbed. I tensed when the needle went into my skin and tried my best to think of home and how much they would appreciate fourteen weeks' pay.

And I hoped. I hoped and prayed I wasn't a Mutie.

"Do you know how hard it is," Penelope asked, "to get into the top ten percent of all these potential Vessels?"

"Yeah. I know exactly how hard it is. I just did it."

Penelope chuckled. "Then you know how proud I am of you."

The nurse pulled out the needle and squeezed the syringe into a bowl. The blood flowed up a tube and made the machine buzz and whirl. "If it turns green, then you're golden. If it turns red...well, let's hope it doesn't turn red."

I held my breath. *Please don't be a Mutie. Please don't be a Mutie.*

The green light dinged, and relief washed over me. I wasn't a Mutie. Now if anything happened to me, at least my parents would be safe; at least they would get my money.

*

I slept like a baby that night. I dreamt of Dad and Mama, and the cool breeze in my hair. I dreamt of flying free over the City. The sweet dreams didn't last long, though. My eyes popped open when I heard a blood- curdling scream.

"Violet!"

The lights turned on and I jumped from my bed. Out in the hall, the shouting continued.

"No," the voice shrieked. "Get up! Get up! *Get up!*"

I pushed open the heavy metal door. The hallway was a blood bath, the white walls and concrete floors covered in blood. Violet's lifeless corpse lay on the ground. Her dead eyes stared into me while Penelope pounded her chest. "Come on...come on."

Penelope tried and tried, but it was no use. I had seen it before on the farm: Violet had lost too much blood. She was dead.

I knelt down in the blood and pulled back Penelope's hand. "She's gone. She's gone."

Penelope shook her head. "No. No. *No!* Come on. Wake up. Wake *up.*"

I hugged her. "She's gone. There's nothing you can do. There's nothing you can do."

Penelope turned and buried her head in my shoulder. She wept. And I wept. We held each other, kneeling in Violet's blood, as military police stormed into the hallway.

CHAPTER 5

Violet was nice. I had liked her. She has such kind eyes, I thought—no, she *had* nice eyes. Now they were hollow and lifeless. They looked like Joan's had in death, the soul sucked out of them--so pointless, so cruel. I couldn't believe Penelope would do such a thing, but the police were convinced.

They interrogated me for hours. I don't say that figuratively, either. They spent over two hours asking me what I knew, what I saw, and where I was when Violet's throat was slit. The whole thing could've taken less than three minutes: I was in bed, end of story.

I didn't mind the distraction though, even if it was a waste of time. It prevented me from thinking about death. I'd seen plenty of it recently and it never got easier. If anything, it was harder every time. Their faces forced their way through my memory into my thoughts: the Muties from the Third Ring, Joan, and now Violet. I didn't want to think about Joan. I didn't want to see her dead eyes when I closed mine, but I couldn't help it.

Each time I went through the interrogation loop, somebody else came in to ask me questions. First it was a beat cop, then an officer, then a captain, and finally it was time for the Constable. She had the same snarled puss from the last time I saw her.

"Don't try to cover up for your friend," the Constable said.

It was a giant leap to call Penelope my friend just because she'd been nice to me. They'd arrested her immediately, because you know, there are lots of killers who try to resuscitate the body of their victims.

"My friend? She's not my friend. She's my Chaperone. And I've only known her a couple days."

They flipped on the security cameras. It showed footage of me in Penelope's room. The Constable circled the table. "Why don't you tell me what you are doing here in this video?"

"I was changing because I pissed myself. I already told you that." I knew it was saucy of me to talk to them like that. I could have been shot by any of the guards at any time, but now I was a Vessel—a legit one, too. You can't hurt Vessels. If they popped me, they would be killed on the spot.

"Why were you in the room, Althea?" she asked again.

"I told you what happened. Penelope took pity on me."

"And now you want to return the favor," she pushed,

I didn't believe Penelope was guilty. She had been nice to me and most people in the Center weren't nice—they were downright awful. The idea that Penelope could be a stone-cold killer just didn't sit right with me. Still, I wasn't dumb enough to lie for her.

"You think I'm lying to you? You guys have big guns and bigger hard-ons to use them. You think my life is worth a new tunic?"

The Constable slammed her hands on the table. "All I'm saying is that it's awful convenient."

"*What* is convenient...that I didn't see anything? It was the middle of the night and I was asleep in a room behind a heavy metal door. The real question is, if Penelope is so good at luring girls into her room, why in the Five's name would she murder a girl in cold blood in the middle of a hallway?"

The Constable stood silent for a moment. "We're looking into that."

"And besides that," I said, "if you have so many video cameras, why don't you just look at those?"

"The ones in the hallway were conveniently turned off."

"I don't think Penelope would think it was convenient."

*

They interrogated me for another hour before letting me go. Guards walked me back to my room, through the hallway that was smeared with Violet's blood. Detectives swabbed the blood, placed the samples into bags, and took pictures of the evidence they didn't need. As if they hadn't already made up their mind and decided Penelope was guilty.

If she was guilty though, why did she scream?

The room was silent when I walked in. I hadn't heard the room so quiet since that first night in the hallway.

Even before the Muties and Joan and the horrific scene in the hallway, I had seen death before, however many of these girls had never encountered death before.

McKinsey sat in the corner, rocking back and forth, mumbling to herself. Almost the whole bunk had circled around her, looking for guidance. Many of them sucked their thumbs or sobbed uncontrollably as they waited. I empathized with them. I remembered what it was like to see a dead body, like Joan's or Violet's, for the first time. Those thoughts still raced through my mind in the quiet moments.

The only one who hadn't been shattered by the sight of Violet was Cam. She knew death all too well. Death was common in the mines; she'd lost her brother when she was three, and watched helplessly as a mine had collapsed, killing her best friend. We gave each other a supportive glance as we watched the others process Violet's death.

*

They made us go to group counseling to discuss our feelings. How are you supposed to feel about somebody you knew being brutally murdered, besides just an overall yuckiness? There was nothing that a fat, bearded man could say that would make it all right.

"I just want to express our true condolences," he kept repeating. "Time wishes he could do more than hear you all out. He wishes he could be here with you, but we all know that is impossible."

The fat man was Time's assistant. Considered as an extension of the Five, each assistant had been hand-picked from the best and brightest in the City and spoke on behalf of their master

"Is it impossible though?" I said. "He is one of the Five. He should be able to come here if he wants."

The man smiled. "Even for the Five, there are rules."

"Doesn't really make them good gods," McKinsey added.

The counselor jotted down some notes. "You don't have a lot of respect for the Five, do you?"

McKinsey snarled. "I used to hold deep reverence for them, but how could they let this happen in their own house?"

The counselor smiled. "They are the light. They are the only reason we are here. We are blessed to be in the same building as them."

"You're avoiding the question. They are all knowing and all powerful, are they not?" McKinsey asked.

"Of course," the counselor said.

"Then how did one of them die, and how did they not prevent Violet's death, huh? Answer me that."

"They work in mysterious ways."

Now it was my turn. "That's a cop-out answer," I scoffed. "Do you think Wind wanted to die?"

"Maybe he did!" the counselor shouted.

"And you think they wanted Violet to die in front of us?" McKinsey spat. "Isn't she a Vessel? Wasn't she equal to them? That's what the Book says!"

The counselor cleared his throat. "None of us know their plans, and sometimes their motives are unclear. You can't speak for them. You must choose to believe they work for the greater good. Death should make us believe even harder. You'll recall Time chapter twenty, verse thirteen: 'Death strengthens those left behind.' Believe me, the Five always have a plan."

McKinsey shook her head. "Sounds like a stupid answer from somebody who doesn't know anything."

The counselor stood. "I think that's enough for today."

I loved McKinsey for that, even if I hated myself for loving McKinsey. On the way back to our room, the counselor's words rolled through my head. *"They have a plan."*

He had a point. They always had a plan, and this was the Five's house. Things didn't just happen in somebody's house without them knowing about it. Wind's death. Violet's death. Penelope's arrest. Was there any chance these deaths were somehow related?

We discovered Earth sitting in the center of our room when we walked through the door. It was really Earth, in the flesh, without guards.

I had seen Earth exemplify the worst in the Five. She was vain, arrogant, and ruthless. She hadn't even blinked when she'd killed those Muties from the Third, or when she'd berated Penelope. She showed no sympathy or humanity.

Still, I was enamored with her. *Had they programmed our DNA like that or was it because she was my great-great-great-great to the tenth power grandmother?* She may not be perfect—and she certainly wasn't a god—but her life was meaningful, and it made me feel meaningful to be in her presence. After all, my mother wasn't perfect either and I loved her.

"Hello children," Earth said with a calm smile. "I came to console you. What happened was a travesty… a complete and utter travesty! I can't believe that Penelope snapped like that…we all knew she was under a lot of stress, but to take a life…we never thought after Wind—"

"What does Wind have to do with this?" I asked.

"Penelope was Wind's personal assistant, duh!" McKinsey rolled her eyes in exasperation.

Earth responded with a smile. "You are correct, McKinsey. Penelope served Wind faithfully for years. They were as close as any two could be. When he died, we thought it would be good for her to be involved with the youth…but now we know…it was Penelope all along.

"It's clear now that she killed Wind in bloodlust, an unquenchable bloodlust. How stupid of us! I am just ashamed it took a second innocent death to make it clear. What a grave mistake and such a true shame."

Cam cleared her throat. "What will happen to her?"

Earth lowered her eyes. "She will be dealt with. Don't worry. Your friend will not have died in vain."

There was silence for a moment until Earth continued. "Now, on to the question at hand. This is a most unusual occurrence, and as such, it needs most unusual manners. So we will allow you all to leave, if you want. You can take your winnings and go. No questions asked."

"Why would we want to go?" asked McKinsey. "Where would we go?"

"Go home to your families. We cannot provide the support you may need. Not now. Not with so much to do. I urge you to go if you feel the need. It is your choice. I do hope you stay, though. You are all wonderful candidates, and I look forward to learning more about you should you decide to stay." She smiled. "But, there's more. If you leave, we will give you six additional weeks of pay in order to compensate you for your loss, but if you stay, we will give you an additional six months for your courage."

We all looked at each other. That was quite an offer. But I had other things on my mind. "Can we see her?" I asked. "Penelope, I mean?"

Earth shook her head. "That wouldn't be wise. She is ill, and it would only upset you. I'll leave you all alone to make your decision. I do hope you stay. I would so like to know each of you."

*

I had to see Penelope. It was the only way I'd know if she had really killed Violet and Wind. Had I put my trust in the wrong person, or had she been wrongfully accused? If I didn't see her, I would always regret it. Since they wouldn't let me see her, I had to find her myself. I made a plan, and while it wasn't elegant, it was a plan nonetheless.

There were eight turns before reaching the outside. At each turn, video cameras pointed down the hallway. Cam had agreed to go in front of me and cover each one with a blanket. Then I would scoot on past them one at a time. We'd keep going until I was out the door, and then she'd go back and take down the blankets.

"You ready?" I asked Cam, as she put the blanket on the video camera in our room.

"Ready!"

"What are you doing?" McKinsey asked. She was sleeping in the bunk next to ours, even though there were dozens of others available. I didn't blame her. I wouldn't want to be alone either, not after what had happened. She rolled over again. "Never mind, I don't want to know."

"Just don't tell on us, okay?" I begged.

"I'm not gonna lie for you," she said. "But I won't tell on you either."

She would never be my favorite person, but McKinsey had come a long way since we'd first met. I wished her change could have been due to better circumstances, but change is change.

Cam sidled up the hall and threw a blanket over the first camera. I ran down the hall and turned the first corner. Cam followed and threw another blanket. We continued like that until we found the door to the outside.

"Good luck," Cam whispered.

I ran out the door with a sigh of relief. I'd made it out without being caught. Then a shadow covered the bright light from the sun.

It was the Constable. "Did you really think that was going to work?"

"Yes. Otherwise I wouldn't have done it. Why didn't you stop me? Or sound the alarm?"

"I wanted to see your end game," the Constable shrugged. "There's not a lot to do in the Center, especially now. The hooligans from the preliminaries have left, the Muties haven't tried to attack since we shot them in the Third, and Wind's killer is in custody. You are the most interesting thing left. I must say I appreciate your tenacity. My people were always stubborn. I miss the Outer Rings."

"You're from the Outer Rings?"

She nodded. "The Fifth. Just like you. I was from a good family, before they found me. I've been in the military ever since." She motioned for me to walk with her. "Now, what to do with you and your friend?"

"Cam had nothing to do with this. It was all me. I forced her."

We turned a corner and there, standing in front of me, was Earth.

The Constable bowed her head to Earth then spoke to me. "It's not up to me, little one. It's up to her."

"You are an adventurous one, aren't you, Althea?" Earth said from the center of the square. The square's fountain framed her majestically.

I nodded, looking down at the floor. "Yes, ma'am."

"I believe I explicitly stated that seeing Penelope wouldn't be wise."

"You did, ma'am."

Earth's lips curled upward. "I'm not used to being disobeyed."

"I wasn't trying to disobey, ma'am. But you did give me an opportunity to leave. I want to stay, but I've got to know if I'm safe first. I can't know if I'm safe until I know for sure you've arrested the right person, you know?"

"I give you my word. We arrested the right person. Is my word not good enough for you?"

"Honestly, ma'am?"

"Of course."

"No. It's not. I'm sorry to say, but one of you just died, was murdered in fact, so the idea you are infallible...it doesn't sit right with me. And if you knew Violet was gonna die, you should've sent her home. And if you had known that Penelope was gonna do it, you should've reassigned her. See what I'm saying?"

"Well then, I suppose we should let you see your friend and remove all doubts, shouldn't we?"

"Yes, I'd like that. If that's what you decide. I don't have much say in the matter."

"And if I don't, are you going to keep sneaking out until I send you home?"

"Probably ma'am, if I'm being honest."

Earth turned. "I suppose I should take you, then."

*

Forty-eight turns. That's how many it took to find Penelope. We turned so quickly I almost lost count twice. I suppose the prison is designed that way for a reason. They didn't want people knowing their left from their right. By the time we stopped I was nauseated and dizzy.

"Go ahead...go inside," Earth motioned toward the door.

"You're not coming?" I replied. "What if she's a murderer?"

The electric door powered down. "That's why I'm not going inside. There's nothing she can say to me that I want to hear."

I walked inside hesitantly to find Penelope kneeling behind a big, electric cage. The glow bounced off of her face, aging it by decades. I sat down in a metal chair in the center of the room. "Do you remember me?"

Penelope smiled. "I'm not crazy, Thea. And I'm definitely not stupid. Of course, I remember you. But why did you come here?"

"I have to know, Penelope. Did you do it? Did you kill Wind and Violet?"

She crawled toward me. Every pore in her body oozed sweat. Her cadaverous face caved under the unflattering light. "It's a tough thing, Thea...life, I mean. We all have things to do. Things that need to get done. It's tough to know how to get them done. That's what they don't tell you when you're young. They never tell you that the trick is knowing what to do and what to leave alone, you know?"

"No, I don't know, Penelope. I just want to know if you really killed that girl."

"That doesn't matter, Thea. What matters is the perception that I murdered her. Make no mistake. I'll be tried, and I'll be killed. It's only a matter of time. Not much time either. They like things wrapped up quickly here."

"I don't want you to die if you're innocent."

"Well, I don't want to die either way, so at least we agree on that."

"They told me I could go home if I wanted."

"Then you should. You definitely should. I've seen how Earth looks at you, like you're a prize pony. Just the fact you're here right now means you have the inside track. And anyone granted an inside track is usually the winner."

"I don't want to win anything. Being zombie-fied is not a win in my book."

"Oh, it's funny to think you have a choice. Wind thought he had a choice, too. Nobody has a choice. That's the biggest lie we live with every day."

"Is that what this is about? Is this about Wind?"

"Don't you *dare* speak his name!" Penelope sat up, her voice bellowing. She softened immediately. "His dear, sweet name. I suppose I'll hear it again soon, if you believe in that sort of thing. I never believed in it, not until he died. Now I try to believe...I try so hard to believe."

"And do you? Do you believe?"

Penelope inched closer to the sizzling electricity, beckoning me closer. I dragged my chair to the edge of the cell. "I believe he was murdered by Earth. Earth murdered my Robert."

Robert.

Wind's name had been Robert. Their names were lost to the ages, but Penelope knew his name. I turned it over in my head. Robert. I wanted to twirl it on my tongue but knew I shouldn't.

The Five have no names. They were gods and gods have no names. If they had a name, they would just be human. Gods can be a lot of things, but human is not one of them.

"Did you kill her?" I asked. "Did you kill Violet?"

Penelope shook her head. "No, I didn't. But that doesn't matter. I'll die either way. Althea, I have to tell you something. There's a way to know the truth, for certain. Do you want to know the truth?"

I nodded. Penelope scooted forward and palmed a greasy piece of paper into my hand. "Read it. Then destroy it. Promise me."

"I promise." I opened the note.

Find Robert's hard drive.

I looked up at Penelope. Then down at the note.

"Destroy it now. You promised."

I stuffed the greasy note into my mouth and swallowed. A voice boomed on the speaker in the room. "Enough. Time to go."

Penelope scooted back to the back corner of her cage. "My poor, sweet Robert."

I left the cell even more confused than when I had entered. Was Earth responsible for Wind's death, or was it Penelope? I didn't know. It was, for all intents and purposes, the ravings of a mad woman.

Robert.

The name brought me pause. Penelope wouldn't have just told it to me. She was proving a point. She was trying to make me believe her—and let me know that she trusted me. She believed that Earth had killed Wind. And if Earth had killed Wind, she had also killed Violet.

"What did the note say?" Earth asked.

I sighed loudly. "It said she was innocent."

I held my breath and hoped she would believe me. A moment passed. Two. Ten. Then a hundred. Earth sighed, and then turned down the hall. "Come. We must get you back to your room."

*

The bunk looked grayer, bleaker, than when I'd left. McKinsey leaned against the wall, blankly staring off into space. The other girls sat with her—everybody except Cam, who ran to me.

"Althea!" Cam shouted. Then she saw Earth and the Constable. "You got caught, didn't you?"

I nodded. "About three seconds after I went out the door."

"I didn't do a good enough job then, huh?"

I shook my head. "That's not it at all. It was a stupid plan."

"A *very* stupid plan," the Constable corrected.

"Girls," Earth said. "I come bearing news. There will be a trial tomorrow for your old Chaperone, Penelope. It will be fair and equitable, and justice will be served. Because of this, I suggest you do not come. However," she continued, "as I've seen today, some of you have an indelible spirit. I doubt I could stop those of you from going if I wanted to, at least not without executing or exiling you." She raised an eyebrow in my direction. "And so, I will allow you access to the trial, if you wish it. However, know it will not be pretty. Justice is hard. We are fair and just in the Center, and that fairness resonates throughout the whole City. What we do here carries weight in every corner of the land. We must set an example. Come if you wish but know you have been warned."

*

I slept fitfully that night, tossing and turning until it was time to get ready for the trial. What did Earth mean by 'justice will be served'? I couldn't even imagine how horrible it might be. I had seen their cruelty and malice firsthand in the Third, where Joan had taught me innocence didn't matter. All that mattered was that there was somebody to blame, and that the whole thing could be swept under the rug quickly. It didn't matter if Penelope was guilty or innocent. She was going to die either way.

*

The trial was short. The Center was nothing if not ruthlessly efficient. The Constable acted as the prosecution. She was full of vitriol and bile. Her teeth gnashed together as she questioned Penelope, who as her own witness, barely mustered a defense. She could only plead that she didn't do it, but she wasn't very convincing. Not even to me.

"It's very convenient to claim you're innocent, seeing as the cameras were turned off."

"That's not convenient at all—because I AM innocent!"

"It's funny how the cameras were turned off at the exact moment a murder happened, don't you think?" the Constable asked.

"It's quite the coincidence," Penelope replied. "Almost as if somebody planned it."

"I couldn't have said it better myself." The Constable paced back and forth. "Tell me, do you know how to turn the cameras on and off?"

"Of course, I do. I worked for Wind for years and he liked...discretion."

"Ah, and of course the cameras were also turned off during his murder. Curious."

"Again, I couldn't agree more. It is very curious."

"And what would you tell this tribunal to make them think you are innocent? After all, you were found in a pool of the victim's blood."

Penelope hung her head. "I know the law. Guilty until proven innocent. And I can't prove my innocence. All I can say is that if you check Wind's records, you'll see the truth."

The Constable looked up at the judges. Arrow, Time, Earth, and Stone sat on a high pulpit watching the proceeding. They left an empty seat in the middle for Wind. "I think you have heard all you need to hear, wouldn't you agree?"

Time looked down at Penelope. "Do you have anything else to say in your defense?"

Penelope looked right at me, her eyes boring into my soul. These next words were for me. Only for me. "Just look through Robert's records. They speak for themselves."

The Five didn't deliberate for more than ten minutes before delivering their verdict. Arrow spoke sternly for the tribunal. "I had a great affinity for Wind. He and I would take long walks through the Center and talk about the world. I thought Penelope was good for him. After all, she was efficient, bright, and funny in her way. Quirky, but funny. However, after hearing her testimony it's clear that underneath a warm exterior, Penelope is cold, calculating, and murderous. It is bad enough she killed poor, sweet Violet, who may have been the perfect Vessel for one of us. That itself would be an affront like no other. But she did so much more. The evidence is clear. She killed Wind as well, and for that, death is too good for her. However, death is her punishment because we are merciful and just. May Wind have mercy on your soul when you meet him."

With that, the trial was over. I heard the stage being wheeled into the square before the gavel banged. I knew what would be next.

I sat still until the courtroom cleared, trying to ease my queasy stomach. I had never seen such a gross miscarriage of justice in all my short years.

Earth walked up to me with solemn steps. "May I sit?"

I nodded. "Yes, ma'am. It's your house, after all."

"I want to be sure you are...okay with our decision. I know you were...close with dear, sweet Penelope."

I wasn't okay with it. No one could be okay with such a travesty. The trial was a joke. The system was a joke. I couldn't say that though, unless I wanted to face the same fate. "Justice was done. She was put on trial and allowed to speak. What more can a person ask?"

"That is a very enlightened point of view. It will serve you well in the quarterfinals. I assume you are staying, right?"

I nodded my head. "I am. I have a duty to do my best."

*

When I walked out of the courthouse, the stage was ready for Penelope's execution. Penelope stood at its center, surrounded by guards. Announcements boomed through the streets. "Justice will be served unto Wind's killer in five minutes. Exit your buildings and head to the square to witness the Five's final justice."

Chaperones marched the remaining vessels into the square. The sunlight blinded the girls and boys who hadn't seen the sun in days as they made their way to the stage. It was a nauseating spectacle.

Despite the gruesome occasion, I was excited to see Henry. I wondered what chance he had of making it through to the semi-finals? He was nerdy and weak, his head filled with books and numbers. And yet, he had made it this far. He bobbed up and down in the crowd without a care in the world, fascinated by everything he saw, his glasses glinting in the sunshine.

I screamed to him. "Henry! Henry!" But he didn't hear. So, I ran to him. I ran through the crowd and pushed people out of the way. "Henry!"

I wrapped my arms around his neck. The thought of Penelope's death was so much harder than I thought it would be, but Henry's embrace made it bearable. He was the only one that knew pain like I knew pain. His heartbeat against my ear lessened my heartache.

"What going on?" Henry asked. "I kept asking but nobody would tell me anything. They just kept saying to come out to the square." I couldn't answer. I would let Earth deliver the answer for me. I buried my head further into Henry's shoulder as she made her way to the stage.

"I know you are all wondering why the quarterfinals have not started. I apologize for keeping you in the dark, but it was necessary. Now, we will tell you everything."

And as she did, she put her own spin on it of course. She announced that Penelope had killed both Wind and Violet in the most heinous way possible; she spoke about leaving us all in lockdown while they searched for the truth, and how vigilant they were in searching out the killer.

Vigilant. What a joke. They barely tried.

"And we finally found her. Now it is time to administer justice."

I turned my head to the stage and caught Penelope's eye. She was crying big, sopping tears— the tears of somebody about to die.

The *Book of Books* tells us that after we die our bodies are brought back to the Origin Point to wait out the days until the Five's return. Clearly Penelope didn't believe that. Maybe she wanted to believe it, maybe she had even tried to believe it, but she couldn't. Her tears were proof of that. She was as close to the Five as anybody could be, and her tears proved she didn't believe she would see Wind again after she died. If she didn't believe, what chance did any of us have?

Military officers pushed Penelope onto her knees as Earth continued. "We cannot condone such horrible actions in the Center and on our own people. What happens here reverberates into the Inner and Outer rings. Those who commit crimes must be dealt with in the swiftest way possible."

My mind raced to Joan. She too had died from their swift vengeance. Now, Penelope would suffer the same fate—two of my friends taken from me. I squeezed Henry tight. He didn't understand what was about to come. I wished I could protect him.

Earth turned to face Penelope. "Criminal, do you have any last words?"

Penelope gathered her courage. She sucked in her tears and swallowed her whimpering. She scanned the crowd until she gazed directly into my eyes. "I loved this life. I regret nothing. I am innocent. This is all a big mistake...all of this and all of us. If you look at Robert's records you will see, I am—"

The bullet went through her brain before she finished. The crowd gasped. Henry flinched but I didn't. I held strong and gripped him tighter as Earth smiled.

She actually smiled. She smiled at the death of her creation, of her child, like a psychopath. What god does that? What merciful god takes joy in the death of their children?

"Now, balance is restored. We will continue the quarterfinals tomorrow. All contestants will be moved to a new facility where they will have increased protection, nicer rooms and better food. Congratulations, vessels. Good luck to you all."

I took one last look at Penelope's dead eyes— just like Joan's, just like Violet's—lifeless and cold. They once sparkled with joy and pain, and so much kindness. Now there was nothing.

This could not stand. I couldn't let anyone else die in vain.

Penelope was innocent. I couldn't prove her innocence in life, but I would do her justice in death. I had to find Wind's records, as she asked, and discover what she knew that was worth killing over.

I released Henry, whose quivering body fought to keep my embrace. He cried and shook uncontrollably. "What...just happened?"

"Injustice. I need your help to make it right. Can you help me?"

Henry looked back at me. "What just happened? I don't—"

I pulled his face toward mine. "They're about to take us away. Who knows when I'll see you again. You can mourn later. Right now, there's no time. I need your help. Will you help me?"

Henry wiped his sniveling nose on his sleeve. "Anything you need, you know that."

BOOK 3

Transference

CHAPTER 1

There is no oppressor without an oppressed.

That quote came from a book I read in elementary school called *The Tail of Guhman the Mouse*. At the time, I thought it was a cute book about a little field mouse, but ever since coming to the Center, it had become so much more.

"A little field mouse isn't supposed to be out after dark," the big, fat owl told Guhman.

"But why not?" Guhman asked.

"It's not a little field mouse's place to question the rules." The big, fat owl scowled.

"This little, old field mouse could do a lot more than just question," Guhman said. "I promise you that."

Guhman was a rebellious mouse. He didn't want to stay inside every night while the owls patrolled the streets "protecting" him. He wanted to play, but every time he left his house a big, fat owl found him.

"Why do you keep coming out at night, little mouse?" said the big, fat owl. "Have I not shown you the night is not safe?"

"I should do what I like," said the mouse, *"without you telling me what I ought to."*

The big, fat owl smiled. *"You may do what you like in the daytime hours, little mouse. But the night belongs to the scary things."*

"Aren't you a big, scary thing too?"

I begged Dad to read it to me every night, and he read it over and over again until the pages frayed and the binding tore. There was something about the little field mouse that I identified with, even then.

"I should very much like to get through," Guhman said on the third night, *"so I can see the beauty of the field at night."*

"This is impossible, little mouse," the big, fat owl responded. *"Lest I should let every mouse into the field."*

"Why shouldn't you? Why should our rights be oppressed for yours?" asked Guhman.

"There is no oppressor without an oppressed, little field mouse." The owl smiled. *"And there is no oppression here. We just want what is best for you."*

There is no oppressor without an oppressed. That line had stuck with me to this day. Wherever there was an oppressor there was an oppressed. They might not say they were oppressors—after all, nobody wants to see themselves as the bad guys—but that didn't stop them from oppressing all the same.

Here in the City, every single person was nothing more than a plaything for the Five. Joan had been innocent. Violet had been innocent. Penelope had been innocent. Yet they were murdered all the same. We were nothing but mice in cages to the Five.

And once I opened my eyes to it, I saw it everywhere. It was in the callousness of the Transference, in the separation of the Rings, in our inability to escape to the Outside, and in the forced labor of an entire people. It was in the execution of a friend after a sham trial.

As I lay in bed that night after Penelope's execution, thoughts of my parents ran through my head and I wondered what they thought about the systematic oppression of our people? Or had a lifetime of work numbed their hearts and minds? Did they even care what happened beyond the Fifth?

Harvest season was coming soon, and I knew they needed me to silo the crops even though it wouldn't be a good harvest by any stretch. Our yield had fallen every year since I was in middle school. And even though we planted the same crops, they just didn't grow anymore. And those that did were smaller and weaker every season. The whole reason I had left home in the first place was to fix our dying farm.

And I had. I had made forty weeks' pay, more than enough to buy a better class of crop. I could leave tomorrow and have enough to save us, but this wasn't just about the farm any more. It had turned into something so much more.

I knew that even if I left, we would be in debt to the Five forever.

We were all in debt to the Five, every last one of us, and we had been for all of recorded history. We were just mice in a maze. They controlled whether we breathed, ate, slept, and survived under the Bubble that protected us from the Outside. Any sense of freedom we had was as artificial as the weather they created.

I had considered that maybe the gods were like scientists experimenting on us and if that was the case, maybe the Five really were gods. Maybe they had just sat and watched as the bomb exploded and sent my train plunging into the river, as the cops shot Joan like a dog for stealing a little food, as all of those boys and girls were tormented in the preliminaries and while somebody killed poor Violet and pinned it on Penelope. I know they had watched while she was executed. I'd seen Earth smile.

And as long as I was here in the Center, they could kill me for any reason and nobody could do a thing. I had to escape, but it wasn't enough just to flame out of the competition and go home. Even at home I was in jail. I had to break the chains for good if I wanted to be free. I had to find what was worth killing Penelope over. Luckily, I had a plan.

There wasn't much time. Even though I'd started in the preliminaries as one of 4500 other girls and made it into the quarterfinals with only 443 left, I had no clue how long things would last. But more than that, Henry and Cam had made it to the quarterfinals too. In order for my plan to work, I needed both of them.

After the preliminaries, they had moved us into much nicer accommodations. Gone were the rustic bunks in the bowels of a building— our new rooms were in twin high-rise apartment buildings towering high above the rest of the Center. One building housed the boys and the other housed the girls. And as an added convenience, there was a sky bridge on the top floors that connected the two buildings.

Each suite had two rooms, and each room contained two beds. Smelling of lavender, I ogled at the rooms' walls accented with gilded marble as I walked inside. They roomed me with Cam, which I loved, McKinsey, which I hated, and some other blonde named Abigail, who didn't matter to me at all, except for her inane prattling about nothing. She and McKinsey squealed, laughed, and giggled until all hours of the night about stupid boy bands popular in the Inner Rings.

"I heard that Jon is going to ask Ashley to marry him!" McKinsey said.

"No way! He'd never do that to me. I'm marrying him."

I shuddered, hearing them titter. The things people cared about when they didn't know what mattered; when they didn't realize big, fat owls waited in the wings to strike.

The days passed slowly during the quarterfinals, which were a lot easier than the preliminaries. The quarterfinals were more about getting inside our heads than trivial games. I didn't have to lift a barbell over my head, or run fifteen miles, or solve complex problems. They just asked me a bunch of stupid questions. Whatever I answered with, they would counter with, "How does that make you feel?"

Honestly, it was all I could do not to snap somebody's neck. I was frightened and on edge. I felt like everybody was out to get me, but I couldn't blurt that out. If I did, they would think me paranoid, or worse, a threat. All I could do was smile and say, "It makes me feel fine."

What was I going to say? That I still had nightmares of Joan's body and Penelope being shot whenever I closed my eyes? Of course not. That was a one-way ticket back to the Fifth, and I wasn't ready to go home yet.

I spent most my free time on the sky bridge connecting the two towers. From there I could see everything: from the warehouse where they'd checked us in that first night all the way to where the Center crested over the horizon to the south. It was there that I focused my attention. That's where the Five slept and that's where we had to get to for my plan to work. Earth walked there each day as darkness set in and left again when the sun rose.

When I wasn't on the sky bridge, Cam and I walked the Center's roads looking for holes in the security system. We watched the sentries move back and forth, studying the shift changes, and taking notice of all the cameras. The Center roads were open to us, with one exception: an old cobblestone path that led up to a mansion guarded by decorated officers at all times. I had an idea of who lived in the mansion but needed to be sure.

Upon doing some research, my suspicions were confirmed; it was, in fact, the road that led to the Residence where the Five had lived since time immortal, and most likely where Wind's important files were kept. If any incriminating evidence existed, it would be up there, on his personal computer.

"Where do you go all day?" McKinsey asked me one night.

"Just around," I shrugged. "The campus is lovely."

"That's stupid," McKinsey said. "You'll be able take all the walks you want when you're back home. You should be resting."

"Why do you care?" Cam asked.

The room was filled with blonde-haired, blue-eyed, beautiful girls from the Inner Rings.

"Look around," McKinsey said. "You think I want these other girls to stick around? I want you train wrecks there with me. Then I'll be sure to win."

I shook my head. "You don't still want to win, do you? Not after what happened."

Her eyes fell to the floor and her voice lowered. "I still have a duty to my family, Thea. Nothing changes that. No matter what I want."

My heart broke for her. She was still loyal to the Five, even though every fiber of her being told her to run. That was an example of some first-class brain washing.

*

The first time I told Henry my plan, how we needed to pretend like we were dating, variations of "I...umm...it...ho boy...well..." stuttered out of his mouth between incomprehensible giggles for at least twenty minutes.

"You can't be like this. If they're going to let us hang out together, it makes sense that we would be young lovers who can't get enough of each other."

"It's...you're right, but..."

"You've never had a girlfriend, huh?"

He shook his head. "Except for you, I've never even held a girl's hand. Besides my mom and sister, of course, but I feel like that shouldn't count for much in the grand scheme."

I placed my hand in his. "Well, you have to get used to it now."

The guards wouldn't suspect three people were plotting against them when two of them were making googly eyes at each other. It would be an easy sell. We'd met through a very traumatic situation before coming to the Center. It made sense he would fall in love with me. What didn't make sense were the real feelings I had started developing for him.

I thought it would be weird pretending to be his girlfriend, but it felt natural almost immediately. I'd never felt a connection to Jake, at least not a physical one. With Henry, I felt a flutter in my stomach every time we touched, even from those first moments.

It wasn't easy to find time to be alone. I mostly saw Henry at meal times. The boys were subjected to different rigors than the girls. Their days were spent in the computer labs that dotted every floor, being tested for one thing or another.

"I have to admit, I could do without all the math," Henry said.

"Math?" Cam asked.

"Oh my god. There is just so much testing. We're testing all day and night: science, calculus, and equations galore. I've never had to remember so much math."

Henry might have hated it, but access to the computer labs was a necessary part to our plan. He needed to find the blueprint for the Center so that Cam and I could figure out how to get into Wind's room and raid his hard drive. Then, he needed to hack into the camera system to reprogram them so that they would malfunction as we passed them. It was a complicated plan, and without him, it all fell apart. He was the only one who knew computers well enough to make it happen.

"Luckily," Henry said, "I always finish my tests first and they're always flawless. It gives me a lot of time to hack into the Center's mainframe and look around for what I need."

"I wonder why they aren't testing us like that," Cam said.

"Oh, they are. Just in a much different way. I heard they're testing your psychological mettle. Earth wants to make sure that you can withstand the enormous pressures of her job. Time and Arrow have different pressure on them, but they're still important nonetheless."

"What about Stone's job?" I asked.

Henry laughed. "That's funny. You think Stone has any power anymore?"

"Why wouldn't she?"

"Because she's crazy, Thea."

After the third day of the quarterfinals, Henry finally found a flaw in the security camera system. "Their security software hasn't been updated in over three cycles. Anybody with decent skills could break through the security firewall and take over the system. Luckily, I am that anybody."

Henry risked being caught every time he went into the system, but he did it with a smile. He really was an amazing—not just an amazing coder but an all-around amazing person.

While Henry worked to hack into the camera system, it was our job to find the flaws in the guard patrols. On the fifth day, we did.

Every night the curfew bell rang at 9:45 PM. At that time, we were put on lock-down while the guards made one final sweep of the building, who, when finished, went back to the guard station across campus for shift change. They were gone ten minutes before a new shift started. That was our window.

*

On the fifth night of the quarterfinals, Cam and I had a group session with McKinsey and a few others before dinner. I thumped my foot on the floor to expel my nervous energy. I didn't care about listening to Abigail prattle on about her feelings. I only cared about the mission at hand.

There were a dozen of us forced together chatting the chit about nothing. I hated these group sessions more than anything. Nobody ever said anything interesting and the chairs were uncomfortable.

"And how does being here make you feel?" the moderator asked Abigail.

"Well, I really want to see Mister Binkles again. I miss him. He used to curl up on my stomach when I slept, and he would keep me warm." Abigail loved the attention. She needed it. She would make a good Earth. They both loved being loved.

Finally, an alarm dinged, and a fat, old woman walked inside. "It is time for session to end and dinner to be eaten, yes?"

The moderator smiled at us and closed his notebook. "Very good, Greta. I think that's enough for today. Good session."

I'm glad he thought it was good, because to me it was a waste of time. How many times could they ask us the same questions before they gave us the ax? How many times did I have to hear the same stupid answers to the same inane questions?

Greta walked us down to the cafeteria. As she opened the door to lead us inside, we got an unexpected surprise. Earth was sitting in the middle of the room, just as she had been after Violet's murder.

"Welcome, children. If you've made it this far, you have survived the first cut."

My heart skipped a beat. Cam and I had made it. Thank God. A lump tugged at my throat. *What about Henry?* Without him our plan could never succeed.

"You will be moved onto a single floor," Earth told us. "And you will be spending time with us personally. We have ranked you according to who is best suited for taking over our consciousness at this moment. If you show up on one ranking, that is fantastic and if you show up on two, then that's even better. Some of you will be pleasantly surprised. Some of you disappointed."

A projector turned on next to Earth's head. A recording began to play. Each of the Five appeared on the screen and took turns naming their top ten candidates. I scanned the boards for Henry's name and found him at the top of Time's chart. My heart settled down. He'd made it through in exemplary fashion. I knew he'd made an impression on the bearded philosopher, but I didn't think he would be first. More importantly, I didn't expect to see myself as fifth on Time's list!

I turned to Cam. "Why would Time choose me? I'm a girl."

"Well, yeah," Cam said. "These people have been alive for thousands of years. You think they've always kept to one gender?"

I did, actually. I'd studied the Five extensively in school and had never known them to switch genders. "I've never seen them switch, actually."

"That's small time thinking, my friend. Besides, even if they know who they're going to choose, it's nice to explore other options."

Abigail jumped for joy when she showed up second on Earth's list. She demanded a big hug from McKinsey, who unenthusiastically agreed.

After further study, I noted Henry had only showed up on Time's list, and Cam had only showed up on Stone's list, along with McKinsey. McKinsey was in first place, of course. She choked back a lump in her throat and plastered on a smile. It was wooden and hollow, but she played the part well. "I'm going to win, you know. It's all but assured now."

I didn't care about that. I was just happy to pass, and although I hadn't placed high on any one list, I was the only person who'd made it onto three lists. It was a weird feeling to be so wanted by people I so hated so intensely.

I breathed a sigh of relief that we'd all made it through. It was sloppy work to have waited this long before executing our plan, but Henry needed time to prep. Now we had no choice but to move forward—I couldn't risk us being separated. We would never have another shot at this. It was time to strike.

CHAPTER 2

I spent the rest of the evening walking the Center, timing the guards, and watching the cameras everywhere I went. It was busy work, but it made me feel useful. When I finally made it back to the suite it was an hour before curfew. I expected Cam to be a little nervous, but when I opened the door to our room, she could barely look me in the eyes.

"What's wrong?" I said, sitting down next to her.

"I don't think I should go with you," Cam said.

I leaned up. "You have to."

"No. Henry does— he's the brain for this operation. He knows how all of this all works. Without him next to you, this plan is going to fall apart. If you think about it for a second, you'll see I'm right."

I had thought about it. Honestly, I had thought about it all evening. I loved Cam. She was dear, and loyal, and brave... but she didn't know anything about computers. If there were a problem, Cam and I wouldn't be able to solve it.

"You're right," I said, flopping back on the bed. "He's gonna flip his lid."

And he did. He squirmed and jittered when I found him in the computer lab fiddling away. "No. Absolutely not. I'm not doing that. I want to help, but no. That's too much to ask." His voice cracked and grew louder with each syllable.

"Keep your voice down!" I hissed through gritted teeth.

He shook his head vigorously. "We had a plan. I designed a plan. I like plans. This plan is timed to the fraction of a second for you and Cam. By adding me, you are adding a new variable to the plan. I do not like variables."

"None of us do," I said, "but this is a better plan. You know it."

"I don't like change."

"Look, run the numbers. You love running numbers. You'll see this has a way better chance for success."

His eyes spun back in his head for a moment. When they flipped back, his face contorted in a scowl. "Okay, fine. You're right. I don't have to like it though."

*

I entered our suite just as the curfew bell sounded. The big, fat owls made it so we couldn't move again until the break of day, but I wanted to see the field. The next fifteen minutes of waiting were the most brutal of my entire life.

"I'm scared," I said for the first time out loud.

"It is scary," Cam replied. "But you'll be fine. It's not like just anybody can make it this far. You're special."

I smiled. Somehow, her words made me feel better. I looked at the clock again as it rolled over to 10:00pm and heard a soft rapping on the door. My heart lit up when I opened the door—it was Henry. "Come on then."

Henry walked Cam and me down the hall and across the sky bridge into the boy's dorm. "Cam, all you have to do is sit, smile, and make sure nothing goes wrong."

"And if something goes wrong?"

"Nothing is going to go wrong," promised Henry.

"Then why can't I stay in bed?"

Henry stopped. "Because I can't stay in bed, okay? Don't think I'm clueless as to where Thea got the idea to send me on this crazy mission. I'm very smart. I can run hundreds of calculations per minute, and they all point to you. Stop here."

He looked down the hallway, waiting for a straggling guard unit to pass. I had never seen him take charge before, and I liked it. This was Henry in his element. Fours were planners and executers. They knew how to keep a schedule. I had never thought that sort of thing would make my knees weak.

On one hand, it was weird the kinds of things you found attractive about somebody once you get to know them. But on the other hand, I hated feeling something for Henry because I knew it could never work between us. In the worst-case scenario, he was going to be one of the Five. In the best case, he would return to the Fourth and we would never see each other again.

"Let's go." Henry walked forward with authority. "I've studied the blueprints of the Center until my eyes bled. Turn here."

We turned into the computer room where a dozen monitors glowed blue in the darkness. Henry sat down at one of the stations where his screen showed thirty-six different camera feeds.

"This is the Center's monitoring system. Thirty-six cameras are active on screen at any one time. They rotate every thirty seconds. I programmed the cameras to use our feed when I signal them. All we have to worry about is getting through a section before the guards come back. Cam, all you have to do is watch and pray to the Five we won't be caught. Okay?"

"Got it."

"Don't forget to turn off the system at 10:29 PM, at which point you'll have thirty seconds to get to your room before the guards come back. If you don't turn it off, they'll trace it back to this site and connect it back to me. If that happens, we all get in trouble. Got that?"

Cam nodded. "I got it."

"Then we're off. Ready, Althea?"

I smiled at Cam. "Good luck sitting on your butt."

Cam smiled back at me. "Good luck risking yours."

*

We moved quickly and quietly out of the building and onto the quad. Henry pulled me into the brush as we watched the guards disappear around a building.

"The next shift will be back out in ten." He pointed up to a nook in a nearby brick building. "Do you see the blinking light over that camera?"

I nodded. "Yes."

He smiled. "Good. So, right before my program overrides the camera, it moves to the far left and jiggles a bit. Then the light turns solid red. Watch for it."

Henry pulled a clicker from his coat pocket and hit the button. "This should send an override to the camera." Nothing happened for a moment and Henry's breath stiffened in anticipation. "Come on."

Another couple seconds of nothing and then it happened. The camera moved far left, jiggled slightly, and the light turned solid red. "That's it," Henry said. "Let's go."

We continued through the streets until they turned from asphalt into cobblestone. This was the furthest into the Center I'd ever been. You couldn't make it behind the cobblestone without a pass, and I never had one, but right now the path was clear.

I smiled to myself. "I was right. It's working."

"Yes, yes. You are very smart." He clicked his button and the cameras jiggled. "Let's go."

*

We stepped onto the cobblestone street and made our way toward the Residence. The buildings became more opulent and gaudy as we walked up the steep hill. The simple brick fell away and was replaced by marble, stone, and gold.

Eventually the houses and buildings cleared out and only one loomed in the foreground, majestic in its eeriness. Behind a heavy wrought-iron fence, the mansion glowed, surrounded by a thick ethereal hue, like it was sent from the Origin Point itself. "That's the Residence, right? It has to be."

Henry smiled. "It is. Follow me." He grabbed my hand and brought me to the back of the complex. The wrought-iron fence continued around the whole perimeter. "Wind was famous for sneaking women into the Residence late at night. Did you know that?"

"No, I didn't," I whispered, thankful the darkness hid the flush on my cheeks.

Henry stopped at a bush next to the fence and then pulled at its roots with all his might. After a few seconds the bush gave way, revealing a manhole cover. Henry placed his palm on the center and it opened to his touch. He threw a smug smile over his shoulder. "It's amazing what you can learn rooting around in the subdirectories for a week."

I smiled as I lowered myself onto the ladder that led down into the tunnels. "And yet you couldn't get into Wind's computer remotely."

"Yeah. That's because it's not on the grid. If it was—"

"I was kidding, Henry. Let's go."

"Oh."

The tunnels under the building weren't ostentatious like the Residence's façade. The rocks supporting the walls, which continued onward in each direction, were craggy and felt damp even though there was no water running through them.

"This used to be an old storm tunnel thousands of years ago, before they could control the rain. They run all over the Center and out into the First."

Before the Incident, the Five couldn't regulate the weather; they couldn't control everything like they did now. For instance, while it was always warm and sunny in the Center, it was usually cold and damp in the Fifth. I'd cursed the weather during storms and wished the thunder would stop. The Five had the power to make it stop. They could make the grass grow or lay a field fallow. Everything was at their whim.

Henry stopped me at another ladder. "Up you go."

When I got to the top, I opened the hatch and pulled myself up into a dark room barely big enough for both us.

"We're here," Henry said. "Wind's room is apparently right outside these doors. He was a sneaky little guy, huh? I am impressed with the level of deception and calculation required to create such an elaborate system, all for the purpose of having intercourse. Fascinating."

When we stepped inside, the room was pitch black, save for a shimmering door with light flowing in from underneath. "We need light if we're going to get anything done."

I heard voices coming from behind the door. Guards. If I turned on the light, they would see it. There had to be a way to conceal us. I turned to Henry. "Take off your shirt."

"Why?" Henry asked, confused.

"To shove under the door, so the guards can't see."

"Oh." He shuffled to remove his shirt and stuffed it under the door until we were in complete darkness again. When he was done, I fumbled across the wall for the switch.

The lights flicked on and the brightness blinded me for a moment. When my eyes focused, I saw a pasty-chested Henry smiling back at me. He was handsome, even though his chest caved in on itself.

"Please don't stare," he begged.

Henry was not classically attractive. He wasn't Jake, but his narrow frame and thick glasses gave him something you don't see on the farm very often. "Strapping" was the best word to describe the men I knew, and Henry was not that—no, he certainly wasn't that. Still, I couldn't help but be attracted to what little of him there was. He had...character.

"Let's get started," he said.

I looked around the room. Hundreds of pictures covered the walls and an unmade gilded bed sat in the middle of the room. As I moved forward to study the pictures, I recognized a tall, bald man from three of Wind's lifetimes ago, and the finely coifed one from his last. Every picture on the wall was one of his past lives.

I studied them all, the most interesting ones dating farther back in time. The frames looked older, and the faces in them were colors I had never seen before— black, caramel, mocha, yellow, and red. Throughout my entire life, I had only seen the same skin color staring back at me in every textbook. Even in the Inner Rings, everybody had the same light brown skin tone. I had just assumed that that was true everywhere and forever, like an idiot.

The rest of the room, though ornate, was sparsely decorated. Across from the bed stood a chest of drawers with a television perched on top, and across the room Henry had sat down at a simple desk already typing away at Wind's computer.

I continued to snoop while Henry worked and noticed the marble nightstand next to Wind's bed. Then I saw it—a framed picture of Wind and Penelope, smiling happily. If I didn't know any better, I would have thought they were in love.

Then it dawned on me. They *were* in love. It made complete sense. That must have been why she was so miserable all the time. It explained the pining eyes she had when talking about Wind. Judging from the look in Wind's eyes in the picture, it wasn't an unrequited love. Was that why they'd both been killed?

"Are you done over there?" Henry whispered. "Because I have a problem."

I walked over to the computer and watched as he typed furiously. "What is it?"

"I didn't account for this computer being an antique. I can't bypass the login screen, and I'm trying to override the password with my program, but it's not working. This computer is so old it won't recognize my code. I have to manually try passwords by hand, but I only get a few guesses before it locks down completely. Any idea what the password could be?"

My brain whirled. "Try...Penelope," I suggested.

He typed away, but an error screen popped up. "That didn't work. We might only get one more shot at this."

"I've got it. Try Robert."

"Why Robert?"

"Trust me."

His nimble fingers flew over the keys and like magic, the password screen faded into the home screen. "How did you..."

"Later. Now, let's get to work."

"Right." Henry pushed a data cell into the computer's port and copied all the files. "I can't believe this worked."

I smiled at him. I couldn't believe it either. As we watched the files fly across the screen, something caught my eye—a file labeled "DO NOT OPEN."

"What's that?"

Henry squinted at the screen. "It's a text document," he whispered. "From...whoa, a thousand years ago."

He opened the file and we read it together:

I shouldn't be writing this, but I can't stop myself. I need to remember exactly how we got here. When I start losing my memory, I need this to be right here where I can read it over and over again. I have to remember it in every lifetime. I have to remember the truth. Over time, truths become half-truths that become lies...and those lies become facts. My mind is already slipping and with each transference, I remember less. But I have to remember this. We destroyed the world.

It wasn't supposed to happen like it did. We were all so happy just a couple hundred years ago. The Center for Scientific Advancement was the best research facility on the planet. The top minds in the entire world were here. That's why I came here to study. That's why Janet, Dave, Sven, and Lin came too, from around the world.

It was all going so well, until it all blew up in our faces. Janet didn't mean to bring the whole world crashing down. She couldn't have known what it would do. She was running a test of her nuclear fusion reactor and it wasn't even supposed to work, but it did. It worked better than anybody could have predicted. It pulled power directly from the sun.

We were elated at first, but then things went horribly wrong when a solar flare took out our dampeners and fried our fail-safes. Then, the shielding I developed wasn't holding because there was so much power coming from the reactor. I somehow redirected power to protect the Center and the surrounding city. I still don't know how I did it. It was instinct.

In the end, we only survived the explosion because of my shield and it's the only thing that protects us now. This stupid Bubble is our prison. The nuclear fallout will last generations. Who knows how far the damage goes, or how far the solar flare reached?

The rescue crews never came, and we never saw anyone from the outside. Years passed, and we were able to cobble together working power from Janet's designs. Poor Janet. She hasn't been the same since. And her poor daughter...no one knows what happened to her.

Eventually, we got Lin's environmental dampeners online so there was climate control and we could make food and Sven helped us rebuild life.

But the power was fragile and only a few knew how to work it. We tried to train others, but nobody else understood. As we aged, people became frightened our deaths would lead to their deaths too.

Finally, we came up with a solution— a horrible solution. We discovered how to transfer our consciousness into new bodies. We were mad scientists. We knew that. But we had to survive to protect the city, and this was the only way. If we could keep our race going, the dreadfulness of destroying people's minds would be worth it, right? That's what we told ourselves.

So, we were chosen. The five of us. We were supposed to protect humanity, not enslave it. I don't know when we chose new names. I don't know when we abandoned the desire to open the force field back up. Maybe it was power, fear, or just greed. But here we are.

Henry and I stared at each other, our mouths agape. This contained the makings of something much bigger than the murder of Wind. This was the dismantling of everything we understood about our lives.

No wonder Wind had been murdered. And no wonder Penelope's death quickly followed. People would go to any length to protect this secret. It went to the core of exactly what it meant to be in this City.

The Five were our saviors, but they were also the ones who imprisoned us in the first place. If this got out, it would destroy everything.

CHAPTER 3

I made it back to my room just as the guards returned to duty. Very quietly I slipped into bed and shut my eyes, trying to get my heart to stop thumping in my chest.

That night, I experienced a slew of strange dreams. I dreamt of being exiled and of being killed. I dreamt of opening the Bubble, being poisoned and jettisoning into space. I dreamt that I was the downfall of society, and I dreamt of the wind in my face as I ran through the fields at home.

I dreamt of Robert and Penelope, about how happy they must have been for a time, and how horrible his death must have been for her.

I dreamt I was a puppet on Earth's string. In order to escape I had to cut myself free from the rope. As I cut away each string, they became chains that grew and grew in strength. By the last string, the chain was so thick it suffocated me. Right at the moment of my death, I woke up.

I was alone. Cam's bed was made up perfectly and she was nowhere to be found.

By the time I'd returned last night, Cam was already fast asleep. Despite wanting to wake her up to tell her everything, I had decided to let her sleep and now I regretted that decision.

I reached under my pillow and pulled out the data cell. It wouldn't be long before the guards discovered what we'd done. They would know Henry had hacked into their system. We had to make it out before that happened, but we had to be cautious. We couldn't bring any attention to ourselves or make anyone suspicious.

When I walked out into the suite, Abigail bopped her head to some crappy boy band music blaring over the radio. "Morning," she yelled. "I needed a break from the craziness. I hope you don't mind."

"It's fine." I couldn't worry about her terrible taste in music—I had things to do.

I prepped for the day like normal, even though it wasn't a normal day. Today each of us met with the Five, one on one. They would size us up and make a decision about our mettle. *How could I look them in the face, knowing what I knew now*? But I had to be strong. We were so close to freedom.

As soon as I failed their interviews, the Five would discard me like old socks and never be the wiser. At least, not until it was too late.

Breakfast was over by the time I came downstairs; the room empty except for Henry and a squad of bored guards sleeping and playing cards. The other Vessels had ravaged the food, leaving nothing but scraps for me.

But it didn't matter. I was too worried to eat anyway. As my stomach swirled into anxious knots, I sat down next to Henry. I breathed easier when he was close. "Hey. Have you seen Cam anywhere?"

Henry shook his head. "No. She must've had an early meeting with Stone. She wasn't here when I came down." He swallowed a big bite of muffin. "Aren't you going to eat? You'll need all your mental faculties to get through today. I calculated that I'll need to consume three thousand calories to make sure I'm in top mental shape today."

"I do my best work hungry. Besides, the worse I am, the better I am, right?"

"I suppose so."

Abigail danced her way into the cafeteria. She was chipper, excited, and I wanted to murder her in every way. "There you are, Thea! They're looking for you."

I stood up. "Who is?"

She shook her head and popped in her ear buds. "I think they said Time. I wasn't really paying attention."

I nodded at her. "Thanks."

I palmed the data cell into Henry's hand as I got up to leave.

"Bad luck!" He smiled as I walked out the door.

*

Time's office was filled to the brim with antique clocks and metronomes, all of which pounded in my ears with every simultaneous tick. I flashed back to the third door. The ticking of that infernal clock would haunt my memories forever.

"I have collected them over the centuries," he said without me asking. "Time is fleeting, yet for me, it goes on infinitely. Having these...it brings me back to the present."

"Do you like it...living forever?"

He stroked his beard. "At times. Then, I remember all too well the many lives I've led, and it saddens me."

"Why? You could kill yourself whenever you wanted."

"Could I?" he said. "I suppose, but then so many would suffer." He cleared his throat. "It's not painless you know. Transference. It's almost like dying, I would imagine."

"Imagine how it would feel for me."

He smiled. "I do. Sometimes I swear I can hear my Vessels in the silent moments. Maybe that's why I like the noise. It drowns out all the minds I've shared with people."

"You mean overridden. It's not sharing. It's commandeering."

"That is such a harsh word," Time commented. "Commandeer? We did not force you to come, after all."

I smiled. "Whatever you say."

The sides of his lips curled. "Of course, you understand that. All too well. That is why you are still here. You know that only your sacrifice can save our species."

"We are not of the same species, though, are we? I mean, not really. You are a human, and we are what you consider humanity. I am a replica of what you think humanity should be. Perfect skin, perfect eyes, but still lacking something."

Time didn't say another word. He turned to his clocks until I decided to leave. He didn't even say goodbye or wave me off. He just sat there, pondering. One bad interview done and two more to go-- I'd be gone before the next round.

I walked back into the cafeteria; just like every other day, a guard napped in the corner. I pitied them. It must have been such a boring job, watching us being paraded around.

I then noticed Abigail at a table, rocking out to her jams and playing cards with two officers. I wanted to turn and run from her, but when she spotted me, I smiled halfheartedly and waved. "Have you seen Cam?"

She shrugged. "Nah. She must've left before I got up."

"That's weird. She usually waits for me to eat breakfast."

Abigail shrugged. I had to admit that even though she was hopelessly annoying, I envied her innocence. She was not fazed by anything at all.

*

Stone was a hoarder—ancient books, newspapers, and trinkets filled every corner, lining her library from floor to ceiling as papers teetered on the edge of collapse. Some of them already had, coating the entire floor in thick layers of clutter.

Stone herself was skittish, afraid, and cowardly. She sat on the floor with her knees tucked into her chest, rocking back and forth. "So...so...so...tell me about yourself."

"Well, I grew up on a little farm in the Fifth. We mostly grow corn, but we have some dairy cows too, and a few pigs running around for pork."

"That's nice. Is it...a place where you live?"

I didn't know how to answer, so I just repeated myself. "Yes, it's a very nice farm in the Fifth. We mostly grow crops, but we also have a little meat as well."

"That's nice for people, to be in places."

"It's nicer for people to be able to leave places, though."

She didn't like that. Her rocking became more erratic. She started to cry as she stared out into the same abyss that had enraptured Time. "Well, I guess that's it," she finally said.

She stood to usher me out, but I stopped her. "Why did you pick me?"

Stone frowned. "You look like my daughter."

It hit me like a lightning bolt. I remembered what Wind had written in the note. *Poor Janet. Nobody knows what happened to her daughter.* Stone must have been Janet!

Poor Janet was right. She was responsible for everything that happened to us. No wonder she went crazy. There's no coming back from destroying your whole race.

Henry waited for me outside of Stone's chamber. "There you are. About time." He hugged me tight. "Follow me."

He pulled me outside and around a corner. I thought he was going to kiss me—I hoped he was going to kiss me, but he didn't. When he let go of my hand, it was all I could do to hide my disappointment.

"Stone's not picking you. She's already made her choice."

"What about Time?"

Henry hesitated. "Him too."

"How do you know?"

"He...told me."

We looked at each other for a moment. It was the quiet desperation of a boy who knew he was about to die.

"Oh," I replied, dropping my eyes from his gaze. "That...sucks."

"It's what I wanted—to give my life for my City and for my family. At least, that's what I thought I wanted..."

We locked eyes again.

"Now it doesn't matter what I want...but you...you can still get out of here and take the drive with you." He grabbed my hand. "Just blow your interview with Earth and you're home free."

"I don't want to leave you here."

"You have to," Henry said, placing the data cell into my palm. "I checked the data on this thing. If it's authentic, and there's no reason to believe that it's not, it could send the whole City crashing down."

"How?"

"The Bubble. We don't need it and we haven't needed it for centuries. That's what Wind knew and was about to tell everybody—remember the video at the inaugural address? He was trying to change things. If we don't need the Bubble, we don't need the to be locked in here and sacrificed like animals just so the Five can keep living. Somebody will be able to destroy the Five with the info on this tape. Find them."

I couldn't say anything. Tears welled in my eyes. My throat closed in upon itself. I kissed him on the cheek and walked away, leaving him to ponder whatever it was he had to ponder. I still had work to do.

*

Earth's office wasn't like the others—it was homey and friendly, but with the elegance you'd expect from somebody who enjoyed the finer things in life.

The interview with Earth didn't go the same as the others, either. She showed no fear. She smiled at me. She laughed with me. She was the consummate professional.

"Where's Cam?" I asked her.

"I'm sure I don't know. I don't keep tabs on Stone's property."

"Are you sure? Because you seem to know everything about everything around here."

"Well that's not entirely true," Earth smiled. "I don't know where you went last night, after all."

"I didn't go anywhere. I was in bed."

Earth smiled. "You are very smart. That's why you've made it this far. But I'm smarter. Plus, I have centuries of experience on you."

"Yes, well you are a god. I suppose you could just read what I was thinking."

"I don't have to read what you are thinking. I can see it all over your face. You went to see that boy, didn't you? Henry, is it?"

I held back a smile, but it came out as a smirk. "You would know."

"I've seen how you look at each other. This happens every time we hold a Transference. It's really tragic. One of you is chosen, the other isn't. Then you have to spend the rest of your life watching a shell of your former love on television."

"Is that what happened to you?"

Earth leaned forward. "Oh no. It's what happened to your father."

I hopped up in my chair. "My father? That's crazy."

"No. It's not. Back then your father didn't love your mother. He loved...me. Well not me, but the vessel I chose. They were madly in love. So, in love, that they almost ruined it all by consummating their union. Luckily your father was released before any damage could occur and she became, well, me. I wonder what your father thinks, when he sees her. Do you think he still loves her?"

I bowed my head. "You're cruel for telling me that. What made you so cruel?"

"Years and years of life, my dear. But this is not cruel. This is just the truth. Everyone—from the exalted god to the lowly farmer—has their place here. Farmers are very near and dear to me, you see. After all, they are my responsibility."

"Yes. We know the story of you bringing grain from the heavens to feed us all."

"Oh, come now. That's a child's story. We both know you are smarter than that. However, I did develop the systems to harvest food, make it sustainable, and provide the mechanisms that allow this City to thrive. I alone control the temperatures, the day, and the night. If control over the world is what makes somebody a god, then yes, I am a god."

"You also control the police and can kill at will."

Earth leaned back. "I do like you, dear. You are funny. Who would you rather see in the center stage? Doddering old Time? He has no stomach for those sorts of things. Or how about crazy Stone, who can barely keep it together these days? Or maybe slovenly Arrow, who can't be bothered to leave his room except to find more food? No. It falls to me, my dear—to carry the burden, to do what must be done. Do you have the stomach to do what must be done, Althea?"

"You have no idea."

*

Cam didn't come back to the room that night, or the next morning. I searched around for her but couldn't find her anywhere. Henry checked through his databases, but all the files were purged. There was nothing. It was as if Cam never existed. Worse, while many of the girls and boys were packing to go home, I was waiting in limbo. I hadn't been dismissed from my duty as a Vessel. My heart thumped into my ears throughout the day as I hid the data cell in darker and darker places to conceal it.

Henry tried to calm me, but I knew something was wrong. Henry knew something must be wrong, too, but was trying to be polite. Eventually I popped. I couldn't take it anymore. I knew Earth was toying with me and I didn't appreciate it. More importantly, I wouldn't stand for it. I banged on her study door over and over again.

"Come in," Earth said pleasantly. Earth was calmly seated on her plush chair when I walked into the room.

"You never answered my question before. I demand you answer it now. Where's Cam?"

"You really love her, don't you?"

"Of course, I do. She's my best friend in here."

Earth chuckled. "What about Henry? I think he would be sad if he heard you say that."

"It's...different with him. Now stop getting off topic and tell me what happened to her."

Earth stood up and walked to the window. The light of the stained glass reflected onto her face. "Well, since you are so adamant, I'll tell you. She isn't who she said she was."

"What do you mean?"

"I wanted to shield you from this. I hoped I would never have to tell you. She is a spy. The Muties, horrible freaks of nature, somehow bypassed all my security and got her access into the tournament. They overrode all our testing and got her through to the semifinals. She was supposed to kill me of all people, but I saw through her."

I stood. "Then what..."

"Luckily, she made a mistake. We caught her last night trying to edit my list, so she could have an audience with me. Very sloppy work. Easily found out. It's a shame."

"And now what?"

"She'll be executed, I suppose. It's all very messy business— the messiest Transference in recent memory."

I sat down again, slack-jawed and stunned. "I don't—"

"Don't worry. She will have no impact on your standing. You couldn't have known, could you, my dear?" Earth bent down and looked into my eyes, piercing into my soul. "Could you, dear?"

I shook my head no and the conversation ended, but as I walked back to my room it all made perfect sense. The Sixth is far enough from the Center that you can blend in if you wanted, just like Joan blended into the background. You could find a Mutie there who hadn't been tested, recruit them, send them through to the Center, and help them pass every test. Every test until the Five had to make a decision.

Too many things didn't add up, though. Why would Cam have helped me? She risked the tournament for me and saved me—twice. Why would she risk being found out?

I had to leave, that was still true. But I couldn't let Cam die, either. I had to bust her out. I had to save her life. Even if it meant blowing up my own plans for survival.

*

I dragged Henry into my room. He was nervous, agitated even, when I told him about Cam. But he was even more so when I told him I needed to break her out.

"You can't just break into the guard station. It's mathematically and statistically impossible. The number of variables you must account for is staggering. They are going to find you and when they do, they'll kill you."

"They didn't last time."

He grabbed my arms. "You're going to ruin everything. Thea, you can escape. You don't have to do this."

I broke free of his grip. "Yes, I do have to. She helped us and now she'll be killed if we don't help."

"What about me? What about all I've done to help you? If you don't make it out of here, all of that will be in vain."

I stroked his face. "Then I guess I won't get caught then."

"You will get caught. That is a certainty. Then, they're going to kill you."

"They're going to kill you, too. At least I won't be a walking skin for somebody else. I can do this with or without you. Are you going to help me or not?"

Of course, he was going to help me. I could see it in his eyes every time he looked at me. He liked me as much as I liked him. I had always assumed that was true, but now I knew it for sure. A fire burned in his eyes for me.

It pained me to look into those eyes, knowing that very soon they would no longer be *his* eyes. It broke my heart to know that one day I would watch him on TV, but it wouldn't be Henry. It would be Time, using Henry as a puppet...assuming I lived to witness it, of course.

But I couldn't think like that. I had to be positive, even if I was only positive that rescuing Cam was a terrible idea. It looked like Abigail's sickeningly upbeat attitude was rubbing off on me.

The first step, before I could even get into the cell, was finding a key into the guard station. I hadn't been there since the preliminaries, but I watched officers stream in and out day and night during my walks through the Center. In order to get in, I needed a key. Luckily, the guards were idiots.

"I still don't like this," Henry said as we walked back inside. "And since I can't talk you out of it, I guess I'll at least help you get the best odds for success."

Sure enough, the guard on the bench was asleep again, and the other guards were nowhere to be found. The timing was perfect.

"Me either. I would rather my best friend not be a spy and the Five not evil, but that's just the way of things now, isn't it?"

"I suppose." He handed me the clicker from his pocket. "I hope this still works. They're watching the system like a hawk after Cam messed everything up. Be careful."

*

I would like to say snatching the key off the dozing guard was a piece of cake, but it was even easier than that. He didn't even move as I swiped the key from his belt. Once I had the key, I strolled into the quad, pointed the clicker at a camera and waited. The camera swayed right, then left. It jiggled for a moment and the light turned solid red. Henry's program still worked.

I didn't need to shut off the cameras until I got closer to the main station, located across from where the preliminaries had taken place.

*

I made my way across the Center to the front door of the prison. I held the clicker up to the three cameras at its entrance and ran inside. The key card worked like a charm.

I remembered the way through the prison. The last time I'd been here was the last time I had seen Penelope before she'd given up hope and Earth had pelted me with questions during our leisurely walk through the halls.

This time I sprinted. There was no one in sight once I'd passed the first few corridors. The further into the belly of the station I got, the darker and more confusing it became.

Eventually, I made it to the cell. I crossed my fingers and looked inside. At first, I didn't see anything, but then a leg kicked from the far corner, through two layers of red electric gates. A figure rolled over and I saw her face. It was Cam!

I swiped the card, certain it would work, but it didn't. Three red lights and a squeal locked me out. I tried it again to the same result as footsteps approached, clomping down the corridor.

"Alright, you filthy maggot," the guard said, carrying a tray. "Here's your food. Don't know why we even bother. After all, you're gonna be dead tomorrow morning."

The guard swiped his card to the cell and walked inside. I tucked in behind him. Cam saw me, but her face remained stoic. She couldn't give me away. For this to have any chance of working, she needed to be silent, unresponsive.

"Ummm...thank you," Cam said. "So, I'll be executed tomorrow then?"

"What's it matter to you, traitor?"

"Please, I mean… I only have you for company now. Couldn't you at least be slightly civil?"

I inched forward as the guard leaned over to set the tray down. The electric fence made his face glow red. "No funny business, maggot."

I saw my chance. I barged forward and shoved him into the bars. He shook and fizzled before he fell to the ground. "Cam!"

"Althea! What are you doing here?"

I ripped the key from the guard's belt and swiped it on the sensor. The bars fell away, and Cam was free. She ran over and hugged me. "I'm so glad to see you."

"You too. But there's no time. We have to go."

We zigzagged through the halls to the entrance of the prison and that's when we heard it. The siren. Red lights flashed brightly down the corridors.

"Come on!" I grabbed Cam's hand and ran outside just as the electric bars sealed the front door. Guards came from everywhere, funneling in toward the prison as we ran around the side of the guard station.

"What do we do now?" Cam gasped. "Do you have a plan?"

"Of course, I do," I shouted.

There were manhole covers all over the city, not just in the Residence. The whole Center had been a research facility before the Incident, and the underwater pipes led everywhere, including out of the Center and into the First. Henry had a wealth of information on the subject and had nearly bored me to death talking about it after we snuck into Wind's room, but the information was coming in handy now.

I ran to the nearest manhole cover and pressed my palm on its face. After a moment, it opened for me and I shoved Cam inside.

"Why did you come back for me?" she asked, making her way down the ladder.

I crawled in after her and forced the cover back into place. "Because you're my friend."

"You know I'm a traitor though, right?"

We reached the bottom of the ladder as the sirens blared over us.

"You're not a traitor; the Five are the traitors." I held up the data cell. "And you're gonna prove it."

I placed the data cell in Cam's hand. She cradled it tight. "I'll guard it with my life," she promised.

I don't know how long we walked, but the sound of the guards' feet came from every direction, clomping through the tunnels and reverberating through the walls. Their sporadic shouting and the sound of their feet thumped in my ears.

"Why did you do it, Cam?" I asked as we walked. "We were so close to finding out the truth about the Five and taking them down for good."

Cam looked away from me. "I had my orders. You...compromised them. I convinced you to go with Henry, so I could get back on mission."

"Which was?"

"To kill Earth. Once we saw that they could be killed, we knew what must be done."

"But Cam, what we found...what we found could shut down the Bubble forever."

"I didn't know that—I didn't even know if you would come back. I'm sorry for putting you through this."

"You can apologize later."

Eventually I saw a light glowing in the distance, the entrance to the First. We ran forward, but as we got closer, the blue light sparked and fizzed at us. It wasn't the outside at all; it was a force field gate.

We could see the First through the translucent blue, but we couldn't get there. The barrier crackled as we inched up to it. I dared not touch it for fear of being knocked unconscious.

"There has to be an electrical box around here somewhere," Cam whispered. "Feel around for it."

I ran my fingers along the uneven bricks until I felt a smooth, metallic divot in the craggy wall. "Here. It's here."

Cam grabbed a rock from the ground and clenched it tight. "Watch out."

"Cam. No!"

But it was too late. Cam slammed the rock against the panel. It fizzled and sputtered before exploding with a loud crash. The blast echoed off the walls down every corridor. Worst of all, the barrier was still up.

I heard the guards' footsteps pivot and rush toward us. Their feet got closer and closer and closer. We inched toward the beam separating us from the outside.

Cam looked through the gate at her salvation. It was so close. "This is it. We failed."

I shook my head. "No. It's on you now. Go."

"I'm not leaving you," Cam said. "You'll die."

I nodded. "Probably, but I'm still a Vessel. They can't shoot me like a dog. I'll stall them as long as I can. Find a way out. Go." I pushed her away. "Go!"

Cam and I looked at each other for a long moment then she disappeared around a corner without another word. She would be caught for sure. I had tried my hardest and I failed.

I stuck my hands into the air as a dozen soldiers rounded the corner with their guns drawn. I thought of my family. I wanted my last thoughts to be of them. I didn't want to feel fear or hate. I just wanted the simple wind on my face. I wanted peace.

CHAPTER 4

They questioned me for hours. This wasn't the type of questioning they put me through after Violet was killed. No. This was far worse. Gone was the crooked smile on the Constable's face, replaced instead by a deep, dark scowl. And screaming. My god, the screaming.

"Is that what you are? You and your family? Are you a splinter cell for those disgusting Muties?"

"I don't think they like to be called that."

Feelings of guilt swirled in my head, not for betraying the Five, but for endangering my family. They were surely being investigated just as intensely for my crimes. They would be arrested and tried. I could never live with myself if something horrible happened to them. Then again, living wasn't on the menu for me. Not anymore.

"And what about your friend, Henry? What did he have to do with this?"

"Nothing. He was just a pawn."

My sweet Henry. I knew he would break. I hoped he would tell them everything was my fault. Because it was my fault. All of it.

They took me back to a cell, beaten down and exhausted, after hours of interrogation. I tried to sleep, but the red glow from the electric bars kept me awake. The light flickered in my eyes and made them twitch.

Hours later, I tensed up when once again the clomping of the guard's boots came down the hallway. I couldn't go back. I'd rather die than have them interrogate me another minute. They opened the gate. I held my breath. *Please kill me.*

"Henry! Oh my god!" I screamed.

They held Henry in their arms, barely conscious and clinging to life and tossed him into the cell. His glasses were gone; his hair matted with sweat.

"Sleep well, traitors."

The guards grinned at me sadistically, the way Earth had when Penelope was killed. Then they stomped away, chuckling.

Henry trembled as I held him in my arms and rocked him back and forth. "What did they do to you?" I asked.

When he spoke, his voice was hoarse. "So many questions. So much yelling. I thought it would never stop. They threw me into the third door, and...and left me there. I don't know for how long. I saw...everything."

The third door...the door that nearly drove me insane during the preliminary challenges. The one that was as close to torture as I ever experienced. Poor, sweet Henry. They had ruined his fragile innocence. He dropped his face into my shirt and cried until he had no more tears.

"What did you tell them?" I asked.

"Nothing. I told them nothing."

"Henry," I groaned, "that was stupid! You should have told them everything. You are the golden boy. They won't kill you."

"Exactly. But they will kill you, your family, and everybody you hold dear. They want the data cell back. I'll bet that's why they have us in here together. Hoping we'll slip up, that the sight of me like this will drive you crazy and you'll do anything to save me."

As I looked down at his face, I knew they were right. I would do anything for him. He was the only person I could still save.

*

Earth sat across from me inside the third door. It didn't affect her like it affected everybody else. I wondered why for a moment, before I decided it was because she had no soul.

It was the door I swore I would never enter again. Now I had no choice. I heard dead skin cells flake off my arm. I felt my hair grow. My eyes blinked, and the sound shattered my eardrums. The clock on the wall ticked incessantly. Every click of the second hand thumped against my brain.

"You are very smart, Althea. It was a very good plan to strike now. Especially after we just admitted to the whole City that we were at our weakest moment. We were in too much shock to look for an attack."

"I don't know what you are talking about."

"Yes. You say that." Condescension dripped from her tone. "No matter. Your part of the plan was for naught. We already checked Wind's computer for sensitive information. Your stunt did no damage to us."

I grit my teeth together to keep my voice from faltering. "I'm glad you aren't hurt. I am a faithful servant of the Five, after all. It's not like they would ever lie to me or keep me in prison against my will."

"Well, maybe I misspoke. You damaged us by helping your little friend escape. And you damaged us by joining a fringe group bent on destroying our way of life. Tell me where your friend is going, and we will be sure your family doesn't suffer your fate."

If I had known where Cam was, I might've told her, just to save my family. But only if I believed a word Earth said. And I didn't.

"Well, if I didn't take anything important, as you claim, then why the manhunt for Cam? And why are you treating me so poorly?"

"You let a traitor and an assassin roam free, my dear. That is a serious crime. We've executed people for less. You know that, of course. You've seen it with your own eyes."

"Is it worse than lying about the horrors of the outside? Is it as horrible as keeping us all prisoners of your will for thousands of years... because you're afraid to die?"

Earth laughed. "That is quite the story. It's a shame you won't be around long enough to tell it to anybody."

"Luckily I don't have to say a word. So that's what it will be then? A trial and execution?"

"Perhaps. We have to finish with your family first. They really are lovely people."

I lunged in my chair. The shackles that bound me cut into my wrists. "You leave them alone!"

"They are being treated very well, for now. They don't know what you've done. I think it would kill your poor mother. But, if you cooperate, you might be able to see them again before the end."

*

Back in our cell, I curled up on the floor next to Henry and told him over and over again that it would be okay.

"What about my family?" he asked. "I never even thought about my family. I never even considered them as a variable."

"Soon, you will be Time, and Time is very forgiving. It'll all be okay, Henry."

He didn't want my support or comfort. He only wanted to complain. It was his right. I had gotten him into this situation and now his family was in trouble. I hadn't thought about my family before recklessly saving Cam and I certainly hadn't thought about his, and I certainly hadn't considered the mental toll it would take on him if we were caught.

There was only one thing I could do. I had to take the blame. I had to make up a great story and convince myself it was true.

*

"Cam recruited me," I told Earth the next morning, "after we got to the Center. Then I recruited Henry."

I started out with a half-truth. After all, I did meet Cam at the Center. Then, I did recruit Henry to help us. Earth's eyes pierced deep into mine, searching. I tried to keep her out, but it was so hard with the fear of the third door grating against my soul.

"And why did you join her?" Earth countered.

"I was angry at you, ma'am, for killing my friend. You represented everything I lost in the process of getting here. You told me to come, and because of that, my friend Joan is now dead. She's dead because of me just as much as because of you. Penelope's death just strengthened my hatred of you. Cam...she took advantage of that."

That was the truth. I did hate Earth. If, following Penelope's execution, Cam *had* told me her plans, I probably would have joined her out of spite alone.

Earth didn't move. "I see. And you didn't think that what you were doing was wrong?"

"Of course, I knew it was wrong, but I knew you were more wrong. Or at least that's what I thought then."

"And now?"

I looked up at her. "Now I know I was mistaken."

They brought me back through the third door over and over again that day. When I would be inches from insanity, they would pull me out and drill me with questions until I couldn't think straight. Then back inside. I saw Joan and Violet and Penelope and my family. I watched my skin flake off and shatter to the floor. I felt my ears twitch and heard my nails grow. I dared not move, because moving made it worse. Every creak of my bones snapped inside my ears. It went on like that over and over. Over and over. Over and over again.

On my fifth time through the door, Earth smiled at me. "Your stories don't match up."

"Excuse me?"

"You and Henry need to sit down and decide the truth, because right now the truth varies depending on which one of you speaks."

"Oh really?" I gasped. "And what does he say?"

"He says he recruited you. That he and Cam were working together since before the Center...that they manipulated you, and that you are the innocent."

"That's not true."

"We'll see. We have plenty of time to learn the truth."

When they threw me back in the cell again, Henry was there, staring off into space. It was the first time I'd seen him all day, but I couldn't even enjoy it. I was too furious. "What are you doing saying you recruited me? You're going to get yourself killed."

Henry just smiled. "Either way I'm going to die. At least this way I can save your life."

"This isn't what I want."

"But it's what I want."

*

They woke me up early the next day. I hadn't slept or eaten, and I couldn't think straight, but I had to maintain. And even though I refused to admit it, they had broken me. But still, I held on to the broken pieces of my soul, pretending I was whole, even though I wasn't.

"He's lying to you," I said through my tears. "He's lying about everything."

"I know," Earth said. "He's not nearly as good a liar as you."

"What...do you mean?"

"Come now, Althea. Let's treat each other as grownups. I know some of what you say is true, or at least half true, but for the most part, you're just lying for the sake of lying. My dear, can we move past that, please?"

"What do you want from me?"

"The truth. Why did you help Cam?"

I sighed. Maybe Earth was a god. Whether she was or not, I stopped fighting her then and there. "Because she's my friend."

"Finally, a truth. Did you care that she was a traitor?"

I looked Earth dead in the eyes. "I counted on it. That's why I gave her the data cell."

Earth smiled. "We will find it. This is not the first time somebody has tried to undermine our way of life. We are very old, and this seems to happen every millennia or so."

"How many millennia is that, exactly?"

"Shouldn't you know? If you have all of Wind's files?"

I bowed my head. "What I know is that you are a traitor and a coward. Why did you keep us under this Bubble for so long? Was it really just your own vanity?"

Earth laughed. "You are so naïve, child. Just because Wind says we don't need the Bubble it doesn't make it so. Yes, he believed that it was safe beyond the Bubble, but what if he was wrong? What if all his data, from all his ancient machines, was wrong? We are the last of humanity. Would you really risk all of humanity on a hunch?"

"I would rather be free to run in the field, ma'am."

"Even if that momentary freedom meant the death of not only you, but your family and your entire race? What would you do to protect those you love? What would you do to protect yourself from extinction?"

"I wouldn't lie about it. I wouldn't lie to everybody. I would let them make a choice."

"And what if they made a wrong one? What then?"

"Then it is their choice to make."

"Just like the choice you made, no matter how stupid, will doom your family? Is that fair to them? One life, dictating the fate of them all? Is that fair to them?"

"Will my family be okay?"

"I don't think that matters right now."

I looked into Earth's hollow eyes. "It matters to me. Please. I've answered all your questions. Just answer one of mine."

"Yes. They passed all their tests. They'll be able to go home soon and live out their days in peace. The shame of being branded a traitor's family is punishment enough for them."

"And what about me?"

"There will be a trial, of course, and we will decide justly what to do with you, as we have always done."

*

The next morning, I was led into the courtroom with Henry. They walked us past several rows of disinterested onlookers bent on our deaths. Then I saw them, for the first time in what felt like years—my family.

Mama screamed as she ran toward me, calling out my name, but a burly guard held her back. I tugged at my chains, attempting to leap into her arms, but I couldn't reach. My efforts were useless.

At the sight of his mother, Henry broke into tears as well, in a fit of shame and fear but they pushed us forward. I walked past my weeping mother, my stoic father, and my brother as he choked back the tears. I looked back at the guard.

"Please. Please let me just hug them one time."

There was no response. I wriggled and weaved, but the guard held me tighter, his fingers digging into my shoulders. The message was clear: *shut up.*

The trial was over before it began. The evidence was presented, and then Five deliberated for less than ten minutes. The moment they stepped back into the chamber, I understood the dread that Penelope must have felt awaiting her fate.

Earth spoke for the group. "Do you have anything to say before we render our verdict?"

I stood up. "I beg for your leniency, not for me but for my co-defendant. I will accept his punishment as mine. I only request I be able to speak with my family one last time."

Earth smiled. "I will take it under consideration. I assume you would like to see your family too, Henry. Is that correct?"

Henry nodded. "Yes, ma'am."

"Well if that is all, then here we stand, ready to render our verdict. The accused are found guilty on all counts. However, this leaves us in a predicament. They are Vessels. Do we execute them, even if their mind is the perfect conduit for one of us? It seems that would be a worse fate for this City than releasing them. But justice must be served."

Earth paused for dramatic effect. "We pondered what to do and have come to a decision. Should either of the accused be chosen as Vessels, only then would their punishment be commuted into a lifetime of service. However, if they are not...then their punishment shall be taken with their death."

The crowd roared thunderously in applause. Intellectually, my brain could accept my fate, but my heart was another story. It didn't want to die. It didn't accept death. But, the Five wanted us both to die. I never thought anybody would cheer for my death.

*

Guards threw us back in our cell immediately after the verdict. We sat together in silence, holding each other. We were dead, one way or another. There was no comfort in that. There was nothing more to be said.

Hours later, the Constable came to us. "Your plea worked. Come on."

She walked me into an interrogation room. This one wasn't filled with screaming and questions. It was filled with the warmth of family. My family. Gone were the tears in my mother's eyes, and the sadness in my father's. Instead their sadness was replaced with great joy at the sight of me, and mine at seeing them.

"Mama! Dad!"

Dad ran to me and scooped me up in an enormous bear hug. Mama didn't wait for him to release me; she came and hugged me even tighter. I could barely breathe, but I didn't care. I savored every second of it. When Dad finally released me, my brother had his turn. They smelt like the farm, like fresh air, and hard work. I had missed them so much. I had missed home with all my heart.

"How are they treating you?" Mama asked.

"Good, I guess. For a prisoner."

Dad shook his head. "We told you not to come here."

Mama scolded. "This is not the time."

Dad dropped his head. "I'm sorry. You're right. It's just—it's a shame, is all."

"I think that's an understatement, Dad." I grabbed his hand. "I know about Earth...why you hate seeing her so much."

Dad lifted his eyes. "I never wanted you to find out. Linda was so...kind."

I looked over at Mama and she smiled sadly. "It's okay, dear. I was there too. I know what happened."

"Tell me about her, before she became Earth."

My parents exchanged a glance. They didn't want to talk about it, but I needed to know. I placed my hand on Mama's. "I'm sorry, but that might be me soon. I have to know."

Mama nodded. I could see her heart was breaking, but she couldn't deny my last request. "I know, dear."

"She was..." Dad started, "full of life, her constant laughter was infectious. We came to the Center together from the Fifth. It was a long trip and we were tired, but she cracked jokes the whole time. She never let our spirits dampen."

Mama smiled. "That's how I remember her. She was just so...nice. I wanted to hate her for being with your dad, but I couldn't. She was impossible to hate."

"She's a lot easier to hate now," I mumbled.

Mama choked back her emotion. "When she became Earth, it broke my heart. Linda...my friend...she had no life in her. The sparkle in her eyes was gone. I don't want that to happen to you."

"I don't want that either. This whole situation sucks." I let out a sob. "Promise me you'll carry on," I said. "No sad funeral. Just happiness. Okay?"

Mama grabbed my hands. "I wish there was a way to carry on without you, my dear, but I don't know if it's possible. Was this all worth it, Althea?"

I looked back at the Constable, who strutted forward to take me away. "I hope it was, Mama. That's all I have to go on anymore. I'm sorry, and I love you all."

I said my final goodbyes to my family. I never wanted to let them go, but I had to be brave. The next time I saw them would either be at my execution or as a hollow vessel. I wanted to forget the horrible feeling in my stomach and shrivel up in a cocoon, a Henry cocoon.

*

When I got back to the cell, there he was, cradling his knees in his arms. I sat down next to him. "How were they?" I asked.

He didn't say anything. He just cried. And I cried with him. We thought we were strong, but we weren't. We were just kids.

All I wanted was to go home— to my bed, to watch TV with my family, and to till the land until I died of old age. But that could never happen. I wouldn't live to see next week.

Before I came to the Center, I thought the worst injustice was marrying somebody you didn't love. Now that wasn't even in my top thousand.

I would never feel happy again. I knew that, but I wanted to fake it, even if just for a second. I had held off kissing Henry all this time, but my body ached for him. So, I kissed him, and he kissed me back. Our bodies molded into one, and we didn't stop. That is where I lost my virginity.

CHAPTER 5

It didn't hurt, having sex. Everyone always said it would hurt. I would even say it was pleasurable, in a way, even quite pleasurable for a couple moments. I wish I didn't have to bite my lip the whole time to stop from crying out, though. I broke the skin on my lower lip and my mouth bled after we finished. That did hurt.

Really, I think it was more awkward than anything. There definitely wasn't a mood and it wasn't the right time. No one thinks their first time is going to be in a prison cell when they're about to die.

But really it wasn't about being magical or perfect. It was a big screw off to the people that were about to kill us. To accept the Five into your consciousness, you had to be a virgin. It was one of the main rules of Transference, and we'd broken it.

I know it doesn't make me a good role model for the stories they're bound to tell after I die. People are going to look at me as a cautionary tale, as one of the Five's all-time worst creations.

But at least then I'll be immortal; I'll live on beyond my days, even if it is in infamy. That's all we were trying to do, in the end— to live beyond our days. And that was all the Five were trying to do. And if I could live on in that way, at least I had something.

After it was over, Henry and I sat on opposite corners of the cell, twiddling our thumbs and trying to think of the right words to say. We'd tried to cuddle, but it just didn't feel right.

"That was...not what I was expecting to happen when we met. I calculated the odds once or twice, don't get me wrong, but they were always statistically insignificant," Henry finally said.

I looked up. "I don't think any of this was what I expected."

"What did you expect?"

"I thought I would come here, get through a couple of challenges, make some money, and go home. I didn't want to stay long. I didn't plan to make friends. I certainly didn't expect to do...what we did. And I definitely didn't want to die."

There was a long moment of silence before Henry responded. "I wanted to be Time's vessel so badly. I thought it would give me some sense of honor, purpose, and duty. It wasn't about my family. It was about me." He cupped his head in his hands and sobbed. "I'm about to get everything I thought I wanted, but now all I want to do is go home."

Before I could comfort him, two guards walked in and flanked either side of the door. My heart sank. It was time.

*

The guards walked us to the Great Hall where the choosing ceremony would be televised live to the whole City. My stomach fluttered. In that moment, all the rebellion fell out of me; I just wanted to live. For the first time, I wanted Earth to choose me. If she didn't choose me, my family would have nothing. I already knew Stone would never choose me. Her heart was set on McKinsey.

McKinsey. It wasn't so long ago that beating her down was the most important thing in the entire world. How stupid I was. How naïve. She was the least important thing to ever happen to me.

I grasped Henry's hand as we walked into the Great Hall, with its ornate gilded columns and domed ceiling. I had seen it before in videos, but never thought I would witness it in person. Even the tittered claps of my feet on the marble floor felt reverent.

We were the last ones to enter. The other girls stood on the left, the boys to the right. They must have culled the herd a couple more times since I'd been imprisoned, because only four boys and four girls remained, among them McKinsey and Abigail.

Earth stood in the center of the room in her most garish tunic, adorned with gold bracelets and necklaces, her hair pulled back in a tight bun. The gold band on her head made her look like a queen. "Please stand with the other Vessels."

I released Henry's hand, lined up with the girls and looked over at McKinsey. For a moment, she seemed to pity me, but her head quickly pivoted to look at Earth. She was about to win, after all. It was all she ever wanted, or at least that's what her family convinced her that she wanted.

Two cameras floated above the floor. A red light flicked between them. The whirl of their thrusters provided a comforting and soothing hum to Earth's grating voice.

"Tonight, we fulfill the most important tradition in our world. For millennia upon millennia, we Five," she caught herself for a moment then continued, "have kept watch over you, provided for you, and loved you. And in return, all we asked was that you provide us with a Vessel, so we may carry out our mission. You have complied in great stead, and we are grateful. We will now take our turns to announce our choice. We hope you understand the great sacrifice these boys and girls have made to be here, what courage their families displayed, and how honored we are. Time, would you begin?"

Earth faded into the background, as much as she could fade into anything. The gilded glint of her opulence still overshadowed Time as he came from behind a curtain and took center stage.

"This has been the most trying transference in recent memory," Time began. "And not just because we lost my great friend, Wind. He was a great man, yes, but we also lost Penelope, his wonderful assistant and the love of his life. Well, of this life. Every millennia or so Wind found a soul mate, even though we argued against it, and Penelope was as strong as any I've seen him court. She also was his final end, in a brutal twist of fate."

"On top of that we had my star recruit, Henry, accused and convicted of being a traitor. And that gave me pause, because his brain is sharp, his mind is agile. I could do great work through him, but could I stare at his face every day for the next several decades?"

I looked over at Henry, who hung his head in shame. I knew how horrible it must be for him, even though he didn't want it anymore, to hear his idol speak that way about him.

"These faces I wear, though, they blend over time. I barely recognize anything but myself in them anymore. Could I do that with Henry's body too? Or should I pick another, who is less able, for my own selfish reasons? It's kept me up many a night."

"However, in the end, I decided to make the sacrifice and look at his face for the next decades, even though it sickens me to do so, in order to give you the best possible Time, because in the end, this is for you. This is for the City. I choose Henry Reyes!"

The crowd's applause echoed through the chamber as Time beckoned Henry onto the stage. The heaviness of Henry's step betrayed the heaviness of his heart as he put one foot in front of the other and climbed the marble staircase to his destiny. He plastered a big smile on his face, as fake as could be, as they shook hands. Time lifted Henry's arm in the air, and they walked off the stage together.

After the applause died down, Stone waddled meekly to the stage. Her hair hung about her face in brittle strands as her makeup free face cowered when she noticed the cameras tracking toward her. I looked over at McKinsey and pitied that she dreamt so low as Stone spoke softly.

"I have been through a lot this Transference. Not only did one of my chosen Vessel candidates plot to kill Earth, but I also lost a good friend in Wind. It makes me wonder if our presence is something you want anymore? Is it what you need? I don't know. I used to think what we were doing was the right thing, even if it felt wrong, but now...I'm not so sure.

"Honestly, I wish I could pick no Vessel at all. These girls are so full of life and love with so many years left in them. They have so much more they need from us than to be taken from their families. Is any of this worth it to them? Is lavish compensation enough to deal with the loss of a loved one? I doubt it."

At these words, silence filled the room. Stone looked back and her posture straightened when she saw Earth's eyes narrowed into daggers. "But this isn't about my hesitation. This is about the City, so I will carry out my duty, and choose McKinsey McAllister as my vessel!"

There was no joy on McKinsey's face as she walked up to the stage, no bliss in her eyes. There was only death, as if she finally realized what was about to happen, and it hit her at once.

*

Arrow was next. I didn't know any of the other male candidates, but it didn't matter. He was going to pick the most handsome one. "I don't have the same reservations as the other two. I know this is important. I know it must continue and I know *we* must continue!"

He lifted his hands in the air. "We are the barrier between you and certain death, and four young teenagers are but a small price to pay to protect your City!

"It is an insult to say otherwise. It's borderline heresy to say that four are more important than millions! We have thrived for generations, and we will do so for thousands more because of this tradition. And we thank you!"

Arrow called out the name of his chosen Vessel and the most handsome boy I'd ever seen walked up to the stage. They shook hands and walked off together.

*

Earth waited until there was complete silence before she took her turn. "A lot has been said tonight that needs addressing. I agree Wind was wonderful, and his loss was tragic, but I also believe strongly in this tradition, for it is all that stands between this great city and utter destruction."

She smiled. "Is it difficult, of course. I look at these women and see beauty, grace, and intelligence in each of them. They could each be incredibly valuable to our city. However, not as valuable as we Five are to it. We have saved this City for millennia and will continue to save it for millennia more.

"It is with a heavy heart that I make this choice. I do wish there was another way; a way to save these girls and preserve ourselves at the same time, so we can make this City great together. But all of our attempts to create a better way have failed, and what's most important is to continue this City's survival. So, I choose. I continue. For you. For us all."

I desperately wanted Earth to choose me. Not just for myself, or my family, but for the other girls. I already had a death sentence. Nothing could change that. But these girls, they could be saved if I was chosen. They could have long lives. I would be dead either way.

"I choose Abigail Norton."

Poor Abigail. She didn't know this was all a sham. She thought her sacrifice was noble. She was giddy and bubbly as she walked up to the stage, smiling gleefully while she hugged Earth and waved to the cameras. The thought of her death never entered her mind. I wish I had that kind of blind faith in anything.

"Thank you all for your service," Earth said.

And then it was over. The cameras cut out, the lights dimmed, and we were all alone. I was alone with my failure. I was going to die. My family would be shamed forever. I was a horrible daughter. I was a horrible person.

*

I bawled when they locked me away. In that moment, I was alone, truly and utterly alone. There would be no more Henry. There would be no more family. There would be no savior. There was only the execution block, the jeering citizens gunning for my head. The Vessel who went bad. I would be a cautionary tale forever.

In the silence of the cell, with nothing but the din of the force field for comfort, I had a lot of time to think. The hum put me in a sort of meditative state. I thought back to all the mistakes I made since I'd learned of Wind's death and all the times I could have turned back.

I should have never left home in the first place, once my family found me on the train tracks. I should have swum away from the Inner Rings after the explosion on the train and walked home. I should have turned back when I witnessed that execution in the Third, or Joan's in the Second. I should have turned back when I met Joan's parents in the First, and they gave me a sinking feeling in the pit of my stomach, just like the one I got when I stood in line at the Center.

I should have turned back when they made me strip down and take that humiliating shower. I should have failed one—just one—of the thirty-six challenges set before me in the preliminaries, and I should have left when they gave me the choice after Penelope died. I should have left with Cam after I saved her.

I should have run away any number of times. But I didn't. Instead, I chose to stay. Stupid Thea, trying to save the world.

After all, would anything really happen if somehow Cam survived and found something valuable on that data cell? Would anything change?

Did I really think the City would trust that the Muties had found an information file, which happened to prove the Five were liars? Of course not. They would think it was made up for cheap publicity. The people in the City were too simple minded and set in their ways to believe that their entire existence, everything they knew about the world, was a lie.

After awhile, a squad of guards filed into my room, flanking the cell on either side before Earth entered. She hadn't stolen Abigail's body yet. She was still the same old Earth.

"I can officially say you lost, my dear Althea."

"Don't look so broken up about it."

"You helped my enemy escape. An enemy who threatens the very fabric of our City's being, a City I have protected for hundreds of lifetimes. I won't say I am sorry to see you die."

"So, what now? You kill me tomorrow morning?"

"Tomorrow evening, actually, once the dust has settled from the Transference and I can look at you with fresh eyes. I don't want it to overshadow the ceremonies. But rest assured, once we have revealed our new forms, the first order of business will be to dispose of you."

"Tell me then. Why do you keep doing it? Is life so grand that you hold onto it with everything, even if it means losing your soul?"

"I wish I could say no, dear. But it truly is. I believe in my work. I believe in the good of this City, and I would have nobody else protect it but me. If it's cruel to want one more life to keep my work going, then that makes me cruel."

That was it. They would dispose of me like I was trash. I was no longer a person created in their image. I was just garbage. I wanted to rail against that thought, but there was no fight left in me. She was right; I had lost.

There was truly nothing I could do except await death.

*

I held off going to bed as long as I could. It was difficult to accept I was facing the last day of my life. I wanted to remember every second I'd lived, to count every good memory. I struggled against it as long as I could, but eventually my exhaustion got the better of me and I drifted off to sleep.

A siren jolted me awake. The loudspeakers shouted incomprehensible gibberish into the ether as four guards stormed into my cell and pulled me out.

"What's going on here?" I shouted. "Let me go! It's not time yet! I have more time!"

I fell to the ground in protest. The guards picked me back up and dragged me outside.

"It's not time. Please don't do this. Please!" I knew it was undignified to beg, but I didn't care. I didn't want to die. My last memory couldn't be blaring sirens. I wanted to be with my family again and live a full life so that my last memory would be lying in my bed surrounded by children I could never have, now… I would do anything for just one more second of life.

*

I continued to struggle against the guards as they dragged me outside. The fresh air hit me like a rocket. I usually welcomed the breeze, but here it smelt like death. It brought me one step closer to the stage. I expected to hear cheers from the crowd welcoming my death. Instead there were only the sirens screaming into the night.

I looked toward the quad, expecting to see an execution block prepared for me, but there was none, and the streets were empty except for a stream of people sprinting for the Great Hall where the guards dragged me.

They rushed me down tight corridors behind the Great Hall. The sirens blared as a haunting, red light blinded my eyes. They turned a corner and we were inside a room few had ever seen. It was the Transference room. Only Vessels, the Five, and a small team of workers had ever seen inside its walls.

The room bustled with activity. A ghostly, white light hung in front of each of the Five as they sat in ornate chairs above the fray, slumped over motionless. On the floor in front of each of them was a Vessel: My sweet Henry in front of Time, McKinsey in front of Stone, Abigail in front of Earth, and the beautiful boy in front of Arrow. They had crowns of electrodes on their heads connected to a huge panel of buttons and levers.

The Vessels lay still on the cold floor, all of them except Abigail, who was seizing uncontrollably. Her mouth foamed as her eyes rolled back into her head. Blood and bile pooled on the ground below her.

"Earth can't remain in stasis forever. We're gonna lose her!"

Workers at the big board of controls pushed buttons and pulled levers frantically. "She's slipping! If we don't get her into a new body soon, we'll never get her back."

The Constable grabbed my arm and pulled me forward. "We got another one! Move that piece of garbage and make room!"

They kicked Abigail away into a discarded corner.

"Kneel!"

They forced me on top of Abigail's blood and bile. The warm liquid squished through my legs.

"What's happening?"

"This is your lucky day, sweetie. Your friend over there was another Mutie plant and we didn't have anybody else to take her place. Except for you that is." They placed a crown of electrons on my head.

Earth slumped on her throne, catatonic. Behind me, the frantic workers shouted orders. "If we don't hurry, this is all going to be wasted!"

The Constable stepped back. "It's on. Start it up!" Then she looked at me and smiled. "See you in another life, Earth."

Excruciating pain surged through my body, as if a thousand lightning bolts had converged on me at once. It lasted for only a second, but it felt like a year, and then it was done.

"Ma'am, are you okay? Are you okay, ma'am?" The Constable helped me to my feet. I watched as Henry and the others steadied themselves on doctors and attendants. "Can you speak, ma'am?"

I nodded. "Yes."

Henry stood upright and stiff. He crossed his arms and spoke in lyrical sentences. His eyes had none of their sparkle. He was Time, now and until his body outlived its usefulness.

McKinsey was different too, no longer commanding and regal. She cowered next to her handlers. The handsome boy Arrow had chosen was asking for pastries.

Everybody had changed except for me. *Why wasn't I different?* I should have been Earth. Yet these were my thoughts. How was I moving my own arm? Shouldn't I be dead?

Before I could search for answers, the sirens sounded again.

"We're under attack!" The Constable turned to me. "Stay here, ma'am."

Gunfire rang out, crackling through the halls and echoing off the walls. The violent pops deadened my senses. I couldn't think or speak. I looked over at Henry, who stared back at me with venom. I knew it wasn't truly Henry, but his vile stare broke my heart.

Two tin canisters rolled into the room. "Grenades! Get them out!"

Before anybody could move, the canisters broke apart. The last thing I remember was coughing as gas plumed into the room.

*

I woke up in a cell but wasn't like the ones in the Center. There were no electric bars, just wrought iron ones, rusted to boot. The stonewalls crumbled to my touch and the floor underneath me was cracked.

Two women dressed in civilian clothes guarded me with machine guns. Behind them, a familiar face emerged from the shadows. It was Cam. She'd made it. She was free. I was so happy I could sing.

"Do you remember me, Earth?" she asked. "I know you have a new face, the face of my friend, but you're Earth, and you tried to kill me. You tried to kill every one of us. Now we know the truth about you. It's ironic, isn't it? The face you're wearing was the catalyst for your downfall."

I was tired, weak, and confused. "What are you talking about? It's me. It's Althea."

"Don't even try to pull that. You may be able to manipulate everybody else in the City, but not us. We see right through you." Cam bent down and looked at me. "We have big plans for you. Just you wait."

Her eyes were cold and furious. There was once a spark of friendship in them, but there was nothing there now.

"Please, Cam. Don't do this."

She pivoted on her heels. "I know what you are, ma'am. We all know who you are." She gestured to the others and they walked out the room together. "Sweet dreams, ma'am."

I was left alone. Again. I said I would give anything for one more moment of life. And I did. I gave up everything. *What did I do to screw it all up so bad?* That was the question I was left to ponder. A familiar feeling grew in the pit of my stomach. The one that told me I was going to die.

BOOK 4

Redemption

CHAPTER 1

"Hello. This is Earth. I'm coming to you after the fifteenth data dump the rebels have released proving we Five are criminals. Everything you've heard and seen from the Muties is true. Every piece of it. These documents were taken from Wind's computer, which were confiscated from his room. We Five conspired to hold you hostage under the Bubble for our own selfish gain. The world outside the Bubble is safe."

A fat woman held up her fist from behind the camera. She was my handler for every video. I made a new one every other day, trying to convince the citizens of the City to believe the data dumps from the Muties but it hadn't been working well.

"Cut!"

The red, blinking light above the camera turned off. A woman next to the camera dropped her cue cards as two brutish men lowered their guns on either side of me.

"You don't have to do this. I want to help you. I gave you—" I began as a swift punch across the face quieted me.

They dragged me from the video room and threw me into the cell I'd called my home for the last three months—they only took me out to beat me, interrogate me, and force me onto TV.

Nobody believed the Muties, even after releasing several videos of me swearing the files on the data cell were true. It came from the Muties that had kidnapped their god and held her against her will.

I used to scream but it was no use. It only made me sick and I needed my strength. They weren't going to let me go no matter how much I begged. They took no pity on me.

Whenever I shouted, they tortured me worse, sticking bamboo shoots under my fingers or shooting water into my eyes until I screamed in agony. They left me alone without food for days. They wanted me to break. They wanted me broken. They wanted me to spill my secrets. The problem was, I didn't have any.

"I'm not Earth! I'm Althea!" I shouted at them over and over. They didn't believe me but why would they? Earth was the queen of all lies. She was the epitome of everything they hated. Why wouldn't she do everything she could to save herself, like pretending she was a child?

They pelted me with questions day and night. More than anything, they demanded to know how to get Outside. They were obsessed with the Outside, wanting to forge their own path beyond the Bubble.

Wind's documents had revealed much but hadn't said exactly how to shut down the Bubble. The documents were mostly confessions about his life. The personal files told a damning story about the history of the Five. If even a tenth of it were true, society would crumble, which is why nobody believed it. It meant everything they knew, and their parents knew, and their parents knew, going back generations, was built on a lie. Nobody wants to believe they are that gullible.

The only people who knew the truth and were willing to believe it were the Muties, who'd been cast aside and looked down on for millennia. For them, the Five were always horrible and the Bubble was always a prison. Convincing Muties there was a sinister plan afoot was easy, because they already knew it. When Cam delivered proof, it was easy to believe. It was easy to get them to lead the rebellion.

It wasn't so easy to convince the rest of the City because they were all people like my parents. They had a good life. They wanted for very little. To them, the

Five's imperfect system was at least pleasant. They enjoyed the veneer the Five created, even if it was a fake one.

My father, though he hated the Five, never thought of them as evil, just as stupid and unnecessary. More importantly, he benefited from their plans. He had a nice home and a loving family. Shattering his world was nearly impossible. Even if he believed the Muties, he had too much to lose by joining their rebellion or even uttering the truth in his private moments.

That's not to say there weren't people in the Rings who believed them. There were citizens from every Ring joining the fight, and more joined every day. Buses pulled up throughout the day and night, full of Muties and citizens alike. They were tired of the lies. They were tired of the Five. They wanted to live free outside the Bubble.

Yes, the movement was growing, but I could tell from my cell window it wasn't nearly enough. The Five had an army thousands strong ready to pounce from any point in the City. The Muties had a couple of hundred maybe, and they didn't know how to fight. In order to stand a chance, they needed to change public opinion.

The only way the public would admit that the Five had lied to them, and accept that it was safe on the outside, was for the Muties to chip away at their confidence inch by inch until the City had no choice but to cave to the overwhelming evidence.

And so, they kept putting me on camera to keep the propaganda flowing. Only after the Muties had pounded the truth into the people's heads would they be able to overthrow the system and find a new life outside the Bubble. Every time they put me on camera, more people turned to their cause.

They should be able to go Outside. That's why I'd stolen Wind's files, hoping it would lead to a solution. But it seems to have only given them more questions. And those questions needed answers. And they believed those answers would only come from torturing me.

They hadn't let me see Cam since the first night. It must have been hard for her, seeing my face, but I knew if she came to me, I could convince her I was Althea, and not a monster.

I sent for her often, but she never came. I gave guards little tidbits of information only the real Althea would know, but it was no use. She'd abandoned me to my torturers. I couldn't blame her. I wouldn't have been able to look at her if she became my worst enemy either, but it wounded me to know she wouldn't see me.

Then one day they dragged me into my cell and there she stood. "Cam!" I dropped to my knees in front of her and wept. "It's so good to see you. I can't believe—"

"Stop sending for me." Cam threw me into the wall.

"Please. Don't do this, Cam. Please. I'm not who you think. It's me. It's Althea."

"Do you know why they wouldn't let me see you, Earth? Do you know why? Because Commander Armstrong knew if I saw you, I would kill you. And I'm going to. I don't care what they do to me. I'm going to kill you for what you've done."

"Cam, please! Can't you tell it's me? Look into my eyes! Earth's eyes are cold and dead! Mine aren't. They're the same ones they've always been! Just look!"

She kneeled down in front of me. "What do you want from me?"

"I want you to look into my eyes," I said, "and if you really don't see your friend behind these eyes, then kill me. If you do...just give me five minutes."

Cam bent down. "Oh, I'm not going to kill you. That would be too merciful a punishment. I'd rather you be tortured over and over again for the rest of your long, miserable life. But okay. I accept your terms."

I lifted my ragged head to meet her glare. She looked into my eyes. Her eyes went wide. There was a moment of recognition; she saw me, if only for a second. Then her face went limp and she grimaced. "I see nothing. Take this worthless sack of crap away. Knock out a couple of her teeth for good measure."

They smacked a molar into the back of my throat. I choked it out a moment before they knocked out one of my front teeth. Then they dragged me back into my cell, bloody and broken, again.

I wanted to cry, but I couldn't. All the tears had dried away months ago. I was sure Cam had seen me, that she knew me. More importantly, I thought I knew her. But that wasn't the girl I knew. It was all just an act. I wondered if she'd ever been that girl, or if she'd been playing me all along.

The creak of the door sent shivers down my spine. I couldn't deal with more torture. Not again. Not today.

"Please, just let me die."

But the guards didn't come. It was Cam. She carried a folding chair under her arm, which she opened and sat down on. "Okay. You want me to believe you. Talk."

*

I talked for an hour straight. I don't even think I stopped for air. I just rambled on about everything that had happened at the Center, hoping some glimmer of what I said would spark something in Cam or resonate with her, or I was dead.

"I slept with Henry," I ended finally, before I fell silent.

Cam had sat steely faced the entire time, never once cracking a smile or moving a muscle. Her eyes scanned my face, never once giving a clue that she believed me.

Not until I told her about Henry. That got her. She blinked and turned away for a moment. Her back heaved. A titter fell out of her mouth and echoed off the walls. She sniffled to keep in the laughter, but it came out despite her efforts. When she turned back to me, it was half laughter and half crying, but all smiles. For the first time in months I saw the Cam I remembered.

"Excuse me? You did what?"

I smiled. "I slept with him."

"You slept with nerdy 'ole Henry?"

"Yeah. And don't say anything about Henry. He was...cute."

"You have Stockholm syndrome, Althea." She regained some semblance of composure. "Why would you do something so stupid?"

"I don't know. I was...about to die. I'm seventeen, and seventeen-year-olds have sex. I guess I just didn't want to die without experiencing it, you know."

Cam stood, and her steely demeanor returned. She inhaled deeply as she looked into my eyes. "That's stupid."

She left without another word, but when she returned, doctors dressed in dirty white coats accompanied her, and not guards.

The doors opened, and the doctors helped me up and Cam walked me out with them. "Do you know why the Five demand that everybody coming into the Center is a virgin?"

I shook my head. "Nope. No idea."

"It's because if a Vessel were to somehow get pregnant, it would mess with the Transference process and, well—," she paused, "this could happen. It was in Wind's notes. Apparently, it happened once or twice during their testing. When you're pregnant it changes your body, obviously. The synapses fire differently. Your body changes and their machines don't like that."

I was stunned, shocked. I only had sex with Henry one time. "How could I be pregnant?"

"Umm... you had sex. It happens."

They brought me to their makeshift doctor's offices built inside a crumbled down hospital wing. It wasn't like my doctor's office from the Fifth. I remembered kind doctors who smiled and gave me lollipops. But these were field doctors, doing their best to keep people alive.

I rubbed my temples. "Where are we?"

"It's war, Althea," Cam responded. "After we got the data cell and saw what was on it...it was the last straw. We've been fighting non-stop ever since."

"And what was on it?"

"Let's just say the charade the Five used to build and maintain this city has reached its end. We've lost a lot of good people, but we've won our share of battles too. We aren't going to stop fighting until that Bubble pops."

The doctors went into action, taking my blood and checking my blood pressure. They hooked me up to monitors and tested my heart. Their equipment was old, decrepit even. Even their pencils were nubs.

Eventually they finished their examination. A young doctor with a scar down his face came in to me. His dour face told me that something was wrong. He cleared his throat and tried to crack a smile. "I'm so sorry," he said with a shallow breath.

"Sorry for what?" I asked.

He swallowed. "You were pregnant...but you aren't any more."

My eyes went wide. "What do you mean not anymore?"

"The torture. What we did to you. You lost the baby. I'm sorry."

I wanted to care, I really did, but I was relieved. I didn't know how to care for a baby. I didn't want to care for one either. Still, my heart broke for it, even though I never knew it was real.

*

If God did exist—a real God, I mean, not the fake Five—then he must be looking down and laughing right now. Who would have thought the way to be treated like a human was to lose one growing inside me?

They moved me from the dank, dark cell into my own private hospital room with real walls and a floor made of linoleum instead of rock. I had real sheets and a towel. They even let me take a shower. Most importantly, I had a bed. A soft, cozy bed.

I sat up late that night staring at the ceiling. I thought about the baby I'd lost. I would have named her Virginia, after my grandmother. The moment I gave her a name it became all too real. I sobbed for her. I sobbed for myself. I sobbed for everything that had happened since I left the Center. I sobbed myself to sleep.

The door opened in the early morning hours, and Cam entered—contrite, her head sunk low. "We have to talk, Althea."

She used my real name. "What? You took my baby and now you care about who I am and want to talk?"

"What we did was horrible. There is no making up for it. But we can try to move on. I have a proposition for you. Do you want to hear it, or should I lead you back to your cell?"

It was as if the last three months had never happened, but they had in fact happened. I hated them all for what they did. Still, if I wanted my freedom, I had to hear her out. "I'm listening."

After she had her say, Cam brought me into a room full of haggard, bruised, and grizzled old men and women who wore their contempt for me on their dirty sleeves.

They all looked as if they'd seen Hell and come back to tell tales of it. One had half an arm. Another propped his one-legged body up with a makeshift crutch. They were all scarred, some on their faces, some on their body, and all on their souls.

A gruff woman, her short hair wrapped in a bandana stood up with strong, determined motions, and spoke, her voice like gravel. "Alright, let's get this over with. I'm Commander Armstrong. I'm sure you've heard of me."

The room shifted from contempt to hostility as I moved to the chair. My voice broke as I spoke. "I have. Why am—" I cleared my throat. "Why am I here?"

Armstrong folded her arms. "I have to admit, as much as I hate you, I respect a woman that gets right to the point. So here it is. One of my soldiers is convinced you aren't Earth. Cam, come over here."

Cam stood at attention, hands behind her back, and dutifully walked over to Armstrong, who barked, "Soldier, did you relay my message?"

"Yes, ma'am," Cam said curtly. "I told her that if she helped us, we would show her leniency after this is all over."

"Thank you, soldier." Armstrong turned to me. "Do you know what the new world order is?"

I shook my head. "No idea."

She sneered. "It's the way things will be when that Bubble pops and we can live wherever we please."

"Aren't you worried you might be wrong? Last time I talked to Earth she said Wind was wrong."

"We read Wind's journals and while we don't have his research, we have his personal thoughts, and he was convinced it's safe out there."

"And you're willing to risk the whole world for that belief?"

"I'm willing to do anything to stop living like a prisoner, Earth."

"I'm not Earth! I'm Althea. Look, Earth...she was awful, but Cam can tell you I found the information on that data cell. I brought it to her. I saved her life!"

"Why should I believe you?" Armstrong said. "I know what you are. I've seen you kill, maim, belittle, and destroy us for as long as I've lived. I've seen you kill families and innocents just to rile up crowds. So, you'll excuse me if I don't believe you. But it doesn't really matter. The deal is the same. The Bubble is coming down. Either it can come down with bloodshed or with your help. So, what will it be?"

I looked over at Cam who looked away before our eyes met. "Of course, I'll help. Because I am not Earth. If it's safe beyond the Bubble, then we should pop it."

Armstrong cracked a smile. "I never liked you, but at least I appreciate your survival instincts." The woman rubbed her hands together. "So, let's go over the plan. We are going to stage a prison break for you and take you back inside the Center. One guard is going to defect in exchange for a pardon of all their crimes."

"I want Cam."

"That's very cute, but you don't get a choice."

"I want Cam." I spoke the words deliberately and firmly, emphasizing them one at a time. "If you are going to send me back inside the Center, I want Cam. I trust her."

"Are you sure you should? She knew about your torture and did nothing to stop it. It seems that somebody like that would hate you."

"I hate me, too. But if you're going to send me back into the Center, I'm going to get Cam, or you might as well kill me now."

It took another hour of convincing, but I eventually got what I wanted. It was such a small request in the grand scheme of things. The fact it took an hour of convincing showed just how much they hated me.

"Why would you ask for me?" Cam questioned as she walked me back to my room. "I don't want to go back to that place. It almost killed me."

"Because you're the only one I can trust. You know I'm Althea and not Earth. And you know this is a suicide mission, and I know you don't want me to die."

"You seem to know a lot of things, Thea."

"And besides, you're the only one that's been inside the Center. We walked that campus a dozen times. None of these other people know anything about the inside. It has to be you."

She sighed. "You're right, but I don't have to like it."

"You don't have to like any of it. I don't. All you have to do is help, even if you don't want to. That's what being a soldier is, right? Following orders."

Cam cracked a smile. "You would make a good Earth, Thea."

*

We made our way out of the encampment in a rusted pick-up truck later that day. I never thought I would survive to see the deteriorating building fade into the distance. We passed by a sign on our way out of the complex that read "Sisters of Mercy Psychiatric Hospital."

"What was this place?"

"There were always wars," said Cam. "Between the Muties—us—and the Five. This was one of the first casualties of it."

"Why wouldn't that be in textbooks?"

"Why would it be? The winners make history. Do you think anybody wants to admit this whole City is a horrible construct borne from the minds of sociopaths? Why do you think we need the military guarding the walls?"

"In case somebody should attack..." As soon as I said it, I knew it was wrong. I was just repeating what I'd heard my entire life. *But who would attack us if the planet was uninhabitable and no one was out there?*

"It's so they can converge on us from anywhere at any time."

I smiled. "I miss being your friend."

Cam looked up at me. "We are friends, Thea. Why do you think you're still alive?"

A smile crept across my face. I was, for a moment, happy. It couldn't last, but I was appreciative that I could still feel happy. I'd spent so long miserable, I had forgotten the emotion existed. Now I treasured every time I felt it.

*

The plan was as simple as it was horrific. Cam and two guards drove me on a prisoner transfer to a new facility across the City. Along the way, Cam would take over the transport and kill both of the guards to prove her loyalty. Then, she would divert me to the Center and beg forgiveness. I would grant her amnesty under my right as one of the Five.

"People won't like it that you forgave Cam," Armstrong told me. "But they'll forgive anything and anybody who brought their beloved god back to them."

Nobody knew the full plan except for Cam and me— not even the two guards driving us across the city. Cam rode in the back of the van with me, making sure I didn't "escape."

"Are you really going to kill them?" I whispered.

Cam gave me a blank look. "I have to."

I didn't try to argue with her. "They say it's harder than it looks."

"'I've watched enough people die. It can't be much different to pull the trigger."

"I think it's harder than you imagine."

"We'll see. It's a shame, you know, that it has come to this. I didn't think I'd be here, right now. I just wanted to work the mines. I was happy working the mines."

"Until the Five found you, tested you, and forced you into the horrible life of a Mutie."

"They never found me, Thea. I'm not a Mutie. I volunteered because I wanted to help."

I gasped. "Why?"

"There are a lot of us that see the injustice in the system. We see how horrible the system is for everybody and we decided to fight back. Abigail wasn't a Mutie either. She just wanted to help. She wanted it to be better and she knew killing Earth was the key to changing things."

Poor Abigail. I'd written her off as an idiot, cringing when I heard her talk boys with McKinsey. I wanted to be rid of her, but she was truly the bravest girl I ever knew. She died to save the world from Earth. She is the only reason I was still alive.

"She was a good soldier. She knew her role. If I couldn't get to Earth, she had to. And she did. Poor Abigail. She saw what I saw, the hatred in the world, the unfairness. We need to be free, Althea. All of us."

"I had some good years in the Fifth," I replied, "before I came to the Center and found out the truth about the Five. There's a lot of people like me who won't wanna be shaken from their cushy lives. People are going to fight back against you."

In fact, they already were fighting back. Commander Armstrong let me watch the news and read old papers to catch up on the world since I'd been imprisoned.

Arrests for Muties were through the roof. The military had been rounding them up at random and executing them as a show of force. Worse, the people from the Inner Rings, normally cool and detached, were lynching Muties at night. They burned effigies of them.

"People will always fight justice, but that doesn't change anything. This is prison, Althea. They tell us where to eat, when to sleep. They change the weather. They kill indiscriminately." Cam looked at her watch. "It's time. Are you ready? Have you practiced?"

"Yes. I'm ready."

"Then I have to be too." Cam stood up, pulling out her gun. For a short moment she closed her eyes. Then, she lifted the gun. It shook in her hands. She lowered the gun, and then raised it again.

The bullets rang out and echoed through the truck. The car swerved as the driver turned to see his partner dead. "What are you doing?"

"Stop the bus. Stop it now."

The driver did what he was told. He put the car in park and lifted his hands over his head. "You don't have to do this!"

"Get out of the car!" Cam shouted.

That was part of the plan. Make it public. I looked up to see a traffic camera pointed right where she led the driver. I didn't want her to do this, but we didn't have a choice.

The next bullets didn't echo. I'd heard firecrackers make louder noises. Seconds later, Cam scooted into the driver's seat, and took one last look over at the driver lying dead in the street. "It wasn't that hard."

That was a lie, of course. You have to shroud lies in the truth. And the truth was that Cam was a girl from the Sixth that was in way over her head, trying to protect a girl from the Fifth who was in over hers.

CHAPTER 2

The military caught up to us in less than ten minutes. I stepped out of the truck first and Cam followed. They cuffed her and threw her in the back of a Humvee and then took me out and examined every crevice of my body.

When they saw I was basically a human pincushion, they dragged Cam out of the car and beat her within an inch of her life. They only stopped because I forced them to and they obeyed because they thought I was Earth.

The soldiers walked me to a limo and lowered me inside. It was plush, velvet, and contained every accommodation I could want. The tinted windows prevented the light from penetrating the inside and the air conditioner blasted the perfect temperature. A cheese plate and sparkling water rested on a table in front of me and I ate voraciously. I'd never tasted anything so amazing in my life. Even on my best day in captivity they'd fed me nothing but oatmeal.

The limo took me to a private train car, where even more food awaited me. It was a long ride back to the Center. Luckily, I had company to distract me. Sitting across from me was a lovely and chatty man with short hair and long sideburns. His name was Sal and his voice danced like music. "We need to talk speeches. Can you give me some insight into exactly what happened to you?"

"Please," I responded. "Can we do this later? I'm so tired."

"I'm afraid not, ma'am. We have to satiate your adoring followers. The City thought you were dead. You are going to have to give a speech when we get back to the Center."

"I can't give a speech!"

"You must. Everybody will want to know what happened to you."

"No—" I caught myself. I was Earth. I had to remember I was Earth. She gave thousands of speeches. She loved giving speeches. She got off on them. *What would Earth say?*

"Don't attempt to dictate my life. I am one of the Five, and you are nothing." That was mean, but Earth was mean. "There will be no speeches until I can put on my face." *That was something people said, right?* "And until a dentist fixes my teeth. You wouldn't want me looking like a hobo, would you? That would be undignified."

Sal caught his tongue. "I'm sorry, ma'am."

"Don't forget your place."

"Of course, ma'am."

It was such an adrenaline rush to tell somebody what to do. I immediately understood how it could go to one's head. It felt good to have absolute power.

"I know you are just trying to help. Now, before we get started, I will need a bath, and you will need to fetch the nice girl who saved me."

His eyes went wide. "The traitor?"

"That's right. It was part of our deal. Everybody deserves second chances, Sal. Everybody."

"I don't think—"

"Don't think. Just do. Have her brought to my room."

*

I hadn't had a bath in as long as I could remember. I am a shower girl, but I have to say that soaking in that tub was as close to Heaven as I'd ever gotten. Every ache and bruise melted away in the warm bath water.

The robe I put on after my bath was the softest satin I'd ever felt. Even though the floors of Earth's room were marble, somehow, they weren't cool to the touch. I walked over to the mirror and looked at myself for the first time in weeks.

My cheeks had caved in, and the bags under my eyes stretched to my chin; my eyes were dim, and shades darker than I remembered. The teeth the guards had knocked out left gaps in my yellowed smile. And my hair— It was so thin.

What had I become? Before I could answer there was a knock on the door, and Sal walked in. "The team is here, ma'am. It's time."

They brought the doctors and surgeons into the Residence and set them up in Wind's old room. It was quite different than the last time I had been inside that room. All that remained from my memory were the pictures on the wall. Gone was the computer and furniture. In their place an operating table, equipment had been set up, along with the six doctors.

"We brought in the best in the City," Sal said. "To make sure you look perfect for your speech today."

I turned to him. "Sal, I told you not today."

He smiled. "No, you said not until you look presentable. These nice doctors are going to make sure that happens."

Earth would never refuse such an offer so neither could I. I sat down on the table and let them prep me for surgery. They placed a mask on my mouth and I was out before I counted backwards from ten.

The next thing I knew, I woke up, and sat up groggily in Earth's bed. I looked over at a mirror. My hair was back to its original luster—no, it was shinier than ever. My cheeks were plump and fresh, and my eyes had lost their bags and shimmered in the light. I looked...hot. I mean I would totally do me. I never thought much of my looks before, but those doctors had made me look...amazing.

"You look good," Cam commented from across the room. Her voice made me jump.

I smiled at her slowly. "Thank you."

She couldn't make eye contact with me. She looked down at the shackles around her hands and feet. "I thought you would never look the same after the torture."

"I really don't though. I look...better."

I marveled at how high they had made my cheekbones and how silky my skin appeared. The prison had made me sweaty and pimply. For weeks, my acne had itched horribly, and I had scratched it constantly. Now, there was no trace of it.

"It's amazing what you can do with all the money and power in the world."

As Cam went to stand a thousand volts shocked her back down. "I'm glad. And I'm sorry. I'm so sorry I never came to see you before."

I glided over to her, feeling graceful in a way I never had before—almost elegant. "There's nothing to apologize for. You didn't torture me. You didn't beat me."

"No. But I should have stopped it."

I shook my head. "I doubt I would have done anything differently."

There was a knock on the door. Sal walked in, a big grin on his face. "Are we happy now, ma'am?"

Out of habit, I covered my mouth when I smiled, but then I let my fingers drop. I turned to the mirror. My teeth were perfect and white. My front tooth, which had always slightly bent in the front, was now perfectly aligned with the rest. "Yes, Sal. Very happy."

He handed me a small remote. "I thought you might like to torture the prisoner a bit before you let her go. Turnabout is fair play, after all."

Cam watched me steadily as I looked at the remote. A deep, primal part of me wanted to press it, wanted to release my rage at what had happened to me, but I fought against it. I placed the remote down. "That won't be necessary. This girl saved my life."

Sal took the remote from my hand. "Then come now. It is time to go. Your public awaits."

*

I didn't realize just how ineffective the Muties had been at convincing the public of their plight until I stepped onto the podium and saw what must have been the whole City chanting my name in unison. Well, it wasn't quite my name. It was Earth's, but the effect was the same. There weren't any boos or hissing; only joy and reverence.

In that moment, I realized that I preferred torture to public speaking. Standing in front of throngs of people who held signs to wish me well, crying, dropping on their knees in prayer, and gathered to hear the sound of my voice made me uncomfortable… that wasn't me. I wasn't ready for something like that.

I saw Henry before I stepped on stage, except it wasn't my love at all. It was Time, wrapped in Henry's body. His posture was different, and he tilted his head differently, but he had the same kind eyes. I promised myself I wouldn't look into them, that it would be too hard, but I couldn't resist. I needed him in that moment, even though I knew I could never have him.

It was the first time I'd seen him since the Transference room. I had thought my heart would flutter at the sight of him, but he wasn't…him anymore. He was Time, and by the scalding look he shot, Time must've hated me, which meant that now Henry hated me as well. I wondered if there was a piece of him left, living under all those layers of consciousness.

I stood behind Sal as he introduced me. "My fellow citizens, this is a great day! After we had already suffered so much tragedy, we thought that our beloved Earth was gone forever too. To think about losing another of our beloved Five was too much to bear. And now we have to bear it no more! Welcome back the mother herself, Earth!"

I walked up to the podium and spoke. "Thank you. Your greeting is most humbling. As I lay almost dying in the dank cells on the outskirts of our fair city, all I could think of was being here with you.

"And all my wonderful colleagues." I turned and smiled at McKinsey, her bravado replaced by a cowering Stone. "Now we can do the business of keeping this City great, of making this City even greater. Many will try to tear us down. They will try to separate us. They are against us. They want us to live apart, but we need to live together. I have seen the other side, and I know now, more clearly than ever, that our path is the right one."

I stopped for a moment and listened to the thunderous applause as two guards dragged Cam onto stage. "I must take a moment to speak about a very brave soul." I looked over at Cam, who hesitantly inched forward from the side of the stage. "Come here, child."

Cam stepped forward, bowing her head reverently. "Yes, ma'am."

I turned to the crowd. "I want to give special recognition to this extraordinary individual. This soldier here saw my plight and worked tirelessly to save my life.

She gave me extra rations of food. She sat with me. She saw through the hatred, and when it came time to strike..."

Two video feeds popped on either side of me. They showed Cam slaughter the driver in cold blood on the side of the road. Cam squeezed her eyes shut and I instinctively grabbed her hand as I finished, "...she acted to save my life!"

I raised her hand in the air and the crowd cheered. "She is proof that the rebels are not all evil. I will grant her a full pardon for her actions, and for all of her courage, I want her to be at my side, as part of my staff."

I turned to Cam. "Please say a few words."

The square fell silent as I stepped down and allowed Cam to take the microphone. "I just wanted to do what was right." She looked back at me. "Althea...we used to be friends...and now she is one of the Five...when I found out she was pregnant there was—"

The entire square gasped. My eyes went wide. I turned around to Time, whose eyes nearly burst out of his head. Sal quickly came up and ushered us all off stage. Behind the curtains I heard chatter flood the City.

*

"Why didn't you tell me you were pregnant?" Sal screamed. "We would have postponed."

"Now, Sal. You are hysterical."

Cam muttered under her breath. "I'm sorry. I'm sorry."

I took Cam's shoulders in my hands. "You didn't do anything wrong. We should have prepped you better."

Time shook his head. For one second, I wanted Henry to be able to comfort me, to know that it was his baby, but it was only Time, glaring at me darkly. "This baby, it was conceived prior to the Transference?"

I shook my head. If the Five found out that Henry and I had conceived the baby in prison, they would immediately piece together the truth. "No. It happened while I was captured."

"Savages. No worries. We can terminate this baby *tout suite* and make it seem like an accident. The child will be a martyr."

"You don't need to worry about me losing the baby. It's already gone. They tortured her out of me."

There was an audible whimper from Stone as the rest hung their heads. They didn't know what to say, which was okay. I didn't want them to say anything. I just wanted to forget it had ever happened.

*

I kept to myself over the next several days to avoid suspicions, and only left my room for official meetings. I brushed off any mood swings and inconsistencies by blaming them on my imprisonment and torture. If anybody pushed, I wept about the loss of my baby.

The City was frenzied over the news of my failed pregnancy and the Center used it to drum up vitriol for the Muties, plastering posters all over the city with slogans such as "Baby Killers" and "We lost the greatest treasure in the world because of Muties."

The Five wanted to discuss the implications of my failed pregnancy, Arrow, the most insistent among them.

"Look, we all know that the food rations will run out sooner or later unless we can get the population back under control. This baby is the perfect thing to distract the public while we work toward a solution. We'll make it a spectacle like you wouldn't believe."

I nearly spit out the water I'd been drinking. "Excuse me. The food rations are running out?"

Arrow chuckled. "Of course! You should know better than anybody."

"Oh yes. I'm sorry. I've been so out of sorts. I feel like I've been gone for a decade. What about the shield, is it still holding?"

Arrow sighed. "This is not my area, but it seems like Stone is keeping it together. Stone? You with us, honey?"

Stone bit her nails. "Yeah. Yeah. It'll hold. For now."

"And how long is 'for now?'" Time asked.

Stone looked at him. "Long enough. We need to vote on whether we still need it. It's better if we vote than wait. The shield should come down. Why don't we vote on it?"

Arrow snorted. He'd already gained fifteen pounds since the Transference. "A vote won't do anything, my dear, except put everybody in the City in danger. Besides, we already know this is the end game. We are at a stalemate, and have been since..."

"Since Wind died," Time said.

"What does Wind's death have to do with any of this?" I asked.

Time and Arrow looked at me quizzically, as if they had never seen me before. Arrow shook his jowly head. "Are you sure you're alright? Did those electrodes scramble your brain?"

I'd said something wrong. I should know all these things, but I didn't. "Do not speak to me like one of your donuts, Arrow. The fact I'm still breathing is a testament to my resilience. If you don't want me to smack that food out of your fat face, I suggest you approach me with the respect deserving somebody in my position."

Arrow scoffed. "Of course. I didn't mean to imply anything."

"Then don't."

*

After the meeting I caught up with Time in the corridor. "May I speak with you for a moment?"

I wanted to grab his hand. I wanted him to tell me it would be alright. "Of course," he said. "I am always here to lend an ear."

"Some parts of my memory are fuzzy—well, most of my memory is fuzzy now. Could you tell me again why we are deadlocked?"

He smiled at me. "Certainly. I couldn't imagine the tragedy you must be going through. Wind was the deciding vote on bringing down the shield. He spent the last century convincing Stone to switch her vote from no to yes. She finally did so right before he died. Then the vote was swept under the rug per your instructions."

I smiled. "Ah, yes. My memory isn't what it used to be. I need to lay down."

I hoped he would want to come lie down with me, to comfort me, to be with me, but instead he looked at me coldly. "That would help, I'm sure."

*

Time had given me the ammunition I needed to lower the shield. If there were to be a vote, we would no longer be deadlocked. Time, Stone, and I would win. We would vote to take down the wall and it would be over. We would be able to save the City and the Muties in one single moment, but the words Earth said to me rattled in my head. What if it wasn't safe beyond the Bubble? What if it was still toxic? If we were wrong, our whole species would be extinct in a moment.

I needed more information to be sure I was making the right decision. Cam was in the archives, gathering information for another data dump, and I asked her to find everything she could about Wind's research. Sal and the other Five didn't like that I trusted Cam so deeply and so quickly, but I wouldn't have it any other way. After all, she'd saved me from my captors.

"I think I found something," Cam told me one evening. "It's the air toxicity levels from outside the Bubble for the last thousand years." She handed me a file folder a hundred pages thick, filled with columns upon columns of numbers.

"What am I looking at, Cam? This really isn't my thing."

"It's not mine, either, but just check out the numbers from the readings outside the bubble. They're going down. Everything is within normal range."

She was right. The first ninety pages were full of red numbers on page after page, but somewhere, around a hundred years ago, the numbers had turned black, and then to green on the last pages.

"What does this mean?"

"It means we don't have to be prisoners anymore."

*

"I want to ask you a question," I said to Time.

I had rehearsed the conversation in my head a hundred times. I had picked Time as my confidante for reasons beyond my love of Henry. He was the most reasoned and welcoming of the Five. Stone wasn't the right person to talk with about my change of heart. She would see me as an aggressor. I couldn't go to Arrow, because he would desperately try to talk me out of it. He might even try to have me killed. It had to be Time.

"This is most unusual, my friend," Time said. "That we speak twice in a single year. It is odd we should meet like this now, when our Vessels were in love. Are you feeling okay?"

The truth was that I wasn't feeling okay. The urge to touch him burnt inside me. "Let's keep this professional, Time, if we could." I was saying it as much for me as for him. Looking into Henry's eyes and hearing his sweet voice sent me for a loop, but I had a mission.

Time smiled. "I would always be willing to be professional with you, if you extend me the same courtesy."

"Always." I cleared my throat. "My months in captivity caused me to have a change of heart."

"I'm sure. So, what? Now you want to destroy your enemies? It isn't enough to relegate half our creation to abject poverty?"

I had the file Cam had found and slammed it on his desk. "Can you tell me what this means?"

Time slipped on a pair of reading glasses and opened the folder. "Well, this is the toxicity report Wind printed out for us every month."

"Of course, it is. And what does it say? Why are the numbers red for so long, and now they are green?"

"They had been red for a hundred thousand years. It meant that we weren't able to go outside because it was toxic. But then a hundred years ago that changed." He held up the folder. "Right here we started seeing breathable levels, and now—well, according to this data, it's livable."

"Couldn't the data be wrong? Or a sensor be broken?"

"Not likely. Maybe one sensor, but we have them all over the Bubble. The military repairs and maintains them. It's one of their core functions. These numbers are right. They've been right for a long time."

"And this is why you think it's safe outside?"

Time nodded. "It is."

"Then I want to set them free."

Time sipped his tea for a long moment. "Set them free. That's a new one."

"Set them all free. Not just the Muties, but also everyone in the City. It's time to lower the shield."

Time smiled. "What is your end game here, my dear?"

I swallowed hard. "No end game. These are my children and they deserve to be free. Being tortured gave me a lot of time to think. I don't think we should turn off the Bubble, but I do think we should allow people to go outside and live freely if they choose. Is that possible?"

"There have always been airlocks to let people outside. They have never been used, but they do exist."

"Then that should be an option. We should allow people to leave out of the airlocks if they choose. We should allow them to exist without us."

"You know what this means, what it really means if you move forward. What it means for us."

I nodded. "I do. This is our last life. Let's make it count."

Time agreed to set up a meeting with Stone. He didn't think it was appropriate for me to talk to her directly. She was afraid of me. I didn't blame her. I was scared of me too.

With Time as an ally, I only had to fend off Arrow until I could broker the peace. He was the most vengeful of all the Five, and if he discovered my duplicity his temper could destroy everything.

I found him waiting for me outside Time's sanctuary. He carried a box of donuts and had powdered sugar all over his face, which he wiped off with the sleeve of his tunic.

"What were you talking about in there?" Arrow asked.

"That's none of your business."

"It is my business. You have been acting very strange since you came back from imprisonment. I hope you aren't getting soft. This City is in a panic and we need to make it great again by taking out these accursed Muties once and for all."

I scoffed. "They are in an uproar because of your propaganda."

"It's *our* propaganda, isn't it?" Arrow grabbed my arm. "Are you still with me? Look into my eyes and tell me you are with me on this."

I gulped. "I have, am, and always will be with you as long as you represent the best interests of this City. Now, can you please tell me why this new body feels so...decrepit compared to the others I've used in the past? All the joints are loose and wobbly. They don't bend to my will as easily as previous vessels. I think you're losing your touch." And with that I walked off. "You know what, never mind. I have better things to do."

*

I needed rest. During my meeting with Arrow, I could barely hold my head up and the walk back to my room took the rest of my energy. My head had barely hit the pillow when the virtual projectors flicked on. Arrow was on camera doing an interview with Sal.

"So, tell me," Sal said. "Why are you concerned about our City?"

"Well," Arrow started, mini-jowls flapping, "I'm concerned because my dear colleague Earth was captured, taken, and returned to us broken." He paused considering his next words. "Look Sal, I'm not just concerned. I'm scared for this City. There is a group present that Earth has allowed to act with almost reckless abandon for years, decades even."

"And what group is that?"

"The Muties. We've never mounted a *real* attack against them. Not effectively anyway. And now Earth is cozy with one of them? I mean what kind of ridiculousness is that?"

"Some have called it...Stockholm Syndrome."

"I don't think that's too far off, honestly. I mean, what do we really know about Earth now that she's back?" Arrow gave the camera a wary glance. "She was pregnant. We don't know who the father is. It could be a Mutie for all we know. And is that the kind of person we want leading this City?"

"She's done a great job as your spokesperson for eons."

"She has, but times change. Look at the data dumps she has allowed the Muties to release. Look at all the times she spread lies for them. Completely useless information, and slanderous to boot, but she's done nothing to condemn them. She's done nothing to say the videos she made in captivity were a lie. She's let them fester."

"Well, maybe she has let them fester because they haven't gained traction."

"Maybe, or maybe she's been brainwashed. Either way, it's time for a new voice. This City could be great, and it's my job to make it great. Muties are destroying this City, and it's time to show them what's what, which is why I'm calling on our military to round up every Mutie they can find and lead them out of the Inner Rings."

Arrow was a cunning political operator. Knowing my weakened state, and suspecting my plot against him, he had acted by driving a wedge between the citizens and me. It was time to act.

*

Arrow's ranting and raving worsened by the day. He was on camera constantly. "This City needs to exterminate the vermin. I take responsibility for creating these Muties, and as their father, I demand they lay down their weapons!"

But, in response the Mutie Resistance grew stronger each day. Arrow exiled the Muties from the Third and into the loving arms of the resistance. These new recruits gladly took up swords against their jailers. They fought against the military in the Fifth and Sixth. They even won a few battles.

They were so effective that people from the Outer Rings joined their cause en masse after seeing how unjust Arrow had become. Soon the resistance would have a bigger force than the military.

But the military was stronger and more powerful. They had the guns and the money. They executed Muties hourly on live TV as Arrow's voice played in the background, condemning them. "We will show these creatures that our City is great, and they cannot destroy it. Many have tried. All have failed!"

The Muties couldn't win in the long run as the Five's soldiers converged and surrounded them anywhere in the City. That was why they had manned stations throughout the Bubble. It wasn't just to fix the Bubble should it fail. It was so they could contain any problem or rebellion with ruthless efficiency. It would only be a matter of time until they exterminated the Muties completely. Luckily, I only needed one more cog to fall into place before I could end it all.

Time brought me to Stone in the dark of night, when the watchful eye of Arrow would be affixed elsewhere. When I walked into her room, the past hit me like a punch in the gut. Not long ago I'd interviewed to be her Vessel. I wonder if she still saw that in my face, or if she only saw Earth now.

Stone was scattered, more so than the last time we talked. She reminded me of a skittish cat, crawling up the walls looking for an escape route. Even before I spoke, she was on edge.

Time cleared his throat. "I think we can skip the small talk, yes?"

I nodded. "That would be best. Stone, I would like to speak with you about allowing people to live outside the Bubble if they choose. I think it's time."

Teeth gnashed, and hems hawed, but eventually I convinced Stone that I was honest and forthright in my desire to bring down the force field.

"Look me in the eyes," she said. "And tell me this isn't some trick."

"It's not a trick. The Bubble needs to come down."

A smile crept over Stone's face. I hadn't seen her smile before. It was unnatural and painful to watch, but the crow's feet in the corners of her eyes told me her affection was genuine.

I smiled back. "I promised myself to keep this City safe until we could enter the Outside again. It's the least I can offer after what I've done."

I couldn't believe Time and Stone were willing to give up their lives for us. It made me think the Five may not have always been so bad. Maybe some of them never were.

"I'm happy to die," Stone told me. "I just want it to end. I want to see my daughter again and get through this waking nightmare. When you're responsible for destroying almost all of humanity, every day is a nightmare. When you made the light leave your daughter's eyes because of a mistake you made...nothing is worth living for. This has been my penance and it's time for it to end."

"Fair enough," Time said. "But without the support of the military there can be no peace. We must convince them their loyalties should lie with us."

I smiled. "Leave that to me. I'll convince them or die trying."

*

Time walked me back to my room. I didn't want him to open his mouth. I didn't want him to say a word. If he did, I couldn't pretend it was Henry. Time's cadence was slower and more methodical. He emphasized different words. He didn't have the wonder that Henry had when he spoke.

"I appreciate you doing this," Time said. "It's been a very long time since I have been excited about anything."

I swallowed my sadness at my broken illusion. "It is the right thing to do."

"Do you believe that, truly?"

"I do. Are you not convinced?"

"I am very convinced, but I am concerned. The first years after Transference are the hardest. Thoughts are cloudy, actions more intense, hormones rage for those our former bodies once loved."

I gulped. "That's very forward, Time."

Time laughed. "Oh, that was not, as they say, a 'come-on.' I just know these years are very hard on all of us, and with your trauma, you might be acting...irrationally right now."

We arrived at my door. "I am perfectly rational. More rational than I've been in many lifetimes, I assure you that."

"Then I am happy my concerns are unfounded."

*

The next morning, I headed out to the Bubble with Cam as my driver. If we were going to take down the force field, we needed the support of the Constable and the military. Without her on our side, there could be a coup attempt; there could be bedlam. We needed a smooth transition into the future of our City.

Arrow had continued making his hate speeches around the clock, riling up the whole City and the people wondered why I hadn't responded. But I was biding my time and would speak out that night. There would be a massive speech at the wall to ask the military for their help.

Cam played Arrow's speeches as she drove me out to the wall. He shouted into the rafters. "We can't allow these people to destroy our way of life."

But in reality, he was the one destroying our way of life. This wasn't the way we were supposed to live.

"Do you think we'll win?" I asked Cam. She had been silent the whole way to the Bubble.

"For the first time, I really do. Just stay low and we'll be fine. We'll get through this together."

The closer we got to the wall, the more burnt out and desolate the surrounding area became. Cam smiled wryly. "They told us not to come this close to the wall when I was a kid."

"Why?"

"They said we'd be shot on sight if we came out this far. We all tried it though."

"And?"

"Some of 'em didn't become adults. Let's just say that."

There was no civilization near the Bubble. More than that, there was nothing at all. There wasn't grass, or trees, or rocks—just a vast expanse. It made sense, if I thought about it. Why would they focus on making this pretty when only soldiers would see it?

We came over a ridge and a great barracks towered in front of us, along with a great wall stretching into the horizon in both directions. From its top the Bubble shot into the sky.

Guards stood in long formations for hundreds of feet along the wall and there she was, in front of them all: The Constable. Since my imprisonment, the Five had promoted her as head the entire military, answering directly to them. Aside from us, she was the most powerful person in the City.

My throat tightened when Cam stopped the car. I closed my eyes, forcing myself to focus. The Constable opened my door and saluted me. She...saluted me. I never thought I would live to see the day. The rest of the troops saluted me in unison as we followed the Constable on a tour of the facility.

"It's been a long time since you've been out here, ma'am," she said. "I can only imagine you're here because you need something from me, but first I need to know something. Is what Arrow said true? Are you really thinking about siding with those pansies Time and Stone?"

"I believe you call them gods, Constable. Maybe show some respect."

The Constable caught herself. "Yes, ma'am. I didn't mean any offense. It's just—out here, things get a little rougher than you remember. We are in a constant battle with Muties for our very lives."

"No offense taken, but please understand your place in this world. It is to protect these citizens. Do you believe this Bubble protects its citizens? After all,

Wind's last studies before his death showed that the outside air is safe to breath."

"Even if that's true, ma'am," the Constable continued, never wavering in her steps, "we don't know what kind of monsters are out there or how they've changed over the past centuries."

"You are strong, powerful, and loyal. You could lead our troops to tame the wide new world."

"That's a great risk. It's safe in here, ma'am."

"Yes, like a child is safe inside his crib, but would we say the child should never explore the outside world, should never grow, should never improve?"

"If the baby tried to step out into the unknown world, I would like to think we would try to stop it...for its own good."

"And what if the crib was too small for the baby? Then what would you do?"

The Constable didn't answer, which was fine, because I wasn't paying attention. I was hypnotized by the translucent blue hue that shimmered and glowed in front of me.

The Bubble was as beautiful as it was deadly. If you stared long enough, you could almost make out the outside world. I ached for it. I wanted to put my hand through the Bubble and pull myself into the great unknown.

But I couldn't. There was work to be done to secure the peace. "I want to tell you the truth, Constable. We are moving to allow people to live outside this Bubble. There will be a meeting in the morning once I return to the Center and we will convene to shut it down. Time, Stone, and I will win. We have the votes. This City is a powder keg right now and getting worse every day. It can't take another revolt. If the Muties want out, we will let them out. We will let everyone out. I can't have us killing our own citizens. I can't have them taking up arms against us."

I squeezed her shoulder. "I need you to be on my side as you have always been. Time, Stone, and myself are all on board. Only Arrow stands in opposition. Are you with me?"

The Constable thought for a moment. "I am in eternal service to the Five's wishes, ma'am."

"Good, because you will be responsible for leading expeditions to show that we are safe. It is a dangerous job. Are you up for it?"

The Constable nodded. "Yes, ma'am."

*

When it was time for my speech, I resolutely stepped onto the stage to the unified salute of a thousand soldiers. Every one of them would be out of a job soon and would be enlisted for a more dangerous one.

"Thank you for being here today," I started as the camera popped on and danced around behind me. "I visited the wall for the first time in generations because I wanted to see why I was kidnapped. It is this wall—the Bubble—that apparently keeps our citizens safe but also causes great pain. People cannot escape. They are ostracized. They are not offered refuge.

"But there is a place where they can find a home. They can find peace beyond the Bubble. They want to take the world by storm and carve their place in it. If we don't want them, then they want to find somewhere that does. My dear Arrow wants to round them up—wants to lynch them—but that doesn't seem like our City.

"I don't agree with the rebel's tactics, but I do sympathize with their end goals. They just want to be happy and free. I want that too. If leaving will make them happy, I will lead the way. I'm heading back to the Center where I will cast the deciding vote to exit the Bubble and enter into a new world, beyond the confines of this City. I would not put you in harm's way. The Outside is safe, and I shall prove it by being the first person to taste the outside air in a thousand lifetimes.

"You do not have to leave the City with us, but you can if you so choose. Hopefully, this will end the fighting. Additionally, I'm asking for a ceasefire until we have a plan in place. I do this not for myself, but for the good of all. Thank you."

As I finished, the cameras turned off followed by a momentary silence. But as the Constable pushed me off stage and into our waiting transport, I heard the screams, boos, and curses boiling up from the crowd.

Cam took the driver's seat. "I don't think those soldiers liked that much."

"I haven't been doing this long, Cam, but I know this. People don't like anything I do, either way."

It was the truest statement I'd ever spoken.

CHAPTER 3

What had I done? I was supposed to convince the military to be on my side, and they were more riled up than ever. The soldiers screamed and hollered behind us as Cam and I sped away. Even if the Constable had wanted to help me, she couldn't control thousands of screaming soldiers. The military would never be able to keep the peace if they protested this proposal so vehemently.

On top of all that, I had placed a target on my back with every powerful person in the City. The soldiers hated me. Arrow hated me. The Inner Rings hated me. Everybody who wasn't a Mutie hated me.

What I just did was suicide. But it was not the first time I'd committed suicide since I'd left home, and I was still alive. Against all odds, I was still here. I won Transference, and yet I was still here. I had beat Earth. There was no person dead or alive who could say that, As the Bubble faded into the distance, Arrow shouted through the radio

"This is a time of great upheaval!" he screamed. "The Inner Rings shall be a beacon for true believers. They cannot bring down the Bubble from anywhere but the Center, and they'll have to pull the levers from my cold, dead hands!"

As we passed into the Fifth, where I used to live and where I used to be happy, I watched the wind blow through the fields where I had played as a child. "I need to make a stop, Cam. Take me home."

Cam looked back at me. "I don't think that's a good idea. I mean, those soldiers were really mad. I want to get back to the Center as soon as possible before something bad happens."

"Cam, I love you, but this isn't a request. Please don't make me pull the god card."

She looked back at me. "I'm just looking out for you."

"Whether it's here, or there, I'm in just as much danger." It was true. Arrow had been spewing vitriol against me on every channel since the moment I left the stage.

"Earth killed every last one of you," he screamed. "She will see you all murdered for her own gains! She wants nothing short of your deaths!"

I watched the thistle sway in the wind as we passed farm after farm. Eventually, the streets looked familiar. We passed by my church and I struggled to remember how long it had been since I'd left.

I remembered being in church, the pastor imploring us to enter the Transference as Dad forced us to leave, red-faced and ready to explode. I understood his anger now. I remember stealing away in the dark of night, and Bobby holding Dad back while I boarded the train. How things had changed since then.

Cam pulled off the main road and down the long drag that housed dozens of farms, including mine. "You're going to out yourself as a fraud by coming here you know."

"Will I?" I asked. "It's tradition for the Five to visit their Vessel's old home and offer the family entrance to the Second Ring."

"Whatever you say."

*

The Reynolds farm loomed over the street as large and majestic as ever. They grew apples mostly, and raised cows, but their land stretched as far as I could see. It dwarfed our little farm and Jake's combined, but they never showed it.

Whenever our harvest was lean, they had always given us some of theirs to make up the difference, even though we could never pay them back. Well, never until now.

I wept when our barn crested over the horizon. I never thought I would see it or my family again and I certainly didn't think I would come back with a limo. Best case, I might've come back with my tail between my legs, begging for forgiveness with a few months' salary to make it better. I still would have been grounded, but the money would have bought me parole.

I'd been imprisoned one way or another for close to a year, and now I was back, posing as a god, about to tell my family the truth about had what happened. This was a conversation I never thought I'd have.

The cameras had been following me through the Sixth, more and more of them swarming with every passing block. By the time we turned off the main road toward my farm, they'd figured out my plans and sped ahead of me to set up and were waiting on me when I pulled up to the house. They must have thought I was trying to save face with my own PR move. Little did they know, I thought.

I hadn't considered that if I saw my mother again, it would be with a hundred cameras watching me, but then again, everyone thought I was Earth now. I was accessible to all.

When I arrived and stepped out of the car, hundreds of flash bulbs went off. I smiled and waved, trying to build up good will. I needed as much good press as possible if I was to outlast Arrow, even if that wasn't my original intention.

Mama and Dad waited for me in front of the house, tears streaming down their faces. The press huddled around them, my house awash in a sea of red and white lights.

I had to keep it together. I had to be Earth. When we were alone, I could be honest. If I broke now, everyone would know. I could barely protect myself as a god, let alone as a frightened child.

"It's good to see you, ma'am. Your family performed a great service for our City." I shook my Mama's hand and stared deeply into her eyes as they filled with tears. My father's handshake was strong and firm.

"Thank you," my Mama sobbed. "We are happy to serve our great City."

"I want to thank you for your sacrifice, and let you know that we look forward to seeing you in the Second." I smiled broadly. "I hear you have foregone your house until after the harvest."

Mama smiled. "There's still work to be done, ma'am. We have a City to feed."

I smiled back at her. "You make our City proud."

After the photo op, the press trickled back into their cars. I asked Mama and Dad to lead Cam and I on a tour through the house. The moment the door closed, and we were away from the cameras, I grabbed my Mama around the neck and sobbed.

Mama stroked my hair. "It's okay, baby girl. Let it out."

Cam pulled out a sonic disrupter and turned it on. It created a low hum. I held both my parents' hands. "We are alone. Nobody can hear us. There's something I have to tell you."

Dad shook his head. "There's nothing to say, Althea."

Mama smiled. "We knew it was you from the moment you stepped on stage after being set free."

"How?" I asked them.

"They change," Dad said. "The walk, the talk, the mannerisms, it all changes. But you never did. The twinkle in your eye never died." Dad choked back his tears. "Before...with...well you know...she changed. It made my heart split in two. I didn't know how I could deal with you changing, but you never did."

"Not to mention the fact that Earth would have come down on those Muties harder than anybody," Mama added. "She wouldn't have cared who she hurt."

"Why are you doing this?" Dad asked. "Why are you trying to go outside the Bubble? Why risk everything?"

"It's not right, Dad. If you saw how they were treated. All they want is to start their own life somewhere else. They should be allowed. We should all be allowed."

Mama rubbed my shoulder. "Why don't you let somebody else deal with that?"

"There isn't anybody else, Mama. Either I do it, or they deal with it when I'm gone. I'm going to be found out eventually. I might as well use my power while I've got it."

Dad nodded. "We taught you too well, huh?"

I smiled. "You did, but I still want your blessing."

Mama smiled back at me. "You got it. Always."

We walked upstairs, and I looked at my old room. It looked so small compared to Earth's. It was dark and narrow. I couldn't believe it was once my whole world.

I lay down on my hard, lumpy bed. "You shouldn't just lay there," Bobby said, walking through the door. "Don't you have work to do?"

I grinned at him. "Don't you?"

He sat at the foot of my bed. "You really screwed stuff up this time, sis. I'm a little jealous it wasn't me."

"Well, I learned everything I know from you if it's any consolation."

"The student has become the master, quite literally in fact."

I sat up on the bed and grabbed him around the waist. "I missed you."

He squeezed my hand. "I missed you too, but you're here now. For a little while."

I wanted to stay there forever, but I knew I couldn't. There was work to be done.

*

Cam and I made our way out of the Fifth. We'd listened to Arrow all the way into the Fourth, where we would catch a train to the Inner Rings.

"The Inner Rings will no longer be a bastion for Mutie scum. They will be locked down. All Muties will be shut out of the Inner Rings and led across the bridges to the Outer Rings. Once there, they will be left to rot until the military has their way with them."

The crowds got larger as we drove toward the river that separated the Outer and Inner Rings, as thousands of workers thronged the streets. All the warehouses were silent, and the factories, usually pluming with smoke, were vacant. Across the bridge—the bridge that blew up when I had first entered the Inner Rings—thousands of people marched toward me, led and prodded by guards. They were packed so tight people lost their balance and fell off into their watery graves below.

"What is he doing?" I shouted to Cam. "We have the votes. We can open the Bubble."

Cam chuckled. "It's funny you think power works like that. He'll grab onto anything that allows him to keep himself in power. He's playing on fear. There's a lot of fear."

Arrow's voice boomed through the radio speakers and hovering monitors; he was there, even as he sat comfortably in the Center. "If the Muties want outside so badly, then we'll give them a swift death in the Outer Rings. It's a far cry better than what they would get Outside, and they won't kill us in the process."

As we neared the train station dozens of holograms showed martial law in the Inner Rings as Muties were rounded up and shot in the street.

"If you are of pure genetic breeding," Arrow said through the monitors, "we will protect you in the Inner Rings. Come where it is safe. We have let the Muties live among us and destroy the purity of our race for too long. I know. I created you. All true believers, you have a sanctuary in the Center. All others...may the Five have mercy on your souls."

Arrow, an expert in evolution, was responsible for maintaining the optimum bloodline so that our species had maintained its strength. He was the reason we couldn't breed at will and needed permission from the government. Aside from that, we could have survived without him. But now he screamed like only he mattered. "I am the one true god amongst you. Without me, you wouldn't exist. Any others besides me are imposters."

I knew we wouldn't make it to the Center. He would quarter off every street, inspect every boat that passed through the harbor. The military was his alone now.

I couldn't breathe. I couldn't think. The walls of the limo closed in upon me. I needed air. I grabbed the latch on my door.

Cam grabbed my hand. "I wouldn't do that."

I crawled out of the car and lay on the ground, sucking in air as quickly as I could. I saw Arrow's end game. Once the Muties were out of the Inner Rings, the military could collapse inward and crush what remained of our resistance.

The world stopped spinning after a moment. I could think again. I heard a voice boom over Arrow's hatred— a sweet voice that comforted me.

"Henry?" I shouted. "Henry is that you?"

I rose to my feet and pushed my way through the dense crowd, through the thousands of people crowded around the river's edge. I didn't care. I needed to be closer to Henry. His voice grew louder as I reached a stage. There he was, preaching to the crowd…Time's words coming from Henry's sweet lips.

"I know you are scared. I know you feel alone, but you are not. You are together in a way you have never been together before. It is time to embrace our togetherness that we Five have not allowed until now."

"Henry!" I shouted, but he couldn't hear me above the throngs of people listening to his message.

Cam grabbed my hand. "Follow me!"

I longed to touch Henry one more time. It wasn't really him, but that didn't matter. I wanted to feel his skin, to touch his hair. I ran forward through the crowd, and they started chanting. "Earth, Earth, Earth, Earth!"

Time saw me in the crowd and beckoned me forward. Armstrong stood next to him. Behind him, on screens dozens of feet tall, flashed pictures of the Five's past lives.

Time continued, raising his arms as he spoke. "You don't have to believe me, but I urge you to look for yourself. The Muties have released every bit of data they have. They are telling the truth. We are nothing but humans, and we have deceived you. But now you can be free."

The crowd shouted and screamed at him. They pushed each other and shoved. Time saw me from the corner of his eye and shouted even louder than before. "And this is the woman who paved the way for your freedom. Please come and say something, my dear Earth."

Even though I knew it was only a pleasantry, hearing him say those words made my heart flutter. *My dear.* He pulled me forward. I resisted the urge to kiss him right then and there. I held up my arms and quieted the crowd. I hated speeches, but now all I did was deliver them. I hoped this one went better than the last.

For the first time since I had exited the car, the crowd was silent. They stared at me, some in anger, others in admiration but all with a twinge of reverence in their eye. Even if they hated me, I was still one of their gods.

I grabbed the microphone. "I understand, in ways you never will, just how horrible this situation is. I know that you have never been heard. Now that I've been to the wall, I know what a travesty it is that we haven't explored more than our little city in so very long. What Arrow is doing is not in the spirit of this City. He wants to make us great, but we are supposed to be greater. We are made for greater things than just surviving. That it isn't enough to have a life! We need to *thrive*!

"But we cannot thrive while our citizens are killed and while we are imprisoned inside this Bubble. Wind wanted us to explore outside the Bubble. He wanted it taken down, and if I have to sacrifice myself to make that happen, so be it. Follow me to the wall. Let us test this theory that we can't go outside, and if we can, let us explore the future together."

*

After my speech, Time led me into a nearby warehouse. The doors were barely closed before I grabbed him around the neck and kissed him. The gathered masses gasped—all except Cam who laughed.

"I think that's enough, Althea," Time said.

I stepped back. "Wait, did you just call me Althea?"

Time nodded. "Five minutes with you and it's clear as day, my dear. I think the only reason Arrow can't figure it out is because we've kept you far from him as of yet."

"Who else knows?" I whispered.

"Just about everybody, on our side at least. If Stone isn't careful, their side will know soon too."

"She's with Arrow?"

Time shook his head. "She wouldn't leave the Center with us. She locked herself in her room with the few loyal guards. She was in a bad way, and worse every day."

"And you? Are you still with me?"

"Always. For too long I've kept this City back, *we* have held it back for our own selfish gain. I don't care if you are Earth, or Althea, as long as you help us give this City back to the people."

I smiled. "I can do that."

Time nodded. "I have a plan for how we can get Outside. After the Incident, we reinforced the Bubble. Wind's initial design couldn't protect us forever. We built a wall around the City, which could power the Bubble for a million years. We built an airlock in every direction the railroad ran so we could evacuate citizens quickly if needed. Since they were the only weak points, we reinforced them with a barracks and sent the military to protect it. If we want to get out, those airlocks are our best course of action. We might not be able to open the Bubble, but we can send you out to prove the air is safe. Once we've proven that, then everything can change." He gave me a searching look. "Are you sure you are willing to risk your life?"

"I'm ready."

"I knew you would be, but there is a problem. Everything I know, Arrow knows as well. He's going to be there, waiting for us to make our move."

"Do you think this is our best shot?"

Time nodded. "It's our only shot, actually. Arrow controls the Inner Rings now. Thus, he has access to the controls, which can shut down the Bubble. We don't have any choice but to make our way to the Bubble ourselves."

"Then we go to the Bubble."

"Yes, but every exit is guarded by hundreds of men."

I listened as the shouting voices of the Outer Rings shook the whole room. "But we have thousands. They have the power, but we have the numbers. Between the Outer Rings and the Muties, we have thousands more people than they do."

Time smiled. "Then we walk. Gathering steam with every foot we move forward."

"We can dance if you want, but I won't let them follow Earth. If they are going to risk their lives, they need to know the truth."

"They know what they are dying for," Time said. "They aren't dying for you. They are dying for freedom."

"Then let them make the choice whether to follow me. Not Earth, *me*. Let them risk death knowing the truth."

*

I stepped outside to the thunderous noise of Muties from the Inner Rings mixed with citizens from the Outers. I saw it in their eyes—they needed justification. They needed answers.

I stepped up to the podium, knowing full well this could be the end of it all. Everybody could fall back in line with Arrow and refuse to follow me. They could maul me, or even kill me. But I had been dead before, and I survived. Death was not so bad.

"I am not Earth." There was a gasp in the crowd. "Something went wrong when they transferred Earth into my body, so...as I said, I am not her. I am not a 'god,' but Earth wasn't, either. She was a person. A very old person, sure, and a person with hopes, dreams, and aspirations just like you. She wanted to live. She wanted to keep going, and she would do anything to make that happen, including imprisoning you all inside this Bubble."

There was a low murmur in the crowd. "So. I am still Althea, a simple farmer from the Fifth who was thrust into this by my own ignorance. All I wanted to do was live a simple life. But I'm here now. Thank the Five I am not Earth, because she would not tell you the truth. She would tell you that everything was fine. She would lie to you."

Boos started to fan from the crowd. "Unlike me, she would not have told you that you *could* go Outside, because she needed you to give her power. You were just fuel to her and to Arrow. But now we have a chance to change that. We have a chance to march to the Bubble and escape, to start a new and better life."

The murmurs subsided. The people were listening to me. *Me*. Not Earth.

"We were meant for more than this complacent life. We were meant for greatness. Our ancestors conquered the globe. They made great things. We can do those things again. And I am going to sacrifice myself to make that happen. I am going outside. I am going to grab the first breath of fresh air we have had in thousands of years. If you are with me, we are headed to the Bubble right now. If it's only me, then so be it. I'm still going."

Time stepped up after a long moment of silence. "It won't only be you." He looked at the guards, who didn't know what to do. "Follow us both. I believe in her, and you should, too."

The crowd cleared a path for Time as he walked through them, followed by Cam. I hopped down from the podium and followed them through the silent crowd.

Then, one by one, they followed behind me. By the time we left the Fourth, thousands of people followed behind us.

CHAPTER 4

At first, I didn't know why we walked to the Bubble especially since we had cars and trucks. We could have transported everybody, but Time insisted on walking. "It's the symbolic gesture," he said. "Even if it takes longer, we will build up more steam the closer we get to the Bubble."

And he was right. The further we walked, the more supporters we gained. The media took notice too. As the crowds mounted on our walk into the Fifth, the floating cameras increased exponentially, which led to more people joining the walk, which led to more cameras.

I didn't care that I was sweaty, that my feet were swollen, or that it hurt to breath. Nothing like our march had happened in recorded history. Of course, Time remembered back before our history.

"Back before the Bubble, the greatest activists the world over protested by walking through the streets, across bridges, and through the countryside. We've taken our place in a great tradition, lost to the ages until now, in standing up to the oppressors and making our voices heard. Together, we are more powerful than even a god."

When it was all over, there would be soldiers and there would be fighting, but Arrow would not dare halt us now, lest public opinion turn against him. He could kill us in battle at the Bubble but picking off helpless citizens and arresting Time would be against protocol even for him. He couldn't risk his delicate grasp on power.

He didn't mind screaming about us though. Video projectors floated just in front of us, so I could hear everything that he was saying.

"This vile girl imposed her will on Time and tricked everybody into thinking she was one of us. This is heresy, my friends. This is the wrong path. She is an imposter, which is proof you should listen to me and that this scourge should be wiped off the earth."

His vitriol kept me going as my blood sugar wore down and his hatred fueled me when my legs burned. It fueled our supporters too. When their vigilance wavered, Arrow would shout something horrible and the crowd hurled obscenities back at him.

My protesters numbered in the tens of thousands by the time we reached the Sixth. We gathered citizens and Muties alike. More importantly, we gathered soldiers. It was easy to convince them that what they were doing was ludicrous. After all, they were from the same homes they were now destroying. Somebody just had to point out the way for them, and I suppose that that somebody had to be me, a farmer girl from the Fifth.

Arrow's rage boiled over as we crossed into the barren wastelands near the Bubble. The fizzing and popping from the force field became louder with each step we took. Even the sounds of Arrow's bluster couldn't drown it out.

"These imposters are criminals against our way of life," he shouted. "This is a fragile ecosystem, and this little girl wants to destroy it!"

I heard the fear in his voice. How could the Inner Rings survive if the Outer Rings didn't do their bidding? Even now, the food ran low in the Inner Rings. There was nobody to mine the coal or feed it into the factories, so their houses flickered into darkness.

The funny thing was, I don't think any of these people following behind me really wanted to leave the city—they just wanted options. They wanted the freedom to make their own choices. They didn't like being prisoners. Right now, they were forced to do the Five's bidding. It's very different when you choose to do a thing as opposed to when you are forced to do it.

My parents always knew they had no choice, but they buried it down deep in the recesses of their hearts until somebody brought it out of them. After all of this, I knew they would go back and tend to their farm because they wanted to—not because they had to.

*

When we reached the Bubble, thousands of soldiers stood against us, their lines long and deep. But our horde dwarfed them ten to one. The Constable stood in front of the line as the soldiers drew guns against us. There, standing behind them like a coward, was Arrow.

"The airlock is next to the barracks," Time said, pointing to a large, circular structure several hundred feet beyond the line of guns. "You don't have to do this, Althea. You can pull out now if you want. There needs to be no bloodshed today. It can wait until we are better prepared. Until you are better prepared."

"No. This ends now," I said. "I'm ready to die for this. There are just so many soldiers..."

"The one downside to building people up the slow way is that the enemy knows where you are going. They must have pulled soldiers from every post in the City to stand against us."

I looked back at my throngs of followers. Our numbers were great. Our cause was noble. But was it worth it risking their lives for my cause? My feet were bloody and blistered. My back hurt and my stomach cried out for food. I knew they fared no different. Was it worth their deaths to see my cause through? Wouldn't it be easier if we just went back to our homes?

Yes, it would be. But that road was impossible. I couldn't go back now that my eyes were opened. I'd seen this City for the prison it has always been and always would be. I used to love this City. Now I see it was all a lie, a fallacy, trumped up by those in charge to keep me doing their bidding. I could not let that stand.

"Are you ready?" Time asked.

I breathed out the last of my fear. "I'm ready."

I looked back at my mother. She and my dad were up front next to me. Bobby stood next to them. They had found me in the Fifth, driven their pickup truck to me and just left the truck there, in the street, to follow me.

That was love. I wondered if I would have done the same for my own child, had it survived. Would I have given up everything for her?

I looked past my parents to the throngs of people supporting me. They followed me, but more importantly they followed an idea. I held up my arms to satiate the growing unrest in their eyes. "Please be patient. Do not incur violence on my behalf."

There would be violence regardless. I couldn't stop that. Still, I wanted to protect them the best way I knew how. I could deal with my own death, but not the death of innocents, gunned down like animals. Maybe this is what it feels like to be a mother.

I walked forward to the front line of the guards. Time walked beside me on one side, Cam on the other. "I think we are going to die now."

Time smiled. "We've had a good run."

"Speak for yourself," Cam said. "I'm still a teenager."

"I mean you no harm!" I shouted to the soldiers.

Over the loudspeaker, behind the army, Arrow shouted, "Well that's not true. You wish to open the airlock, which hasn't happened...ever. And that endangers everybody."

"I'm not stopping, Arrow. If you think your soldiers will shoot two of the Five remaining alive, then you're crazy!"

"Ah, my dear, but there are no longer Five, there are only Three. Wind and Earth are gone. Without Time, there will be two—Stone, and I—who wish to keep this City safe. We can be rid of those of you who wish to do it harm."

I stopped at the front line. The guards kept their guns trained on me. "Let me pass and I will do you no harm."

The soldiers stayed steadfast in their aim. Months ago, this would have caused me to crumble, but I was forged from steel now. Time stepped in front of me. "I order you to move. Is Arrow really the only one of the Five who can issue a command now?"

"He protects us while you seek to destroy us," the Constable said.

"Let me tell you something," Time said. "We were all chosen together, and it was not for our good nature. It was because we hid our secrets so deep that you needed us to survive. We kept them to ourselves so you had to sacrifice your children to us. This was not charity; it was evil and wrong. What we do now is an attempt to right that wrong, even centuries too late."

The Constable's eye twitched as her brain worked to process this new information. Arrow shouted across the loudspeaker. "Oh, just let them through, already. What can they do to a god?"

The crowd behind me screamed. I held my hand to calm them. The guards parted, and the Constable led us toward the barracks. Arrow waited for us next to the airlock. He smiled and grinned at us as if we were old friends. "This is so interesting, Time. We've been at odds for so long, fighting against you, Stone, and Wind for so long, and I finally won. I thought it would feel delicious, but I never knew just how delicious."

"You haven't won, Arrow. You've brutalized everybody who doesn't agree with you. You used the military we designed to protect this City against our citizens. But look out there. There are more of them than there are of you. They want freedom, or at least some choice in how they run their lives. So honestly, why won't you let them have it?"

"Because they will destroy us."

"No," I said. "They will destroy you, and the Five. They will make it so you are irrelevant, and you will have to train them to fend for themselves. You will have to reveal your secrets, and you will die."

"The Five will never die!"

"But they have," I shouted. "Wind and Earth are dead. You plan to kill another." I glanced at Time then back at Arrow.

The Constable snarled. "Watch it, kid."

"Look at you," I wheeled on her. "When I met you, your job was to protect this City. Isn't that what you said?"

"I do protect it!" she shouted.

"Do you? Look at your men, drawing weapons on this crowd who are peacefully trying to fulfill their birthright to step outside. You are nothing but a jailer."

"I protect freedom!"

"From where I sit, this whole Bubble is a prison, and your job is to keep us docile, so the wardens can carry on getting fat and playing god. Aren't you more than that? Look behind you. Don't you want to see what's out there, beyond the Bubble?"

The Bubble fizzled in agreement with me, but the Constable shook her head. "No. It seems foolish to leave safety."

"It is foolish. We are foolish beings," Time said. "But that does not mean we should be left in here. Don't you want peace?"

"We are trying to maintain the peace!"

"No," I said. "You are a soldier. But if you let me go outside, maybe we can be so much more. Just ask yourself this: why does Arrow care? Let's think about this. It's safe out there. Wind knew it, Time knows it—even Stone knows it. And I know it too. Even if it's not, you can just watch me die and seal it back up. All of this can be over if I'm wrong. So why does Arrow care so much? Only one reason. He knows I'm right. And if I'm right, then you don't need him."

The Constable looked up at Arrow. I could see the confusion in her face for a moment, then her snarl returned. "Lock them away!" she screamed and grabbed my arm. "Let's go."

"The whole data cell, with everything from Wind's computer, is available to the people. All I'm asking is for you to look at it, Constable. If you still think I'm crazy afterwards, I'll accept my fate."

She didn't speak. She just squeezed my arm harder.

*

"It's not so bad," I said to Time from the floor of the grimy cell we shared. "I've been in much worse."

"Yes, that's how this whole thing started, isn't it? Imagine if we had just put you in two separate cells."

"Yeah, why didn't you do that?"

"Oh, Earth convinced us that it was a better tactic to have you together talking and giving away secrets. She figured you were just dumb kids who would slip up eventually." A devious smile crept across Time's face. "She couldn't have known this was going to happen."

"And that mistake cost Earth her life. She was too busy worrying about me to even see Abigail as a threat. Really though, who could have seen Abigail as a threat?"

"Her need to find that data cell and prove her omnipotence clouded her judgment."

The door to the holding cell flung open. The Constable walked in with a bloody forehead and mud on her clothes. "Your protesters are out of control! What is wrong with them?"

I stood up. "They want freedom and you're keeping them from that. It's amazing what people will do to live freely."

"You have to talk to them. I don't want more of my officers killed by your protestors. Their blood is on your hands."

"Fine. I'll talk to them."

I stepped out of the cell and into a war zone. Soldiers were fighting protesters and the protesters fought back, taking guns from guards. Their sheer numbers had overwhelmed the military. Casualties from both sides lay dead on the ground. I hadn't wanted any of this. *What have I done?*

The Constable walked me up to Arrow's loudspeaker. He was nowhere to be found.

"Where is Arrow?" I asked her.

"Does it matter?" the Constable replied. "He won't be trouble anymore."

I knew what had happened. The Constable had sided with us. Something I said had finally gotten through to her. "What was it that convinced you?"

"I just looked at the evidence. It told me everything I needed to know."

I turned to the microphone and shouted, "Stop! All of you!" And they did. They turned, in unison, and looked up at me. "It's over. There is no need for more bloodshed today."

*

It was amazing how fast things changed after Arrow was removed from the picture. The soldiers and the protestors dropped their guns and the fighting was over. I watched over the battlefield as enemies talked like old friends. Then, eventually, it was time to do my part.

I wasn't scared of death, but I didn't welcome it either. I'd been a friend with it for so long I had forgotten to be nervous. Life never tasted sweeter than in those moments after I'd survived. The air was fresher, the grass greener. My life was better. In those moments, I could accomplish anything. If you've never faced death before, it's impossible to describe the rush you feel after cheating it. And every time you bump into death, the same horrid feeling comes back, but there is also the joy of knowing if you survive it will make your life so much sweeter.

The Constable led me down into the cells. I found Arrow wallowing in his own hubris. He was sweaty and defeated, but no less angry. He shouted vile slurs at me when I entered the cell, but I ignored them.

"I have to know," I said to Arrow as he sat in the cell. For the first time, I was on the outside of his prison cell looking into the darkness. I smiled at him. "Was living longer worth it? Worth the cost?"

"Yes," Arrow responded. "I would do anything for one more moment of life." I had been there before and sympathized with the feeling if not the method. "But that doesn't change the fact that what you are doing is wrong. We have everything we need right here. We can make this City great again."

"No, we can't. This City isn't the problem. We're caged mice that need freedom. We need to wander in the field. We need to free ourselves from the big, fat owls."

Arrow laughed slowly and for a long time. "I fought against that book's release. Guhman was a stupid mouse. The big, fat owls protected him from harm."

"Until they bit his head off! We are made for so much more. We want to see the field!"

"That is not how we designed you."

"But you didn't design us. You modified us. We were here way before you came along. You took the best of us, the parts you loved, and you spawned those, but our little subconscious brain was always there, fighting to escape."

"That was an error on our part. I will be sure to correct it."

"Why would you want to correct it? Why can't you just enjoy that you made us in your image. You allowed us to grow for thousands of years, and now we are ready to leave."

"Because then you won't need us, and we will die."

"No. You won't die. Not really. You'll live forever because we will live on after you." I stood up. "I hope you know how grateful I am to you for my family, and for keeping us safe."

"You have a funny way of showing it."

I couldn't stand looking at him anymore. His hatred blinded him to the truth. I wanted to leave his presence before his contempt choked me, but there was one more question I had to ask.

"Who killed Wind? Was it you or Earth?"

Arrow chuckled. "It was a joint decision, but my man pulled the trigger. It was her decision to call you brats to the Center though. I thought it was a stupid idea. I guess I was right."

"Not from where I stand."

*

Next, I went to my mother, father, and Bobby. I was sick of saying goodbye to them and fearing I would never see them again. Yet, here I was doing it again. They grabbed me in a big bear hug the moment I entered the room. "We are so proud of you."

"I know."

My dad looked at me, tears in his eyes. "You don't have to do this."

I nodded. "Sure I do. Otherwise, what is there to be proud of?"

"We just got our little girl back. We thought we'd lost you...so many times." Mama choked back a sob, her hands touching my hair and my face.

I nodded. "You'll never lose me, Mama. But this is bigger than us. It's bigger than this City. Can we just hold each other for a while and forget what could happen to me?"

Bobby nodded. "Yes. Let's do that. It sounds nice."

When I finally finished crying, I wiped my face and walked outside where Time waited for me. I collapsed into his arms. I knew he wasn't Henry, but I didn't care. I needed his comfort to believe everything would be all right. I'd faced my past and present, now it was time to face my future, and the future of all our people.

"I am so proud of you for doing this," Time said. "It's everything Wind would have wanted. It's everything we designed you to be."

*

I stood in front of them all, soldiers and protestors alike, as the airlock loomed at my back. My people. I had been chosen to lead them not through divine right but through force of will. They wanted to follow me. I told them all my shame and they still stood behind me, thousands upon thousands of them, stretching as far back as the eye could see.

On my left stood Cam, on the right was Time and behind me was Stone. She'd agreed to leave the Center after we secured the peace. I turned to her first. "If this works, it means that all of your mistakes will be forgiven. You know that, right?"

Stone shook her head. "So many dead. So many dead. So many dead. No forgiveness."

"Yes, there is. You saved all these people. You job was to keep them safe until we could venture Outside again. And you accomplished that. Do you understand? "

Stone looked at me and nodded. "I do." For the first time since I'd known her, a peace washed over her face.

Throughout the crowd, I saw faces I recognized—from the Fifth, from the Center, from the Mutie's hospital, from moments in my life I couldn't fully remember. They smiled at me, full of hope. I didn't want to let them down, but it was out of my control. All I could do was step into the airlock. The world would do the rest.

I took the microphone, hoping it wouldn't be the last time I spoke. "Thank you for being here to see this historic event. I hope that it will be a glorious victory... and that you haven't come to watch me suffocate and die."

The crowd gave a combination of groan and uncomfortable laughter.

"Should we succeed here today, it will be the dawn of a new age—an age where we can venture outside into the wilderness and move beyond the confines of this great City and into the vast world."

The crowd chanted my name—soft at first, but then it reached a crescendo, rising into the heavens. My heart swelled at the sound of it. I turned to Cam. "Wish me luck."

Cam opened the airlock. She grabbed my arm and whispered fiercely, "What you are doing is beyond what we could have imagined."

I nodded at her, took another breath, and stepped inside the airlock. For a moment the chants grew to a fevered pitch, then the door closed, and they dropped to silence. I was alone with my thoughts. I thought about the entirety of my journey here and how far I'd come.

Would they tell stories about me? About the naïve girl who grew up to become a god, then threw it all away to set them free? Would they turn my story into a song, a song that would live on long after I died, a song that would show new generations of little girls that they could do anything? Or maybe it would be a cautionary fable to scare children into submission?

I still didn't know if I was doing the right thing. I hoped so, but everything I'd worked for could blow up in my face in a couple of seconds. Maybe Arrow was right. Maybe it was too dangerous outside the Bubble. Maybe this rebellion was a horrible idea.

I did know one thing above all else: I chose this path. I chose the path to freedom. I might not have known I wanted it, but I made every choice to keep going. And now I would be the first person in thousands of years to taste the fresh air of the Outside. Even if I died, it would be worth it.

The airlock opened, and I inhaled my first taste of real air. It was glorious. It tasted like freedom.

THE END

ALSO BY RUSSELL NOHELTY

NOVELS AND CHILDREN'S BOOKS

My Father Didn't Kill Himself
Sorry for Existing
Katrina Hates Everything
The Little Bird and the Little Worm
Gumshoes: The Case of Madison's Father
The Katrina Series
The Lobdell Chronicles
The Freeman Files
The Pixie Dust Series
The Invasion Saga
The Marked Ones
The Vessel

GRAPHIC NOVELS AND COMIC BOOKS

Ichabod Jones: Monster Hunter
Katrina Hates the Dead
Gherkin Boy
Pixie Dust